MW01631997

SHANKS CROSSING

Gary Jay Pool

Published by Pool Publishing

Tabor, Iowa

Shanks Crossing

This is a work of fiction, written solely for my entertainment, however Henry Shanks, Shanks Crossing, Ben Crane, the Rousch family, the Pool family, and Mary Dimmitt were real people of the period 1900-2000. Most are members of my family and would never sue me because they know they have nothing to gain. The story of Shanks Crossing is fiction, but the glory hole, the outlaw trying to cross the Yellowstone at flood stage, the Indians, the steel bridge, Pool draw and baby Helen's grave on the hill are all real. The area around Grey Cliff, Big Timber, Reed Springs and Billings, Montana and the Yellowstone River valley do exist. It's a beautiful country populated by warm, generous people molded in the image of Henry Shanks. Maybe this is not a work of fiction after all. Besides, I have written so much in this disclaimer that I feel it only fair that I raise the price of the book.

Published by Pool Publishing, Tabor, Iowa 51653
Printed in the United States of America

Library of Congress cataloguing in publication data

ISBN: 978-1-7321574-0-8

Dedication

This book is dedicated to Kitty Hause, a very dear friend of ours who challenged me to write a story about a Cowboy, a Bar of Gold and a Train.

Contents

SHANKS CROSSING

It was late in the spring of 1917 when Henry Shanks began cutting hay from his lower forty. That small alfalfa field, his pride and joy, was bordered on the north by the Bear Tooth Mountains and on the south by the beautiful fast flowing Yellowstone River.

This morning, like every other for the last fifty two years, Mr. Shanks, as he was known locally, began his waking ritual by peering out the south window of his log cabin to assess the water level in the nearby river. As was his habit, Mr. Shanks did not merely estimate the depth of the clear cold water rushing by some quarter of a mile away; instead he carefully opened the four piece brass telescope, which hung by a leather strap from his bedpost and examined the large red boulder that rested midstream of the rocky riverbed. A large granite boulder sat just north of the area's safest ford, and for the last fifty two years had been the best way for travelers to judge the level of difficulty to be expected in attempting to cross the hundred and fifty yards of churning water. The great granite monitor rock had a number of deep chisel marks, courtesy of a then youthful Henry Shanks. He had cut into its hard sides with deep grooves to be closely examined by any pilgrim wishing to traverse the bridgeless natural obstacle.

This morning's viewing stunned Mr. Shanks, as his seventy four year old eyes indicated the boulder was nowhere to be seen. That magnificent way-sign had been in the middle of the Yellowstone River's on-rushing waters for as long as the old man had lived in the log cabin. His brain insisted the boulder, even in these high run-offs, could not be washed away. The shock and disbelief of what his aging naked eyes had reported, caused the old man to recklessly throw the heavy telescope to his eye in hopes of locating the massive sign. Unable to accept the loss of the marker, Mr. Shanks feverishly slid the four sections of telescope back and forth, struggling to focus on the area of the ford, only to discover a great wake forming downstream by the totally submerged boulder. The old cowboy dropped the telescope from his eye to gaze in disbelief at the inundated boulder, something that he had never witnessed in all of his fifty two years of living beside the river crossing. Mr. Shanks stole a peek through the spy glass periodically as he dressed and prepared his breakfast.

A resounding knocking at the cabin's only door jarred the old man from his trance-like concentration on the disappearing boulder. "Come in Ben, just finished breakfast, but there's coffee and flapjacks left if you're hungry," Mr. Shanks called out to his young helper Ben Crane.

Young Crane was the son of Jeremiah Crane, who had taken up a homestead in the hills to the east, in what was known locally as Pool Draw. Both the Crane and Pool families had given up good farms in the Midwest, after being enticed to Montana by newspaper articles extolling the virtues of the fertile 'free land' ready to be claimed. The rich well-irrigated bottom lands had all been taken up years before, so the newcomers were forced to settle in the hills where the only dependable crops were rocks and rattlesnakes. The Pool's had already relinquished their claim and Henry Shanks knew the Crane's would soon follow suit.

"No thank you sir, mother fixed a powerful big breakfast this morning, and I'm full to the gills," Ben replied, turning his head to look away as he disliked telling falsehoods, especially to Mr. Shanks.

"That's a shame, you know how I hate waste, and if you don't eat these flapjacks, I'll just have to throw them out to the chickens," the old man smiled, knowing the Cranes were short of provisions.

"I never was fond of chickens except when they're fried in a skillet, and I figure feeding flapjacks to a dumb bird would be just plain wasteful," Ben replied eagerly, as he stepped through the cabin door after wiping his worn leather work boots and removing his oversized hand-me-down straw hat.

"Just sit yourself down at the table son, here's a clean knife and fork and some butter and honey. Sorry, I don't have any syrup left," Mr. Shanks apologized, as he placed a tin cup of hot coffee before the youth's plate.

"I've always been partial to honey myself Mr. Shanks," Ben beamed as he began to devour the leftover breakfast.

"Good, you eat your fill and I'll start the chores," Mr. Shanks instructed as he hurried out the door. "I see old Gladys is up at the barn wanting to be milked," he added.

Henry Shanks retrieved the galvanized steel two gallon milk pail from where it hung beside the cabin door, then made his way to the barn where his Brown Swiss milk cow, Gladys waited patiently to be relieved of the uncomfortable load in her swollen udder. The two were good friends, Gladys happily ambled along behind the old rancher to a wooden feed bunk, which he filled with tender first-cutting hay to appease her during the milking process. He spoke in a soft reassuring tone as he positioned his short three legged wooden stool near Gladys' right rear leg and began to gently massage her teats. The Brown Swiss was by nature a gentle creature that never kicked nor tried to wander off before the milking was done, which the aging rancher greatly appreciated.

Henry Shanks had always tried to run an amiable ranch; he didn't keep mean dogs, rank horses, wild cows or rowdy cowhands. It was common knowledge throughout the area that everyone was welcome at Henry Shanks's ranch as long as they toed the mark. It was also common knowledge that any infraction of the rules of decency and the congenial old man would quickly reprimand the offender. Early on Shanks named his spread the

Rattlesnake Ranch or the R-R due to the large number of the poisonous reptiles, which inhabited the land but noisy serpents aside his self-built kingdom was his idea of heaven on earth.

When the last spurts of the warm white liquid splashed into the foamy milk filled pail Henry Shanks rose from his squatted position and hung his three legged stool on the fence. He opened the wooden corral gate that would give Gladys access to the fenced-in grassy pasture where the loyal animal would graze at will until evening when nature would once again call her back to the milk pail.

"Thank you Gladys," the old cowboy declared with a gentle pat on the cow's rump, signaling the task was completed for the morning. Careful not to slosh any milk out of the better than half-full pail, Shanks headed for his hand-dug well, which was strategically located allowing animals kept in either corral to access the small metal stock tank. A wooden framed windmill tower rose directly above the well's steel pump that rhythmically produced one blast of sparkling clear water for each rotation of the fan-shaped blades located some twenty feet above.

Henry Shanks sat the milk bucket on the well platform for safe keeping as he opened a heavy trap door in the three inch thick oak well cover. He then draped a white cotton cloth over the bucket to exclude the entry of dirt and insects before attaching a lightweight line to the buckets bale and began lowering the precious pail of milk into the cool black abyss below.

The hand-dug well was only 54 feet deep, counting the three feet of stone rim extended above ground level. Henry Shanks had dug the well the year after settling the R-R Ranch, once he discovered the inconvenience of driving his stock to the river twice daily for water and the difficulty in hauling enough water to the house for personal use. Fifty feet was not particularly deep for a well in this area due to it being located within a quarter mile of the Yellowstone River. Still quite proud of his well, the old cowboy kept a constant watch on the water level and had never seen it drop below 10 feet in the driest summers, nor ever climb above 15 feet in wet years like this spring.

While the water's depth was indeed important, the fact that difference in temperature between ground level and water level could in the summer be near fifty degrees cooler and as much as 50 degrees warmer in the dead of winter. This time of year the milk, cheese and some meats were suspended near the top of the water to prevent spoilage while during the winter it prevented the foodstuffs from freezing solid.

With the milking chores finished, Henry Shanks looked up and smiled to see Ben Crane had fed the horses and had opened the henhouse door and was in the process of scattering loose grain on the ground within the chicken wire fence. The old cowboy preferred to allow his fowl to roam free around the ranch house where they could feed freely on insects or any other tasty morsel that caught their keen eye, but the hens would be deprived of such privilege today as he and Ben would be some distance away in the hayfield and would be unable to offer protection from prowling varmints.

The old rancher and his youthful hired man met just outside the cabin's door where they made plans for the day's work ahead. "Do you want me to hitch up the team Mr. Shanks?" Ben inquired anxiously because he always enjoyed working with the animals, especially the R-R Ranch's fine pair of work horses.

"I thought we would start our day by walking down to the river and trimming around the rocks and trees. It seems to make mowing easier if you can miss those things with the mower bar. Let's get the hand scythes, the hand file and a jug of water and head down that way," the old man said with a smile.

Ben quickly gather up the named items and the pair, old and young began to walk side by side down the two-track road, which led to the hayfield and the river crossing. "Notice anything different?" Henry Shanks asked in an unconcerned tone.

"No sir, I reckon not," the youth replied after making a halfhearted glance around the river bottom. "Why do you ask?"

"Something has changed and I just wondered if you had noticed," the old rancher replied with a chuckle.

"Oh!" Ben exclaimed. "The monitor, it's gone!" he announced in a loud high pitched voice as if the old man hadn't any knowledge of the missing boulder.

"Do you really think it's gone?" Shanks asked.

"I can't see it and I don't ever remember when it wasn't setting there," came Ben's excited reply while he half bounced and half skipped down the two-track road in a manner intended to hurry his employer to increase his pace.

"I'm of a mind that the boulder is still there, we just can't see it," Henry Shanks stated in a self-assuring declaration.

"But it would mean the river is above flood stage," Ben argued.

"That's why I'm in no great hurry to cut this hay, if we get it down and more water comes along it will all wash away. But of course, if the water gets high enough and runs long enough it will destroy the sweet clover plants."

"That would be a shame Mr. Shanks. I know you have worked hard to start this hayfield, it's known as the best hay in the area," Ben praised the old man's efforts to build up his ranch.

"Yes, it would be a shame," Henry Shanks agreed mournfully, then sensing his young friend's urgency to inspect the river, he increased his pace. They covered the last hundred yards to the rocky riverbank in short order but each successive step of the last twenty yards proved to be softer and wetter.

"Since my feet are getting wet up here on the bank I'd say the river is above flood stage for sure," Henry Shanks announced, stepping back out of the cold river water. "And it's still rising," he added.

"How do you know the river is still rising Mr. Shanks?" Ben inquired, as he eyed the rampaging river.

"I was raised and worked on both the Mississippi and Missouri Rivers before the war and we went through a lot of floods. On those big wide rivers it was easy to tell if the water was coming up because you can see the center of the channel is higher than the outside and the trash floats near to the bank. When the water starts to fall, the main channel appears lower than the edges and the trash floats closer to the center," the old cowboy explained. "Take a close look and tell me what you see."

Ben Crane bent over at the waist trying to get a better angle on the churning water. "I see it, the main channel is higher and the leaves and limbs are floating right near the bank," the youth answered.

"That's right, and if you will look close you can see a ripple in the water just below where the boulder sets. It's still there only the water has covered it for now," the old rancher stated, pointing to the V shaped pattern forming below the marker.

"Can you swim Ben?" Henry Shanks inquired rather off-handedly.

"Yes sir," after a fashion the youth bashfully replied.

"You may already know this, but if you ever find yourself caught in a strong current like this and become too tired to swim, just turn your body at an angle to the bank and the water will take you into shore. Just keep your head above water and float along with the current and you will come to the bank. Now you may be as much as a mile downstream when you land but it's a lot easier to walk a mile up stream than it is to swim a mile up stream," the old man explained.

"I never knew that Mr. Shanks, but I will certainly remember what you said. And thank you for the advice." Ben smiled then returned his attention to the area of the river where the boulder should be visible.

"I reckon you're not paying me for watching the river Mr. Shanks so I'll sharpen the scythes and get to work," the youth announced, eager to keep a job that paid good, hard currency.

"Well, it may prove to be a waste of time but you're right, that's what we came here to do." Henry Shanks was delighted to hear his hired man was willing to earn his pay.

Ben willingly turned to the work at hand because he knew jobs and money were hard to find in the Yellowstone River Valley. The bad financial times had driven several local people to a life of crime, which Henry Shanks mentioned during a rest break. The old cowboy was sharpening his small hand scythe when he divulged that a late evening traveler had related a story of four men who had stolen two hundred pounds of gold from a mine up near Helena. The gold had been cast in a single ingot, hoping to discourage would-be thieves. But it seems there are always men desperate enough to try even the impossible.

The two men found a seat in the shade of a tall stately Cottonwood tree for a brief rest and to sharpen their tools. The tree's large green leaves rustled loudly overhead as they caught the rising morning breeze, but the pair managed to continue their friendly conversation about the brazen robbery far to the north.

"The traveler said the outlaws killed a guard during the holdup so they must be running for their lives," Henry Shanks stated with a disgusted shake of his head.

"Do you think they might come this way?" Ben inquired anxiously.

"I doubt it, if I were those boys I'd be headed for Canada and the tall timber," Shanks replied confidently. "They need to avoid people and civilization; what they need is the high lonesome like the north woods offer," came Henry Shanks's serious reply.

Ben Crane remained silent for several minutes as he rhythmically stroked the coarse file over the hand scythe's metal blade.

"Has your parents considered my offer?" the old cowboy asked breaking the silence.

"I know they talk about it, but I don't think they have made a decision sir," young Crane answered, not knowing what to say.

"I didn't mean to put you on the spot, but I'm getting on in years and I don't have any family to leave my ranch to," Henry Shanks began to explain his offer, but the words were more for himself than for Ben. “If your folks would agree to take care of me until I die, they can have my land, livestock, buildings and all my money. I'll stay in my cabin and we can move your house down here from the draw. I don't want to die in some smelly, noisy town. I want to go right here on my own land and I want to be buried on my ranch. That's what I want and I'm willing to pay for it,” Shanks stated firmly.

“I understand Mr. Shanks,” Ben stated in a consoling voice, then he once again fell silent waiting for his employer to speak if he desired. But several minutes passed while Ben waited patiently, carefully filing the scythes and occasionally glancing at the water level in the roaring Yellowstone River. The youth paused for a moment to examine the sharp edge on the scythe he was working on then said, “May I ask you a question sir?”

“Why yes, of course Ben, I hope we're friends enough for you to ask anything you like,” the old rancher smiled.

“You were in the war and I guess what I'm trying to ask is, well, did you have to kill anyone?”

“Why,” Shanks paused, then began again, “Why yes, it was my duty, my job as it was the enemy's job to kill me, but why do you ask?”

“Father says there is a war coming and we are going to be in it,” Ben began, not sure of what to say.

“I'm sure your pa would know more about that than me, he always keeps up on the news and what's happening.”

"I'd like to start a ranch and maybe get married someday, but I'm as poor as jobe's turkey so I have been thinking of joining the army, we could use the money and I'm just taking up space and food at our place. But I'm not sure if I could kill a man. My friends say it's easy in war but they ain't never killed anyone either. I guess I'm asking, is it really easy to kill another man when you're in a war?" the inexperienced youth finally blurted out.

Henry Shanks pushed his battered sweat stained western hat back on his forehead then took a long drink of water from the water jug. It was clear to his youthful companion that the old man was carefully weighing his answer to what is an unanswerable question.

"I must disagree with your friends Ben," Henry Shanks paused, inhaled deeply, his troubled eyes focused on the distant hills to the north. "I have taken life in the war that's true, but I have also found it necessary to defend my own life and property right here on this ranch." Once more the old cowboy hesitated before continuing with his answer, "I have clashed with both red and white men not far from this very spot and I can definitely say extinguishing a human life is never easy for a true Christian. You are a good Christian aren't you Ben?" Shanks inquired as an afterthought.

"Yes sir, we say grace before each meal, we go to church most Sundays or mother holds service at home in case of bad weather. Oh, and father reads aloud from the Bible and repeats the Ten

Commandments every night at bedtime," Ben's words were clear, concise and filled with pride.

"Good man, Ben Crane, however unlike some other religions the Christian faith teaches us not to kill one another. A man must search deep in his soul for justification when that fatal moment of truth comes. Must I kill this person or is there another way to settle this confrontation?" The old man, his eyes closed, was speaking in a near whisper now and it seemed to Ben his friend was in another place and time.

The youth remained mute and unmoving for several long intolerable minutes waiting for any sign that Mr. Shanks was still in the conversation. Suddenly the old man's eye lids snapped open and he announced in a normal tone. "Someone is riding this way and he seems to be in a hurry."

THE TRAVELER

"I don't hear anything," Ben countered, looking all around the hayfield.

"It's a lone horse galloping down the road from the east," Henry Shanks advised as he sprung to his feet, turning to look down the trail towards his cabin.

"I can see him now," Ben stated after gaining his feet. "Can't tell who it is though. He's not stopping at your cabin Mr. Shanks," the youth continued.

"I know who it is," the old cowboy's voice dropped to a low growl as he announced the identity of the approaching rider. "It's Doc Walker."

"You mean Doc Walker, the gunman from up around Bozeman?" Crane's youthful exuberance was obvious in the tone of his voice and his excited demeanor.

"Yeah one in the same, he's mean as a rattler so let me do the talking when he stops," Henry Shanks ordered in a parental manner.

The thudding animal's hooves grew louder and more distinct as the horse and rider drew nearer and nearer to the hayfield. The sound of the animal's heavy breathing fell on the men's ears, a sign both boy and man recognized as exhaustion.

The notorious outlaw reined back sharply bringing his mount to a sliding halt. Outfitted in a knee-length gray duster and big black hat, he paused for a long moment staring intently at the rancher and his hired man, then turned in the saddle to look back over his shoulder. Doc Walker pulled a worn 1873 Winchester rifle from the saddle scabbard with his right hand then balanced the weapon across the horse's sweaty neck, muzzle toward the rancher. Years of experience from riding the outlaw trail told Walker that the two men standing in the hayfield ahead were probably not a threat, certainly not as great a threat as the men behind him.

Responding to a hard gouge in the ribs by a pair of sharp spur rowels, the still blowing horse reluctantly began to walk down the two-track lane. The gunman, his approach carefully thought out, allowed his mount to walk slowly in the northern most side of the rudimentary road which was calculated to keep as much distance as possible between the two unknown men and himself.

Clop, clop, the weary animal's steel shoes hammered against the rocky dirt of the track as the pair drew near the Cottonwood tree where unarmed Henry Shanks and Ben Crane awaited the arrival of one of the area's most feared men. At fifty yards the gunman stopped his mount once more, stood up in his stirrups, shielded his eyes then called in a questioning voice. “Shanks?”

“**Mr**. Shanks if you please,” the old man called back.

“Mr. Shanks,” Walker corrected himself. I thought you’d be dead by now,” he added.

“I thought the same of you,” Henry Shanks countered the insulting remark.

“May I approach Mr. Shanks?” the outlaw asked, placing an emphasis on the Mr.

“Yes,” came the old rancher’s blunt unfriendly reply.

“Yes siree, I thought someone said you’d up and died Mr. Shanks,” Walker chided the old man.

“Well it ain’t for lack of trying, you know that better than most,” Shanks retorted.

“You? Hell fella, I’m still sporting a big red scar across my back where your pistol ball cut me the last time we met!” the bad man roared out indignantly.

“You shouldn’t have been trying to steal my mare!” Shanks scolded, the volume of his voice equal to Doc Walker’s.

“That was one fine animal,” Walker said with a shake of his head and a wide smile, the first such civil display since he arrived at the hayfield.

“She still is!” the old rancher announced proudly but it was the wrong thing to say as the news that the mare was still on the R-R brought Walker to set up straight in his saddle.

"You still got that bay? How bout we make a trade? I could clearly use a fresh horse and I'd make the trade worth your while." The renowned tough guy sounded like a kid begging his parents for candy.

"No, absolutely not! I've seen how you treat your mounts and I'd never let you ride a horse of mine, let alone own one!" Henry Shanks shot back in no uncertain terms.

"Damn you Henry Shanks, you know I have a weakness for fine horse flesh, but you are just a mean spiteful old man!" Walker roared as if in pain while lifting his Winchester rifle from where it rested on his horse's neck. "I don't see any guns on you or this snot nosed kid so I reckon I could take that mare without...," the outlaw paused then turned to look Ben square in the eye before saying, "just who the hell is this pup anyway?" he demanded with a snarl. "I'll bet he ain't even weaned yet."

"He's my hired man," the old cowboy replied, not wanting to reveal the youths name fearing future reprisal.

"What the hell is your name kid?" Walker demanded once more. "You see I have a thing about killing people whose name I don't know. It doesn't look good in the tally book you understand."

"Ben Crane sir," the youth replied in a shaky voice.

"You're not going to kill anyone Doc," Shanks said confidently.

"I'd gladly kill both of you for that mare," Walker snarled.

"I'm sure you would but something tells me you don't have the time to kill us, find the mare, get her saddled and still get away from whoever it is on your trail," Henry Shanks argued without a second's hesitation.

The killer's demeanor quickly changed while he spun his exhausted mount around to view his back trail easier. "Oh hell I don't want that mare anyway, besides it would be a waste of bullets to kill a feeble old man and some half-baked kid. It would look bad to my friends if I shot the two of you," he added lowering the Winchester down on the horse's neck once more.

"Do you have any friends Doc? I mean anyone who would really care?" Shanks asked.

"We used to be friends Henry, maybe could be again," the hard man's voice turned soft for the first time as his body sagged forward.

"No Doc, you crossed that line long ago, we can never be friends again." Shanks showed no pity only firm resolve in his belief.

"Oh," Doc responded in a low tired voice. "Can I still use your river crossing?" he asked halfheartedly.

"You know, there is a new steel bridge across the Yellowstone about three miles upriver?" the old rancher half stated, half asked.

“I’m in kind of a hurry and the bridge is too far out of my way,” the bad man responded.

“Too far out of the way or are you afraid that a posse is at the bridge waiting for you to cross?” Shanks snapped.

“May I use your crossing Mr. Shanks?” Doc Walker inquired in his most polite mannerly voice.

“That crossing has always been open to anyone from murders to millionaires and I suppose you fall in that group somewhere,” the old cowboy smiled softly.

“Well Henry, I’m close to being both at this very moment, so I thank you for letting me use your crossing and thank you for being my friend once upon a time,” Doc Walker announced with a wave of his large black hat before he turned his mount in the direction of the flood-stage Yellowstone River.

“Before I go, Mr. Ben Crane let me give you a good piece of advice. There are many trails for a young man to follow but if you’re smart you will follow the tracks of Henry Shanks here, and not those of Elmer Doc Walker.” The outlaw stated in a fatherly tone as he inserted the Winchester 73 back into its saddle boot.

“Thank you sir, I will take your advice, now if you will take some from me, don’t....”

Henry Shanks interrupted the youth by shouting out his name, “Ben, you have work to do, besides it’s not polite to presume to tell grownups what to do.”

"Well, I'd better be going and you have hay to cut Henry. If my plans work out this will be the last time I'll have to use Shanks Crossing." The outlaw laughed then spurred his mount into a trot as they headed for the well-known crossing.

"But Mr. Shanks," Ben blurted out as he moved close to where his employer stood quietly watching the outlaw Doc Walker ride toward the bank of the Yellowstone River. "Shouldn't we tell him about the water level?" But the old rancher didn't respond. "I don't think a person could cross that river with a fresh horse let alone one in the shape of that black," the youth continued his desperate plea to warn Walker.

"That's his decision, he knows this crossing as well as anyone. I don't know why exactly but Doc's in big hurry and nothing we say will prevent his trying to cross."

"But shouldn't we try to stop him from drowning?"

"To tell you the honest truth Ben, I can't think of a better man to let drown in that river than Airless (Doc) Walker." Henry Shanks's voice never wavered as he condemned his old friend to near certain death. "Still we'd best walk on down there we might be able to save the horse," he declared turning to walk slowly to the river's edge.

As the pair moved hurriedly toward the riverbank they could clearly see Walker trying to force his balking mount into the raging debris-filled waters of the flooded river. The black horse, driven by sharp spurs and repeated lashings from the end of the long leather reins would enter the cold water up to its knees, then rear up and jump back to solid ground. This scene was repeated several times and each time Doc Walker's anger grew as did the amount of force he employed to drive the horse into the dangerous waters.

"This is one case where the horse is smarter than the rider," the old rancher quipped as he neared the riverbank. "Hell of a way to treat an animal," he added.

Then suddenly the abused, frustrated and frightened horse plunged far out into the rapids. Its powerful unexpected lunge nearly unseated the still flailing rider. Doc Walker's tormented mount's desperate dive into the river had caused them to land in deep water; water deep enough for both horse and rider to disappear completely beneath the turbulent surface. The black mare slowly rose to the surface with Doc Walker clinging tenaciously to the saddle horn.

"Hold onto your horse or grab one of those tree limbs Mr. Walker!" Young Crane shouted out through cupped hands. "This way, swim this way and I'll try to reach you," he added, but the current caught Walker and pulled him under and carried him downstream.

"Help, for God's sake help me!" The outlaw cried out as he broke into the air once more, his arms slapped the water erratically one second then flailed about in the air the next. It was obvious to both of the men on the bank that Doc Walker had lost control of his mental faculties and would be lost without an intervening miracle. However the powers that dispense lifesaving miracles denied Doc Walker his last panicked plea for clemency.

The spry youthful Ben Crane ran down the riverbank shouting encouragement while staying abreast with Walker's movements. Henry Shanks moved at a slower pace than his hired man because he had little desire to aid his old antagonist, but the excitement of the moment swept him along in anticipation of the climax.

Once more the swirling waters closed over the bad man's head causing Ben to believe the famous Doc Walker had met his end. The youth stopped near the water's edge trying to peer through the floating debris into the engulfing flood for any sign of the man.

"I think he's dead!" The youth shouted excitedly to Henry Shanks when the old cowboy finally caught up. "He went under right there!" the youth indicated, pointing to a large swirling eddy, which like a tornado in the water was pulling everything caught in its powerful vortex down to the bottom of the river bed.

"There he is!" Henry Shanks yelled out as the desperado's hatless head shot above the punishing current.

Doc Walker, who continued to struggle, was obviously nearing his physical limits for he had stopped calling for help and his arm movements were restricted to feeble splashing actions. The undeniable current had spun the hapless victim to face downstream. Doc could see what lay ahead but not what was coming from behind. Being so disorientated prevented the well-known scoundrel from seeing a large Cottonwood tree that was catching up from behind.

Ben Crane had taken up his escort duties as he ran full tilt down the riverbank hoping to prevent the inevitable disaster. As the youth ran head long downstream his feet splashed through the cold over flowing river water, a fact his overwrought brain failed to register.

"Look out for the snag coming up behind you!" Ben shouted out with all his might just as his heavy wet boots became entangled with a submerged tree root that caused him to fall face-down in the water. Ben scrambled to regain his feet in time to see the root end of the tall Cottonwood tree collide with the back of Doc Walker's head.

The impact between log and outlaw was tremendous and from his vantage point Ben saw Walker's head snap violently backwards then disappear below the river's choppy surface. The runaway log traveled only a short distance before its large root-ball caught on some submerged obstacle, hesitated briefly and turned end for end. The large leafy top branches swung towards the shoreline where they caught on a large rocky outcropping. Once the mighty tree trunk lay across the current, the immense force of the cascading water began to crack and break away the smaller limbs which allowed the top of the Cottonwood tree to pass the still trapped roots. All this massive water pressure dislodged the roots from their entanglement, driving them toward the bank where they too became trapped against the rocks. But not a trace of Doc Walker had come into view since the man and tree collided just minutes before.

"I'd say he's finished son," Henry Shanks admitted as the pair stood side by side staring at the Cottonwood tree's massive root-ball. "I haven't seen him surface anywhere downstream and if he's caught under that tree he doesn't have a chance."

"Yes sir, I'm sure you're right. It's just that I hate to give up on a human life," Ben replied softly.

"I'll help you look for him but the strong current could wash a body a long ways downstream before it surfaces or gets snagged on anything," the river-wise old man stated in an explanatory manner.

"I know but I just have to give it a try."

The Cottonwood tree with its roots trapped by the rock ledge made an impromptu dam that the torrent of flood waters battered and pounded trying to drive it along the river's winding course. The powerful maddened flood waters struck the massive Cottonwood tree's rough bark trunk like a ramming steam locomotive then slipped under the blockage to make way for another fluid attack. The struggle raged on for several minutes until the inevitable happened, a resounding crack indicated a large limb had given way which weakened the trees foothold on the river bed. This warning sound was quickly followed by what can be best described as an explosion when a massive limb succumbed to one of nature's most powerful forces, that being irrepressible water. Next the tree emitted a loud groan as it began to spin like a waterwheel on its center axis in a slow counter clockwise direction. The two men watched in amazement as the tangled knurled roots rotated like a wheel lifting rocks and silt as well as the limp body of Doc Walker. His battered lifeless body had become ensnared by the grasping fingers of the tree's many flexible, yet strong roots.

"Careful, watch yourself, don't get hooked by one of those roots," the old cowboy warned in futility, being unable to prevent his young friend from diving into the raging current to recover the slowly moving body, a body that was not only moving up but away from the bank as the waters of the Yellowstone River were, once more, victorious over an immovable foe.

Ben Crane's initial frantic jump from the bank had propelled his body to a position where his left hand could grasp one of the longer and stronger lower roots. He fought to gain a handhold with his right hand, but the current slammed the left side of his body against the root-ball before trying to sweep him under the tree. The battle of wills raged on and it seemed the human's muscles would tire long before the relentless strength of the inexhaustible will of nature, but a sudden surge of willpower energized Ben's youthful muscles, driving him to make one last desperate lunge. His right hand was thrown upward and to the right where it contacted the tree's large center tap root. His right hand clamped around the slick wet piece of wood with a death grip that even Mother Nature could not break.

"Hang on Ben!" Shanks called out. "You're headed out into the main channel!" he added before turning to hurry back upstream where Doc Walker's black mare stood, head sagging nearly to the ground in a state of total exhaustion from its brief struggle in the river. The dripping wet mare appeared near the point of collapsing but Henry Shanks, the wise old animal man that he was, spoke softly and moved slowly as he approached the strange horse. Although the horse trembled from exhaustion and fear it still had enough stamina to shy away from the old cowboy, and a foot race was the last thing Henry Shanks wanted at this point.

"Easy girl," the old cowboy whispered, his right hand extending from his waist as a sign he meant no harm. "Easy now, don't be afraid. I need your help and all you have to do is stand still until I get the rope off your saddle," he whispered confidently as he watched the mare for any signs of resistance. The battered horse found some soothing solace in the man's voice and remained sure-footed as the old cowboy patted her neck and stroked her wet matted mane. "All I want from you is this rope," he explained gently, untying the slippery wet leather thong that held the hemp rope to the saddle.

With the rough rope coiled in his hand, Henry Shanks turned to run downstream as fast as his aged legs and over worked lungs would permit. The Cottonwood log carrying Ben and Doc Walker's body had fallen into the unrelenting grip of the Yellowstone River's destructive flood waters. The very act of catching the speeding tree and trapped men presented a Herculean task that the weary

Shanks immediately recognized as impossible. The black mare might be the answer, but not an easy one so the decision was quickly made to run on in the hopes some miracle would intervene and Ben Crane would not perish in the frigid mountain runoff.

The water propelled log had now passed the boundary line of the R-R Ranch's alfalfa field which made travel along the uncleared riverbank even more difficult. But Henry Shanks reached somewhere down deep to tap an unknown well of strength that compelled him to save young Ben Crane's life even at the peril of his own. It was with renewed vigor the old man leaned into the near futile race, he jumped small trees and gracefully hurdled over piles of rocks and brush. It was clear to see he had narrowed the gap between the runaway log and himself, however that sudden spurt of energy was fading and if something didn't happen soon all would be lost.

The old cowboy's leg muscles felt like rubber and his feet began to slap the ground uncontrollably with each step. He stumbled slightly once, managed to recover only to trip on a small round rock, this time nearly falling to the ground. "Jump Ben!" Shanks ordered realizing no matter how much he desired to pull his young friend from the log, his aging body would not respond to these heavy demands.

Just when the rescue seemed the most likely to fail, a large fork half way up the Cottonwood tree's trunk straddled a large submerged boulder. The impact combined with the current turned the roots toward the rock strewn riverbank. Shanks knew that

Ben would be within throwing range of the bank for only a second or so, just possibly enough time to make one desperate toss of the golden hemp lifeline.

Henry Shanks forced his numb legs to take several more halting steps while willing his burning lungs to take at least a few more breaths. His mouth opened wide as he tried to cry out Ben's name but nothing escaped his lips, darkness cloaked his vision which was accompanied by an indescribable pain in his chest and the old cowboy feared the grim reaper would pay him a call before the lariat could be thrown, but death and Henry Shanks were old acquaintances; an acquaintance he had defeated before and fully intended to overcome once more. The tough old frontiersman shook his head, then with polished professionalism spun out a big loop in the end of the lariat, made one fast spin overhead before casting the lifeline at Ben Crane.

The spinning rope whistled as it raced through the air on its errand of mercy. Shanks's left hand played out all but the very last six inches of the coiled rope as the loop miraculously landed around a large root just above Ben's head. The hemp loop instantly cinched down around the root, snapping the rope rigid as the tree resumed its race downstream. The stunned Henry Shanks managed to grasp the tail end of the rope with both hands an instant before being yanked off his feet. He so feared losing his grip on the end of the lariat that he broke one of the first rules of cowboy life, to never allow a rope to coil or wrap around your body. However, realizing that his strength was gone and fearing he might die at any moment, it was sheer desperation which drove the old cowboy to throw a half hitch around his left wrist.

The two rope loops around his wrist pulled tight cutting off the flow of blood to his hand. Understandably excruciating pain from the rope digging into his wrist was more than he could withstand. The old cowboy fainted from the exertion and pain only to be awakened by the shock of his head striking a solid object. The impact to the old cowboys head was a glancing blow that tore his hat from his head and turned him briefly crosswise to his path. Shanks suddenly had an unrestricted view of the riverbank ahead, a view that disclosed scores of small rocks plus the usual tree limbs and trash from previous floods. The stunned and exhausted brain ordered his bleary eyes to focus on a large round object lying about twenty yards straight ahead. Could it be a rock, no it's a boulder, a big boulder. Shanks's brain screamed out in hope and desperation. He knew without thinking this would be his and Ben's last chance to survive their battle with the Yellowstone River and the runaway Cottonwood tree. There wasn't any time to think or form a plan of action. Whatever happened now would be driven by instinct and years of surviving in the wild.

Ignoring the pain, not to mention the distinct possibility that placing more pressure on the rope coiled around his left wrist might sever his hand from his arm, the old cowboy pulled back hard on the rope while planting the heels of his boots into the rocky bank. A scream of pain accompanied the valiant effort, a sound which filled his ears and stimulated his brain to fight even harder than before.

With both feet under him, Shanks pulled on the rope with his right hand which threw his body into a position where he had to either run or fall face first once more. Henry Shanks mustered up sufficient strength to take one long step then another and before he knew what had happened the old cowboy was running headlong in the direction of the huge boulder. Tripping and stumbling he managed to outrun the now slack rope reaching the boulder in time to run around its circumference, falling flat on his face on the upstream side. He watched, mesmerized as the rope slithered, hissed and skipped across the rough rock covered bank, his brain in high anticipation of the point where the tethered lariat would snap taught.

The Cottonwood tree with its two passengers raced onward, propelled by the river's angry current until the lariat which was looped around the tree roots on one end and coiled around a huge boulder on the other gave off a sound like the crack of a rifle shot. It instantly became straight as a tempered steel rod. The enormous energy given off by the rope's change of state from limp to rigid threw small rocks and debris in every direction, driving Henry Shanks to take refuge at the boulders indented base.

"Please God let that rope hold," the old cowboy prayed openly before rising from his sanctuary to examine his hand work. "Thank you Lord," he added, watching in amazement as the hemp rope danced and sang in protest to the tremendous abnormal pressure being exerted on the long piece of braided plant fiber. Pleased that the Cottonwood trees downriver race had been restricted for the time being, the old cowboy rose to his knees, anxious to remove the rope's cutting loops from his painful wrist. This was the first time he noticed the cuff of his long sleeved shirt was shredded and soaked with bright red blood. But it was no great discovery to learn the thick life giving fluid ran down the old cowboy's hand and dripped steadily off his fingertips. The act of releasing the lariat's constricting pressure from Shanks's wrist led to increased blood loss, as well as an intense pain that shot up his arm coming to a sudden stop in his arm pit. Henry Shanks pulled the red bandana from around his neck and wrapped it firmly around the pulsating wound, for there wasn't any time to think of personal discomfort at this point.

The old cowboy tapped into a renewed strength that came from the pride he received in conquering the massive runaway tree and its deadly accomplice the mighty Yellowstone River. He ran to the bucking taut lariat and grasp it firmly with his good right hand. The rope would serve as a guide and crutch leading the old man from the boulder to the base of the tree and Ben Crane.

Now tethered hard to the riverbank and incessantly battered by flood waters the Cottonwood tree riled against the flimsy restraint accorded by the half inch lariat. Still its tightly woven fibers held firm against the onslaught of violent jerks and snaps that tend to fray a rope to the breaking point.

"Get ready to jump Ben!" Henry Shanks called out as he raced towards the lunging mass of roots. But the youth refused to jump to safety, instead he grasped Doc Walker's remains by his heavy leather gun belt. He hung on desperately with his left hand while straining to hoist the dead outlaws body out of the entangling roots with his right. Struggle as he might, the stout young man could not drag the limp body free of the imprisoning tentacles. Finally, without serious study on the results of his actions, Ben Crane braced his feet against the tree roots, grasped the gun belt with both hands and threw himself up and backward. Ben's extra effort broke the cadaver free of its captive state, propelling it straight at the youth's upper torso and their bodies collided with a resounding thud. The momentum combined with the extra weight drove the youth off his feet and the pair toppled backwards into the thrashing waters.

Henry Shanks watched in fear and disbelief as Ben fell backwards into the water with Walker's dead body across his chest, both sinking immediately to the rocky river bottom. The old cowboy lunged forward in a valiant attempt to grab hold of the pair but made only momentary contact with Ben's disappearing arm.

"Ben Crane!" The high pitched scream came from Henry Shanks, but the old cowboy did not recognize his own voice as it echoed across the river valley. "Ben Crane!" The second call was low and plaintive as if the youth had already met his fate. The last call had no more than passed Shanks lips before the old cowboy jumped feet first into the fray. He had not stopped to consider his own safety, his exhausted condition, nor his injured left hand. It was time to act, regardless of the consequences and act he did. Shanks landed feet first in the river with his back to the roots facing upriver. He hoped by taking up this position he might prevent Ben from being swept beneath the tree trunk where he would become trapped and quickly drown.

Henry Shanks's left hand had been badly damaged by the rope wrapped around his wrist and was now ineffectual; the shearing pain drove him to hold the shattered appendage folded across his stomach. The old cowboy's right hand was instantly deployed to grasp the straining lariat, which now passed just over his head; the popping and heaving rope served to keep Shanks from being washed away. The powerful current pinned the old cowboy against the slowly deteriorating root-ball as the rocky dirt melted away, disappearing into the passing water. This violent washing action caused more and larger roots to appear. The old cowboy cursed aloud, which was completely out of character for the man, but losing the use of his left arm prevented him from searching for the men in the water. Then a plan formed out of desperation drove Shanks to turn his injured arm to the left where the bandana-wrapped hand became entangled with one of the larger and newly exposed roots.

The old cowboy gritted his teeth against the blinding pain that began in his wrist and radiated up the arm past his shoulder finally terminating in his chest cavity. The words heart attack flashed through Shanks's brain but there was no time to think of what might be, only what could be. He yanked on his arm twice to make certain the bandana would hold some pressure, then quickly lowered his body up to his neck into the rolling surface.

Henry Shanks thrust his right hand straight down into the frigid water but was unable to touch the rocky bottom where he had hoped to find Ben Crane. Finding it necessary to dive below the churning surface, he inhaled deeply just as something slammed against his legs. That was all the motivation the old cowboy needed to dive into the raging dark abyss. This time his right hand came in contact with something manmade; it felt like leather and metal. His powerful hand seized the object, then began to wrench upward against the pressure of the intense current.

The old cowboy jerked and strained on what he assumed was Doc Walker's gun belt, but his best efforts were rewarded with only slight movement of the heavy weight. Precious time was wasting away and the old cowboy knew he must bring Ben Crane to the surface in the next few seconds if his life were to be spared. There remained in Shanks weary and battered brain, only one chance to prevent his young friend from drowning and that would require the use of his injured left arm. No counter arguments were brought forth; no debate was presented, just the act of Henry Shanks allowing his damaged hand to slide through the bloody red bandana, leaving it still entwined in the ball of roots. It was not necessary for Shanks to swim below the river's broiling surface for as soon as his anchoring left hand was free, the powerful undertow sucked him straight to the bottom. There was no fighting the rolling undertow, which relentlessly fought to cram the old man's body underneath the downstream Cottonwood tree. He fought wildly, both arms and legs searched in desperation for any hand or foothold that would prevent his being drug into the waiting death trap.

Shanks's flailing arms and legs windmilled with the fast moving turbid water which prevented his seeing or purposely touching anything, especially Walker's leather gun belt. Try as he might the old cowboy was only able to remain in place a short time, his strength was quickly waning as his oxygen starved muscles failed to obey his brain's directions. The old cowboy sank lower and lower as he weakened and the irrepressible current drove on and on. He knew that once swept beneath the tree's massive trunk his limbs would become hopelessly entangled with the myriad of tree limbs beyond and drowning was his inevitable fate. The end was near as the old cowboy felt his resistance fade while his body slid slowly down between the riverbank and the root-ball.

"Surrender!" his tormented brain screamed. "Surrender," his brain whispered. "You fought a good fight now it's time to rest." Henry Shanks's entire body went limp as he recognized the end was near. He allowed the rushing waters to take complete control of his body. Henry Shanks was near death, his body began to shut down, his brain filled with a grey fog but the last breath of air remained in his aged lungs. Those heavily exercised lungs were now beyond the incendiary state, they now merely hurt and even that sense was fading quickly. The man's faithful but tired old heart beat slowly, if only sporadically on.

The old cowboy was now face down, drifting downstream just inches off the rocky river bottom, his next stop death's door. A sharp distant pain slipped by the morass of indifference that his brain process had become, his dulled senses now relayed infrequent messages of danger or pain. Still something sharp was stabbing at his chest and stomach, something that imparted a familiar and repeated pattern of pain, then nothing, then pain once more.

Henry Shanks' right hand shot out in a primeval reaction, one intended to stop the discomfort on his chest, and instead it drew sharp pain to the palm of his hand. It was indeed the unpleasant contact that stimulated the old cowboy's mental process for one quick instant, just long enough to signal the strong right hand to engulf the offending object. That wicked pointed object that had raked so unmercifully down the old cowboy's chest and stimulated his brain was the cruel rowels on Doc Walker's spurs. The tips of the star shaped rowels were intended to punish animal flesh and indeed they had punished the flesh of Henry Shanks.

Years of hard labor had forged the old cowboy's muscles to a steel-like consistency and now that metal band had formed a death grip around the dead man's spur. The combined mass of the two men's bodies had increased resistance to the water's flow providing more lift while raising Walker's body off the river bottom. Both Shanks and Walker were swept around the grounded root-ball into the waiting arms of the Cottonwood tree's out stretched limbs.

Ben Crane who had been trapped on the river bottom beneath the dead outlaw's body, bobbed to the surface once the massive weight had been removed. He had been accidentally freed from a watery grave by the old cowboy's unconscious actions.

The youth's head erupted through the frothy river surface into the clean life-giving air, his mouth wide open, arms flaying about for any source of support. He gulped in the sweet air, choked, spit and sputtered before attempting to suck in more air. This was one of the most difficult fights of his young life, a struggle Ben Crane was determined to win. The river's hurried flow slammed the breathless youth against the root-ball, which would have normally knocked the wind from his body but in this instant the force of the impact expelled the water that was blocking his airway and preventing normal respiration. The youths choking and spitting up river water continued for a full minute while at the same time his hands clawed at the slick muddy root-ball in order to keep his head above the current. Crane waged a desperate struggle against impending death until his eyes fell on the taunt lariat just an arm's length above his head. The youth understood he would have but one chance to propel his body high enough to grasp the rope and pull himself to safety, a miss for any reason would spell disaster.

Young Ben Crane realized there was a pulse to the pounding current that swept everything in its path below the root-ball. A surging wall of water would engulf Ben with such intensity that it would nearly drive him under but then the pressure would slacken for just an instant before striking once again. He knew he must time his attempt to grab the overhead rope with that slight lull in the plunging water.

The struggle with the river and being deprived of oxygen for several minutes had left the youth in a weakened state, still remaining in his current position was taxing his strength even more. He must take the chance immediately, so without any more deliberation Ben counted one, two, three and jumped. His timing with the ebb and flow of the current had been perfect as his right hand snagged the rigid rope. His left hand followed with a good grip on the elusive hemp line but his feet still dangled in the water, the currents pressure still trying to pull the young man back into its cold wet grasp. A second lunge brought Ben's feet free of the current as he swung upward he managed to hook his heels over the lariat.

Ben's wet weary muscles throbbed from the strain of inching hand-over-hand along the rough rope that led to the riverbank and safety. His legs were the first to slip off the lariat then in utter exhaustion his left hand relinquished its grip which shifted all his body weight onto the right. The youth hung on for several seconds suspended by one hand just above the waterline on the rock strewn riverbank. All of his reserve strength was gone, there was nothing left to do but command his right hand to release its death grip on the rope and fall to the ground. Ben whispered a quick prayer asking God to allow him to fall on solid ground and spare his life.

The taut rope twanged like a bow string when it suddenly separated from Ben Crane's weight. His limp body fell to the ground in one large heap that was accompanied by a resounding thud as well as a loud groan. The ground, although covered by two inches of water was indeed solid without any current to fight.

"Thank you God," Ben said aloud as he rolled onto his back and straighten out his legs. "Without your help I would have certainly died down there at the bottom of the river," he added in a weak breathless voice. But God didn't answered, the only sound filling the young man's ears was the splashing of the river water against the large Cottonwood tree. It was a soothing lullaby that enticed the completely fatigued youth to pass out for an unknown period of time. A violent case of the shivers raced through Ben's cold wet body. The convulsive muscle action snapped his brain back to reality and drove him to regain his feet.

The young man slapped at the cramped muscles of his upper legs and lower torso that were preventing him from walking to a higher and drier place on the riverbank, but he soon discovered that hobbling about, as painful as the action was, brought the most relief from his discomforts. As the pain induced fog cleared from his brain, several question began to form, but the most pressing of these was, *"where was Mr. Shanks?"* The more his thoughts cleared, the more the question of Henry Shanks burned into his conscious thinking. He managed to stand erect, place a cupped hand to his mouth and call out the old rancher's name.

"Mr. Shanks!" the words reverberated up and down the defiant river but there wasn't any reply. "Mr. Shanks!" the youth called out once more as he began to painfully hobble down the riverbank in the direction of the floating Cottonwood tree. "Mr. Shanks!" Ben called again as he limped past the tree's root-ball which had held all three men captive only a short time before. "Mr. Shanks!" he cried repeatedly, but his voice tapered off as his eyes fell on the old man's upper torso, still clad in his blue work shirt draped over one of the large lower limbs of the massive Cottonwood tree.

The sight of his old friend in such distress brought the young man to a complete stop. He watched intently for any signs of life from a distance of roughly fifty feet, finding it emotionally, as well as physically difficult to approach any nearer. Ben knew that the only way to ascertain the man's condition would require his moving farther down the riverbank plus wading through the rivers current again. He dreaded the thought of ever entering fast flowing water again after being trapped on the river bottom by Doc Walkers body. Still he was obligated to inspect the old man's body with the thought of recovering the remains. How could he ever explain that Mr. Shanks' body had been lost downstream while laying on top of a floating Cottonwood tree? No, this was a task he must bear, which was formed in friendship. It was what Mr. Shanks would do if the tables were turned and he lay dead on a log in the river.

"I must be strong," Ben Crane told himself as he began the torturous walk down the riverbank. His

every step induced pain, every breath came raw and raspy; it was the longest fifty feet the young man had ever traversed. He noticed by the trash stranded along the riverbank that the water level had begun to drop, however he also realized the few inches of fall would be of little help on his mission.

Henry Shanks' body lay face down, stretched out across the tree limb as if he were laying over a barrel. From the riverbank the old man appeared to be dead, there was no movement of his extremities nor any signs of respiration. Ben Crane shook his head trying to summons up enough courage to enter the turbulent river water once more. He turned his face to the heavens for strength but he remained silent, no prayer was forth coming, no request for divine guidance. The young man knew that bracing the deadly waters was a challenge he must face alone.

One painful step brought him to the ever moving water's edge, the next step planted his foot in the swirling water up above his ankle. Now with both feet in the water, it seemed easier to continue his trek to the tree trunk which bobbed up and down some twenty feet from the bank. That would be a long threat-filled twenty feet for it was impossible to know what hazards might lay below the rivers rampaging surface. Two more steps found Ben up to his arm pits in cold rushing river water and he was still ten feet from his objective. This was the breaking point for the nervous youth; if he remained stationary the current would surely wash him downstream and if he attempted one more step the water would be over his head forcing him to swim. He inhaled deeply then using all his strength, pushed off the bottom with his feet. The powerful lunge shot Ben halfway across the narrow track of water but without any footing he immediately sank like a lead weight below the surface of the Yellowstone River.

Natural instinct directed Ben to throw both of his hands out in front of his body in hopes of snagging a tree limb or some other solid object that might serve as an anchor, preventing him from being washed downstream. The youth's right hand fell on the familiar large leaves of the Cottonwood tree, while his left hand fell on wet cloth. Once again natural instinct came into play as both hands eagerly grasped at what they had discovered, the fingers of his right hand engulfed a clump of leaves and small branches which would hold him stationary for a few seconds. The left grappled with the wet fabric that encased Henry Shanks' left leg. On the first attempt the young man's strong finger tips merely slipped across the slick cotton material used in manufacturing common western work pants. However on his second try the left hand blindly grasped the seam on the bottom of the left pant leg cuff; here was a real hand hold.

Ben wadded up a ball of the material and gently began to pull himself across the narrow stretch of water, his head finally breaking the surface as it came in contact with his old friends leg. He released his right handhold on the fragile tree branches, then extended it over head to find a more solid handhold on Henry Shanks' belt.

Once his right hand had a firm grip on the belt, Ben's left hand released the pant leg and thrust it out of the water to find a solid anchorage among the many small branches of the Cottonwood tree. It was in this hand-over-hand manner that the battered Ben Crane managed to haul his exhausted body out of the water. He lay breathlessly draped over the rough bark of the tree trunk just inches from Henry Shanks' body. The idea of looking at, let alone touching his old friend's body was more than the youth's brain could handle at the moment. He took long deliberate breaths while his eyes remained focused on the wild water's action as it rushed by the side of the tree. A few minutes rest and the discomfort of laying on the Cottonwood tree's harsh bark drove the young man to roll onto his side to face the inevitable.

The youth suspended his hand over the old cowboy's body but hesitated, unable to actually make contact with any part of the cadaver. "This has been one hell of a day," Ben said to himself in a louder than normal voice.

THE SURPRISE

"Er, what?" came a low faint reply from Henry Shanks' mouth that was partially hidden by his arm.

Those completely unexpected words from a dead man caused Ben Crane to rear back in shock. "My God you're alive!" he exclaimed in a shrill voice.

"Yeah," Shanks responded, "but I can't take much more of this day."

"My God, I can't believe you're alive!" the youth cried out once more. "I mean, how did you ever come through that underwater maze of tree limbs and trash?"

"I just held my breath as long as I could, then passed out I guess. I came to laying on this log, then of course, I blacked out again. You started talking and woke me up," the old cowboy stated as if in a daze. "How did you make it through?" he asked with a loud groan as he tried to move his badly abused body.

"I pulled Walker's body off the root-ball and it landed on me and the dead weight drove us clear to the bottom. He sure is heavy 'cause I couldn't get out from under him until all of a sudden something ripped him away and I popped to the surface."

"I think I pulled Doc's body off of you as I was trying to save myself from being washed under the tree," Shanks admitted with a shake of his shaggy wet head.

"I don't know what happened, but thank you Mr. Shanks, and thank you God for sparing our lives," Ben stated, still in shock at what had transpired in the first few hours of the morning.

The two men, both of whom were completely spent physically and mentally, lay quietly in the warm morning sun trying to recuperate their faculties. A silent half hour passed as clean fresh air filled their lungs and rejuvenated their muscles. "It's time we move on," Henry Shanks announced as he sat up on the tree trunk. "I have a feeling that this day ain't over yet," he added belatedly.

"Where do you suppose Doc Walker's body is now?" Ben inquired somberly while looking all around the area.

"Don't know, reckon he was washed on downstream, may never see him again," Shanks replied grimly, then paused to point at what appeared to be a booted foot sticking out of the water. A soggy brown leather boot as well as some of the bad man's leg could be seen poking through some small limbs near the top of the tree.

"I don't recall what the man wore for boots, but I guess his foot would be the only one sticking out of this here tree," Ben deduced quickly. "I suppose we should drag him out of there but I ain't sure just how to go about it without drowning," the youth added, trying to work his way further up the tree's trunk. After a couple of bouts with the river, Crane was showing a mature respect for the power of running water.

"Yeah," Shanks agreed then paused, "I would like to recover Doc's body, been too many people buried by this river," he added mournfully.

"Your banged up hand will keep you from being much help, but I'm willing to give it a try if you tell me what to do," Ben announced reluctantly.

"All right, but remember this, pulling his remains out of this river ain't worth dying for, so don't take any more chances like you did before!" Henry Shanks ordered his young hired man. "As for getting him to the bank, I'd like to have the water do the work for us, but I'm afraid we'd lose him. It might be awhile before the water level drops enough and it could be the rope holding this whole shebang in place might break and he'd go right along with it," the old cowboy stated flatly as if he had been studying the problem for some time. "The way I see it, we must wade into the water and try to untangle his body from the tree limbs. It could be a tricky move and if the rope should break we most likely will be caught up in the branches and washed downstream. What do you think?" the old cowboy asked doubtfully.

"Like I said before, I'll do whatever you want Mr. Shanks," Ben reiterated.

"Good, you're young and spry so why don't you try to work your way up the trunk while I use the rope to reach the bank," Henry Shanks said with a weary smile.

As directed Ben started to inch his way up the tree trunk by using the small limbs as hand and foot holds. The old cowboy on the other hand moved in the opposite direction down the trunk to the root-ball and the end of the lariat. He clamored over the muddy roots until he finally reached the ropes end. His mangled left hand would be useless trying to hand-over-hand the rope to the bank, so he dangled by his left elbow and boot heels while his right hand did all the pulling. It was, of course, a very slow and painful maneuver but hard-headed stubbornness and perseverance saw the old man through.

Both men converged on Doc Walker's visible foot, Ben in the tree branches while Henry Shanks hobbled along the riverbank. "Do you think you can reach him?" Shanks called out as he began to wade into the river.

"Yes sir, I can see his arm and head," the youth replied, pointing into the rolling water. "I'll try to grab hold of his arm then maybe I can pull him towards you." Ben Crane's voice was filled with apprehension remembering his earlier near-death experience with the river, but he had committed to recovering the bandits remains and that's what he fully intended to do. The determined youth realized after a bit of probing with his left foot, he could stand on the same submerged limb that held Walker's foot in place. He inched closer and closer to the protruding boot but no matter how hard he stretched, his goal remained just an inch or so out of reach. "I'll have to get into the river if I hope to get ahold of him," the youth called out to Henry Shanks.

"You're taking a terrible risk Ben, I say it ain't worth it," the old cowboy argued. "Maybe we can find another way," he added trying to persuade Ben to reconsider his actions.

"I think I can make it if you can wade in a couple of feet, I'll free his leg, which I hope will spin him in your direction. Are you ready Mr. Shanks?" Ben inquired bravely as he began lowering himself into the swirling water.

Saving his waning energy for the battle ahead the old cowboy didn't reply, instead he stepped cautiously into the river's powerful current, a current so strong that it might sweep both men to their death.

The rushing water pushed Ben along as he made a desperate bid to free Walker's body from the imprisoning Cottonwood tree. Holding his breath, the youth sank beneath the river's writhing surface only to be slammed against the dead man's body before being forced into the same forked limb that had snagged Doc's boot. The youth thrashed and fought like a hooked fish with every ounce of his remaining strength to dislodge the impinged boot. He pulled on the man's ankle and knee while twisting the appendage in every direction with no effect; but just as Ben's lungs were ready to burst, the bad man's sockless foot dropped out of his boot. Doc Walker's body suddenly rose up and twisted toward the riverbank, his right arm broke the surface just before striking Henry Shanks' leg.

The sudden impact shocked the old man into action causing him to grasp Walker's right hand with his own good right hand. The old cowboy pulled and tugged on the cold dead hand but with only one arm, was unable to move the body; in fact just preventing it from being washed down stream became a concerted effort.

Ben Crane, intent on survival, would not be denied life so he clawed and splashed his way through three feet of dark water finally emerging in the clean sweet Montana air. But the struggle continued on as the youth fought to extract himself from the ever surging current. He flailed about until his hand made contact with a large submerged branch jutting straight out from the tree's trunk ending near the water's edge. The tremendous water pressure pinned the young man's body against the Cottonwood tree's course bark that tore at his flesh as he slid slowly down the limb towards the riverbank. Trying to shinny along the branch proved to be not only exhausting but also painful, still Ben persevered until reaching a point where the limb became brushy and covered with numerous leaves. The slender twigs would no longer support his weight, submitting him to the whims of the waters flow.

Ben was only a couple of feet from solid ground and safety, so close yet so far away. The youth was nothing if not stubborn and strong, unwilling to give up and perish. He summonsed together all of his determination before launching his body into the air, much as a fish breaches the surface of the water in an attempt to dislodge a fisherman's hook from its mouth.

Henry Shanks, while still struggling to land Walker's body, had silently witnessed Ben's heroic attempt at traversing the submerged limb, not to mention his unprecedented flight through the air, but it was clear to the old cowboy that the valiant endeavor would come up a bit short of its intended goal. Without a thought for his own safety, the old cowboy spun sideways until he faced the water and extended his left leg. Both men were at the end of their endurance, but it was clearly a live or die proposition for both young and old. The timing was nearly perfect as Ben extended his arms over his head while Henry Shanks kicked his leg out far enough to make contact with the youths searching hands.

Ben Crane's hands automatically closed around the old cowboy's leg like a sprung steel trap would snap shut on a varmint's leg. The results however were predictable as Ben's body collided with the off-balance old cowboy's leg, causing both men to plunge into the shallower but still surging water. Henry Shanks' right hand held fast to Doc Walker's right hand while both of Ben Crane's hands fought to get a better purchase on the old cowboy's leg. The three bodies were like a human chain flexing back and forth in response to the wild current.

Ben forced his head above the surface long enough to realize he was being swept in the direction of the riverbank; at that point he planted both feet on the bottom and once again jumped towards shore. He landed hard, his knees slammed painfully against the rocky bottom but without thinking he repeated the powerful lunge, which rocketed high in the air a split second before splashing down face first on a small boulder that was above the river's surface.

Ben Crane's upper body gave off a resounding thud when it landed on the exposed rock but through the pain and cold the youth managed to maintain a grip on the old cowboy's leg. It was an unconscious reaction, which triggered the youth to wrap one arm around the boulder and at the same time began to pull Shanks' leg and body closer to his position. It was a herculean effort on Ben's part as he strained every fiber of his being to retrieve Henry Shanks and Doc Walker's body from the grasp of the Yellowstone River.

Henry Shanks, now being nearly torn apart by the dead weight of Walker's remains on his right arm and the constant pressure of young Crane pulling on his left leg, made keeping his head above water all the more difficult. Stubbornness being a common trait among pioneering people, the old cowboy refused to release his grasp on Walker while the thought of drowning was completely unacceptable to a man who had spent his youth on the great rivers of America.

"Grrr," the youth groaned out as if trying to cheer himself on in the struggle to land the heavy weight. Many words of profanity filled the youths mind but it was not in his nature to use bad language and he was certain Henry Shanks frowned on such behavior. Mother Crane professed that cussing indicated a person of low moral's, not to mention a weak intellect, still the hard words bounced around in his mind. The youth had heard many an old mule skinner, as well as farmers and miners spew out long strings of hot fiery rant's that would make Satan himself blush.

"Damn it to hell!" young Crane blurted out in shocked surprise at his own weakness, he looked around at the old cowboy's still submerged head and prayed the rushing water had obscured the vile oath. He pulled once more before the thought entered his mind that for some reason the repulsive words seemed to make his impossible task possible.

"Damn!" Ben exclaimed at the top of his lungs as he threw his arm around Henry Shanks' waist and began to drag him to shore. The weight seemed horrific, but once Ben started for the safety of the riverbank, he refused to stop for any reason short of sudden death. Youth and good health favored Ben's success, while a childlike naivety prevented his realization that such exertion had killed or crippled many a lesser man. One more "Damn it!" inspired Crane to propel his upper body, as well as that of Henry Shanks clear of the rivers ever-moving water line.

THE RECOVERY

"My God," the old cowboy whispered as he looked all about, "Solid ground. I was beginning to think we'd never see solid ground again."

"I was having the same thought, but we're here now," Ben agreed. "But are you all right?" he inquired of his employer.

"I think so but I can't hang on to Doc's hand much longer."

"I'm sorry, I forgot you still had him in tow," the youth apologized while rising to his knees. He quickly separated the two men's hands, then began the long fight required to beach the outlaw's body. Ben groaned and tugged until the deceased's remains lay high enough on the riverbank to prevent the rushing water from reclaiming its victim. "I have heard men talk about moving dead weight," Ben declared, "but I had no idea of just what they meant until this very moment." With those words the completely exhausted Crane lay down beside his equally spent employer. The two men lay absolutely still for the better part of an hour while their bodies tried to regenerate and replenish their over-taxed muscles.

"It's getting close to noon," Ben Crane groaned out as he sat upright on the rocky riverbank. "I hate to disturb you Mr. Shanks, but I think we should take a look at your arm."

The old cowboy followed suit rolling onto his back before sitting up. "All right Ben," Henry Shanks agreed, "but I have been laying here thinking about what happened this morning. As I see it Doc was in a hurry, either running from the law or his partners. Take a close look at his body and tell me what you see," the old cowboy directed.

"I don't see anything," the young man began then paused in his assessment of the drowned outlaw's remains. Still weak and battered from his exposure to the river's might, Ben rolled onto his hands and knees before crawling the short distance to where Walker lay. He respectfully placed his hands on the dead man's chest and stomach before rearing back in surprise. "He's hard as a rock already," Ben announced.

"He ain't been dead long enough to get stiff, open up his duster and let's see just what we're dealing with," Shanks suggested, rather than ordered.

Ben shot his employer a questioning look, then without a word, leaned forward and began unbuttoning Walker's knee-length grey duster. He threw the soggy cotton duster open before shaking his head in disbelief. "He's wearing some kind of harness, lot of leather straps and canvas bags."

"What's in the bags?" Shanks inquired, but Ben was in the process of opening the flaps on the bags before the old cowboy could finish his question.

"Some metal blocks," Ben replied, holding one of the samples at eye level for a better inspection.

"Why that's gold boy, gold! You're holding part of a gold bar, most likely stolen in the mine robbery we were speaking of earlier. Looks to me like Doc chopped that bar into pieces to make traveling a bit easier," the old cow boy added. "Now you know why Doc drown so easily and why it's been so hard for you to drag his body around."

"I bet it was all this extra weight that pinned me to the river bottom!" Ben exclaimed, closely eyeing the chunk of precious metal.

"If I don't miss my guess, there's about fifty pounds of gold in each of those bags; one fourth of the 200 pound ingot those fella's made off with." Shanks grinned as Ben passed over the gold for his boss's closer inspection. "This is what dreams are made of or so they say." The old rancher's grin spread across his face becoming a wide smile.

"Every one of these canvas bags is filled with big hunks of gold!" Ben announced waving both of his gold-fill hands in the air. "We're rich!" the youth shouted out as he rose to his feet and began to dance around Walker's body.

"But it ain't ours Ben, it belongs to the mine owner," Shanks said in a calm easy matter-of-fact voice. "I know just how you feel, that much gold can change a man's outlook, especially a couple of poor men like us. But it ain't for us to keep, you'll make your own fortune someday Ben, if you earn it yourself you'll enjoy it more. If you keep this gold you may live good but you'll feel guilty all your life 'cause your folks raised you right."

Ben let his hands droop to his side before slowly wilting to the ground. "You're right Mr. Shanks, guess I was day dreaming about all the things I could buy for my family. I'm sorry for having such evil thoughts. Reckon I'm not any better than Doc Walker and his men," the youth's voice was filled with shame and recrimination.

"I've known the man for years and you're a far better person than Doc Walker ever was and don't you forget it," the old cowboy said plainly, as he casually tossed the gold sample back to Ben.

"And as far as money goes," Shanks continued, "I'm sure there will be some kind of reward for the return of the gold. As far as I'm concerned it's all yours; you did all the work hauling it to shore and nearly drown in the doing!" the old cowboy declared.

"That's not fair Mr. Shanks, I could never have done this without you," the youth argued with his friend's generosity.

"Let's not count our chickens before they're hatched, any number of things could happen before this gold is in the owners hands," Shanks warned. "Something tells me we should get back to the house so if you'll catch up Doc's horse we can load up his body."

Ben easily caught the thoroughly exhausted animal and led it in a large circle , which ended beside its master's lifeless body. The black mare took little note of the man's remains, showing little interest in running off. Henry Shanks showed his advanced age as he rose in a slow shaky motion to join Ben in loading the body. "Let's try to remove any extra weight, like the gold, guns and ammo or anything else that might prevent us from throwing Doc across his saddle. I don't want either one of us to bust a gut trying to get it loaded.

Following his employer's suggestion, the youth unloaded the remaining gold from the robber's home-made money belt before making a thorough search of Doc Walker's body. He removed the heavily used gun belt and revolver, a wad of green backs from a shirt pocket, a gold watch from one pants pocket, followed by a Remington Derringer from the other pocket. He also discovered a six inch sheath knife hanging from Walker's belt plus a smaller four inch blade that appeared from the top of his right boot.

"Looks like the man was ready for trouble!" Ben declared as he made a pile of Walker's belongings.

"Doc was always ready for trouble, or should I say he was always looking for it," the old cowboy hesitated for a second before adding, "in all fairness, trouble just seemed to find him, 'course he was never one to shy away from a bad situation," Shanks stated with a shake of his head.

"Let's see if we can stand Doc up and then boost him head first over the saddle," the old cowboy suggested. "All right here we go, one, two, three," Henry Shanks counted out loud as both men strained to lift the outlaw's remains high enough to fold over the saddle. "That did it, now we'd best use his belt to tie him on. I'd hate to have him fall off and we would have to load him up again. Once was enough," Shanks quipped as he watched Ben use the man's leather belt as a makeshift binding.

"Now let's see if we can put the gold back in his money belt and hang it from the saddle horn, that way we won't have to carry anything but ourselves," Shanks suggested. The two men managed to find a place for all of Walker's belongings including his water soaked Colt revolver.

"Do you think we should cut the lariat and let the tree float on away?" Ben inquired as he placed Doc's six inch belt knife in the man's saddle bags.

"We could, but I think we should save our strength just in case," the old cowboy advised. "You know, Doc never was much of a thief, but it seems he was a good judge of which rope to steal," he added, gathering up the black's hanging reins with his good right hand and turned towards home.

"Let me do that sir, you must be in enough pain with your hand so tore up," Crane offered pleasantly. "I think we should get you to Doctor Bacon's in Billings or at least to my mother; she has a real talent for doctoring."

"We'll see, but it's a long way to Doc Bacon's and I hate to trouble your mother with such a minor thing," Shanks politely refused the youth's offer of medical help. "Anyway, I have a feeling this ain't over yet and my predictions are usually right."

The two men, the old and the young walked one on either side of the black mare's head. Their pace more of a shuffle than a step, their conversation was nonexistent as is often the case between two men who just survived a very trying, near death experience. Words come hard to strong men, men who know deep inside they have accomplished the nearly impossible and that bragging of such is for small weak men.

Round stones and accumulated drift wood on the riverbank forced the men to step high to avoid tripping while traversing the riverbank. While high stepping is a natural task, their weary leg muscles refused to comply. Henry Shanks stumble first and nearly fell to one knee but reclaimed his footing with Ben's quick assistance. A few more steps and the black horse caught a right front hoof in a forked piece of drift wood which threw the trembling beast to its knees.

"I don't know about you Mr. Shanks, but I could use a rest and I think this animal could too," Ben suggested, not wishing to hurt the older man's feelings.

"I guess you're right, so let's stop up there, where my hayfield meets the riverbank. That river water was mighty cold, so let's sit in the sun on that log up ahead," the old cowboy pointed with his right hand at a large pine log, which lay just off the riverbank. "I have intended to cut this tree up for wood for the last six months, now I'm glad I didn't," Shanks chuckled slightly. The old cowboy found a place to sit on the nearly barkless tree trunk while Ben tied the mare's reins to an extended limb.

THE REVELATION

The midday sun warmed the pair and began to relieve their miseries. Feeling better Ben leaned back on the log. “I could run up to the house and bring back the team and wagon if you want,” the youth offered, wanting to be helpful without offending his boss.

“No thank you, if you remember the wagon axle is broken. Besides, I can make it to the house under my own power, but I wish you’d get Doc’s revolver and rifle off his saddle and give them a once over,” Shanks directed his young friend.

Ben Crane hurried to where the mare was tied, removed the soggy leather gun belt and rifle from the water-logged saddle scabbard. He pulled the Colt single action revolver from its holster, cocked the hammer back to the halfcocked position and opened the loading gate before extracting cartridges from each of the cylinders six chambers.

“Doc was ready for business with all six chambers loaded,” the rancher quipped.

"I don't know if these bullets will fire, they look awfully wet," Ben declared placing all six of the 44-40 cartridges plus the revolver on the log next to Henry Shanks. The youth then turned his attention to the Doc's lever action Winchester rifle, also chambered in 44-40. Throwing the weapons lever open, a live but wet cartridge was ejected high enough in the air that Ben managed to catch it in midflight. Drops of water rolled down the rifles steel lever ring and fell to the ground, which encouraged a tipping and through shaking of the weapon. The action threw water around like a wet dog shaking his rain-soaked coat. Ben began working the Winchesters lever in a very smooth but fast manner until he had ejected all of the remaining live rounds from the tubular magazine. "I'm not sure either one of these would fire even if we had dry cartridges," Crane announced with a sad shake of his head.

"It takes a lot to stop a Winchester," Henry Shanks replied with a knowing smile. "Look in the saddle bags, there might be some dry ammo in them," the old cowboy suggested in a kind gentle voice.

Ben leaned the Winchester against the log, then began searching the black's water-soaked saddle bags. The youth unbuckled the strap that held the leather bag closed, then blindly inserted his right hand. "Something bit me!" he cried out after jerking his hand from the bags interior. A trickle of bright red blood was already dripping from the end of his right thumb. After a cursory investigation Ben wiped the blood on the tail of his wet shirt. "Just looks like a small cut," he reported to Henry Shanks, before untying the leather thongs that secured the bags to the saddle. He carried them to a spot just in front of Shanks, then taking no further chances, proceeded to dump their contents on the ground.

All of the late Doc Walker's worldly procession tumbled to the ground in a jumbled pile for the two men to examine. A large sheath knife clattered against a large rock and an extra shirt soaked with river water plopped on top of the knife. A couple of vigorous shakes of the bags produced a soggy cardboard box of 44-40 cartridges, which broke open upon striking the ground. A straight edge razor landed squarely on top of the bullets, but it was the half dozen chunks of pure gold, which fell to the earth that caught both men's interest.

"Open the other bag," Shanks directed his young hired man.

"I'll bet that razor cut me," Ben stated as he lifted the flap on the second saddle bag and turned it bottom up. A limp deck of cards tumbled out, followed by a small worn Bible, then a small metal whiskey flask clattered to the ground. This odd assortment was followed by more irregularly cut pieces of solid gold. "Other than the stolen gold, it ain't much to show for a man's life," Ben nearly whispered. "but I'm not sure what to make of this extra gold."

"It's just what I was afraid of," Henry Shanks growled.

"I don't understand Mr. Shanks, you said he robbed some mine shipment," the youth questioned the older man's words.

"Yes, the four bandits stole a two hundred pound block of gold bullion from up around Helena, that's fifty pounds each. But I'd say Doc had over fifty pounds of gold on his body, probably not the full two hundred pounds, but all he could carry. That's why he drown so easily, and why he pinned you to the river bottom," Henry Shanks suggested.

"But why take so much?" Ben inquired.

"Gold!" Shanks replied. "Gold makes honest people greedy, and outlaws are naturally greedy. Doc just couldn't help himself," Shanks explained. "So the way I see it, this gold from his saddle bags belonged to one of his partners. My guess is Doc took his share of the loot and some from one or all of his accomplishes. I would also guess he was on the run, not only from the law, but from the other three men as well, and that's why he was in such a hurry. I don't think he would have tried to cross the river at full flood stage unless the Devil himself was on his trail," Shanks presented his theory of what had transpired.

"I see, then you think Doc's gang will be showing up here pretty soon and that's why you wanted to check out the guns." Ben turned a complete circle as he scanned the area near the river for he had quickly analyzed their position.

"You catch on quick Ben, that's one of the things I have always liked about you," the old cowboy praised the youth with a pleasant smile. "So what's your opinion of the weapons?" he asked.

"Well sir," Ben started his appraisal of the firearms as he eyed the weapons and the water-logged ammunition. "I been around guns all my life and I'd hate to bet my life on what we have here," he responded seriously.

"I'm of the same mind. Hard to trust bullets that have been under water very long, but it's all we have until we get back to the house. If Doc's gang should show up before we reach the house we'll just have to bluff our way through."

"Yes sir, I understand," Ben replied solemnly.

"I'll tell you another thing, I don't intend to get killed protecting the gold of someone I don't know. As I see it, it was the mine owner's place to guard their valuables. You may not agree with me at your age but you'll find with age, that gold and money and such are not what brings true happiness," the old cowboy philosophized.

"Then what is?" Ben Crane asked, taking a seat on the log beside his employer.

"To my estimation the real treasure in life, is being free, having good health and good friends. It's having food to eat and a place to sleep, but most of all its having loved ones like your family who share your joys and sorrow, your aches and pains, your wins and your losses," the old cowboy's voice trailed off as he turned his head to gaze at Kitty Rouch's grave on the hill to the east of his cabin.

The two men sat without speaking for several minutes until Henry Shanks turned back to the matters at hand. "You might try breaking down a couple of those cartridges so we can have a look at the powder."

Always a willing hand, Ben began to pry the soft lead bullet from its copper shell, but the projectile resisted his thumbs pressure. Realizing his efforts were futile the youth located a crack in the log that fit snuggly around the 44 caliber bullet and he began to wiggle the casing to and fro until the case mouth stretched far enough to easily separate the two components. He poured the clumped propellant into the palm of his hand before declaring the powder wet. The test was repeated time after time and each time the finely milled gun powder grains stuck together in a clump.

"I don't think there's a good round in the bunch," Ben said, with a shake of his head. "I thought this stuff was supposed to be waterproof." He threw the empty brass cases on the ground. "I'll be glad to try some of the rounds that came from the box." The youth slid off the tree trunk and began testing before Henry Shanks had time to reply.

"You were speaking of family Mr. Shanks, were you ever lonely living out here by yourself all of these years?" Ben asked without looking up as he busied himself dismantling the 44-40 cartridges , which had fallen out of the collapsed cardboard box.

"Well," the old cowboy began, then paused, "well to tell the truth, only a crazy person can live alone without craving companionship. But I ran a pretty large spread back in those days; had a big bunkhouse and four to six hands year around. As the people moved in we had a lot of good neighbors, close friends and reason to gather. "Find any good ones?" Shanks inquired turning away from the past and back to the present.

"A couple might be dry enough to fire, but like I said they might be good enough to hunt rabbits with but I hate to use them on a skunk," Ben stated with a smile.

"All right, load the rifle and the Colt but don't shoot them no matter what happens." Realizing Ben had a strange expression on his face, the old cowboy began to explain, "have you ever seen a gun barrel explode? A lot of things can cause such a mishap, one of them being an underpowered cartridge that doesn't push the bullet out of the muzzle. If a bullet sticks in the barrel then a full power cartridge is fired behind it and the barrel can blow up. Just mind what I say and don't fire either of these weapons while loaded with these wet bullets," Shanks warned in a stern voice.

"No sir, I'll remember," the youth promised as he began to follow his instruction and load the firearms.

"I know it's impolite to ask but I have a feeling you knew Doc Walker before today." This was a statement, not a question, which the youth knew the old man would have a difficult time passing off.

Henry Shanks eyed Ben Crane up and down as if sizing him up for a new suit of clothing, but he was actually trying to judge the young man's maturity. Now that the question had been asked the old cowboy felt the need to answer but only to someone who was adult enough to understand.

"Yes," Shanks began in a flat nearly monotone voice, "I knew Doc Walker before our meeting today. In fact he worked for me on this very ranch nearly twenty years ago. His real name was Airless Tarquin Walker you can see how much simpler the nickname Doc was around a ranch," the old cowboy smiled and shook his head. "Doc was a veteran of the Spanish American War; he fought in the Philippines, most folks don't remember that our boy's fought over there," Shanks stated as if he were proud of Doc's service.

"Doc was discharged in 1899 in St. Louis and like so many of those boys, he headed for the big gold strike in Alaska. But again like many, he ran out of money here in Montana and needed a job. I hired him and another veteran named Bates to work on my spread."

"The men were from the east but they caught on quickly and became good ranch hands in no time. Bates stayed about a year, saved up a stack and moved on. Doc worked here for nearly two years, he was a bit wild but he made friends fast with his quick smile and glib tongue. He was a fair singer and story teller, so he was in demand for all the parties and shindigs."

"I had been seeing a neighbor lady by the name of Kitty Roush, she was a beautiful red head who taught Sweet Grass County School just over the hill from your place. We were planning to marry after the spring roundup, that way we could take a long honeymoon in warm weather while she was not busy teaching." The old cowboy paused for a long moment and even a callow youth could sense the turmoil his friend was experiencing. The silence was finally broken when Henry Shanks swallowed hard then said. "We were friends, Doc and I. I trusted him with my money and my ranch but he went bad one night after what was really an accident."

When Henry Shanks once again paused in his story, the dead silence compelled the youth to speak. "Are you saying Walker wooed your lady away?" he asked in surprise.

"No no, it was nothing like that, in fact, Doc had encouraged our romance and was to be our best man. The whole area had been invited to an engagement party at Ezra Pike's place that set on the south side of the river straight west from Grey Cliff. It was the middle of May," Shanks continued, "and there were still patches of snow on the ground but the weather had turned warm and pleasant. We finished the evening chores early and everyone got cleaned up for the party, as usual Doc was ready before anyone else. He hurried out to the barn and hitched the trotters to the buggy then tied them outside at the hitch rail. A few minutes later Doc reported to me that my favorite saddle pony Hob Nob was favoring his right front foot and thought I should take a look. I examined the animal's leg closely and discovered a small cut, which I thought best to treat right away. Doc offered to take the buggy up the draw past your place to the Roush house and bring Kitty back here so we wouldn't be late for our own party. I agreed knowing they would soon travel by here to use the crossing to reach the Pike place," Henry Shanks paused his narration long enough to rub his injured wrist, which drew a sympathetic inquiring look from Ben. The old cowboy shook his head in answer to the youths concerns, then took up his story once more.

“When Doc reached the trail at the base of the hills he encountered none other than Clarence Bates, my ex-hired hand. I understand they talked for a moment until Bates agreed to go along to the party and they rode up the draw towards Kitty’s house. They picked up Kitty and her mother, headed down the trail with everything going fine until they approached the old Pool homestead and baby Helen’s grave on the knoll. It was at this point that Bates began to tease Doc about the trotters and challenged him to a race. I guess it was too much to resist and all of a sudden Bates whipped his saddle horse into a fast trot. Naturally Doc followed suit. The racers remained even until they reached the bottom of the draw where Doc cut the last corner too short, the buggy’s left front wheel caught in a snow drift which flipped the rig over. Mrs. Roush and Doc were thrown clear but Kitty was trapped under the rig while the excited team drug the whole affair another hundred yards before Clarence Bates managed to halt the runaway. When they finally untangled the wreckage Kitty was dead from a broken neck. I know all this to be true because Kitty’s mother confirmed the two men’s account of the event.” Henry Shanks sucked in a long deep breath obviously trying to keep his composure in front of his young friend. He once again rubbed his bleeding wrist then turned his eyes to the hills and the Crane home. “We buried Kitty beside little Helen

Pool up by your house," he stated softly, certain in his mind the youth didn't know who was interred in the small cemetery.

"What happened to Walker and Bates?" Ben asked in a very uncertain tone.

"Bates raced his horse to my place and tried to explain what had happened, but it was all so confusing that I didn't understand until arriving at the wreck. Kitty was still laying on the ground, her new light blue gown torn and dirty. Someone had covered her face with Doc's best coat. Mrs. Roush was nearly in hysterics while Doc paced back and forth mumbling something about the whole thing being his fault."

"As I knelt down beside Kitty's body I heard the distinct sound of a Colt revolver being cocked. I looked up in time to see Doc, his eyes shut tight inserting the barrel of the cocked weapon in his mouth. I sprung from my position beside Kitty in time to knock the Colt from his mouth just before the cartridge exploded. As a matter of fact, if you look close at his body you'll see two upper right teeth missing as well as a notch in the upper part of his right ear where the bullet clipped him. The barrel of the Colt knocked out the two teeth as I batted the revolver from his hand," Shanks explained with a shake of his head. "I'm still not sure I did the right thing that evening. Might have been better for all concerned if Doc had killed himself in those moments of anguish."

"We had a big gathering at Kitty's funeral, Doc and Clarence Bates, hats in hand attended but stood off some distance. Just as the minister said his last amen the pair donned their hats, swung into their saddles and rode hurriedly away," the old cowboy reported in some detail, his memory quite clear about the day's events.

"I feel rested now so maybe we'd best start for the house," Shanks suggested, rising to his feet possibly trying to wipe the image from his mind. "We've got some business to take care of before this day ends," the old cowboy added, turning towards the house.

"Yes sir," Ben replied solemnly as he gathered up the reins of Doc's pony. Deep inside the youth felt there was more to the old rancher's tale, however manners and propriety prevented his broaching the tender subject any further. The dutiful young employee followed one step behind the old cowboy with the pony bearing the bandits body lagged further behind. It was an impromptu funeral procession at best, for it lacked a big shiny horse drawn hearse followed by weeping mourners, while in the distance someone would fife out a proper dirge.

After searching his young agile mind for a few moments, Ben thought he had hit upon the perfect way to reopen the conversation. "When you said we had much to do before sunset, do you mean we must bury Doc's remains?"

"That and several other tasks, most of which I hope you will be able to handle in my place," Shanks answered, stopped in the middle of the road, then added, "I feel you want to hear the rest of the story of Doc Walker life."

"Well, yes sir," Ben responded as he quickened his step coming up abreast of the old cowboy.

"You certainly rate a full explanation after what you have done today. Truthfully there's not much more to tell, but here goes. Some fool spread the word around that I would shoot Doc or Clarence Bates on sight, although I never said that. Still, many people believed the threat and refused to hire either man or give them food or shelter, they became outcasts. Both men left the area, trying to make a new start but the story of Kitty's death followed close on their heels, often times it was twisted to sound like murder. As you can imagine, the pair turned to petty crime; stealing to eat or for some necessity but as so often happens, they became bitterer and bolder until they began to rob travelers and rustle cattle. The red welt Doc referred to earlier was the result of him and Bates trying to steal my saddle horse from the corral. I heard a disturbance one night so I jumped out of bed, grabbed my rifle and raced outside just in time to fire a shot at the two men. I hit Doc, causing him to fall from the saddle but Bates raced in and Doc swung up behind him. They rode off pell-mell toward the main road and I got my horse back. In all of these years, I have not laid eyes on either man." Henry Shanks became very quiet, his steps faltering, his eyes locked on the distant hillside where his beloved Kitty rested.

The old cowboy suddenly stopped and turned to face his young companion. “I have never said this to anyone before, but I could have done more to explain the accident. That’s what it really was, a wild crazy accident, which is likely to happen when two young high spirited cowboys break lose at a celebration. But I was bitter and carrying a grudge so I kept my mouth shut thinking it was fit punishment for my two friends.”

“I understand how you must have felt Mr. Shanks, and I’ll bet Doc understood too. He didn’t appear to be angry when he rode into the yard this morning, he was armed and we weren’t, he could have easily taken revenge on you.” Ben’s soothing words made sense to the old cowboy and he resumed walking to the house, a solemn “Maybe” his only reply. Silence, golden therapeutic silence ended Henry Shanks’ narrative, of course exhaustion played a role in the quiet. Ben was still tasked with dragging Doc’s weary pony, while the old cowboy kept his attention fixed on the tiny graveyard on the far hillside.

WALKER'S GANG

The weary trio were approaching the ranch house when the old cowboy pulled up short one final time, his attention still fixed on the hillside over a mile away. "Will you be so kind as to run to the house and retrieve my spy glass?" he asked of his young friend in a calm somber fashion. The youth glanced first at his employer, then to the spot on the hill that so magnetically held the ranchers attention. Seeing nothing unusual, Ben broke into a fast trot, which carried him to the house and the bed where the old cowboy's worn brass telescope hung. With eyeglass in hand, the youth ran at full speed back to where Henry Shanks waited, still calmly watching the narrow draw that led down from the little graveyard.

Ben, stunned by what he saw reduced his speed to a fast walk before extending the telescope at arm's length. "Are you all right Mr. Shanks?" he inquired earnestly, "you have taken a real beating today."

"I'm all right," Shanks replied in a dismissive voice, "why do you ask?"

"You're covering one eye with your hand," came the youth's inquisitive response. The old cowboy was standing, feet spread shoulder width apart, his injured left hand tucked inside his shirt while he used his good right hand to cover his left eye. "Oh this? It's an old plainsman trick. Most people have one eye which works better up close and one that works better at a distance. In my case my right eye is sharper at long distance than my left, so if I cover my left, the right one becomes even clearer," Shanks explained dropping his right hand as he reached for the telescope.

"I've never heard of the eye thing before, but I have never known anyone young or old that has a better set of eyes than you Mr. Shanks," Ben stated with a touch of envy in his voice.

"Actually I've known folks with better eyes but they are all dead." The old cowboy began wrestling with the telescope's collapsing brass tube. "I'm going to need your help with this thing," Shanks declared in a usually gruff voice. "Please turn your back to me, then I can rest this spy glass on your shoulder." Ben quickly spun around to face the hillside that the old cowboy was so intent on viewing. "Now hold on to the big end of this glass while I slide this end back and forth to make it focus," Henry Shanks instructed. "Good, now turn just slightly to you left," the old cowboy directed.

"Whoa, damn!" Shanks blurted out.

"What do you see Mr. Shanks? My eyes must be weak 'cause I don't see a thing," the youth demanded, his voice trembled slightly at hearing Henry Shanks swear.

"I see just what I feared. Three mounted men are carefully working their way down the draw past your place. I can tell they are tracking by the way they keep stopping and circling back," Shanks explained.

"Who are they and what do you think they're tacking?" Ben asked trying to hold the telescope end steady.

"I can tell you, even at this distance, the man in the lead is Clarence Bates and as to what they are tracking, if I were a gambling man I'd put all my money on Doc Walker," Shanks snarled out.

"I see, they were part of the gang that stole the block of gold and now they are trying to find Doc," Ben half way whispered. "I guess you were right, Doc must have somehow made off with their share," the youth was just beginning to fully grasp the situation. "That means those three will be riding in here pretty soon and I'll bet it won't be a social call," Ben Crane grimaced.

"You're right, they will have blood in their eye. We have a great deal to do and not much time to do it." Shanks lowered the scope from his eye, while shaking his head in disbelief.

"They seemed to track Doc thru the little graveyard; do you think Doc Walker stopped to pay his respects to Kitty Roush?" Ben asked in surprised voice.

“Yes, yes, I wouldn’t be surprised. We were all good friends once, and some bad people do have a good side. Now run to the barn and bring back the two wooden buckets hanging just inside the door,” Henry Shanks directed, then suddenly called Ben back, “hold it, wait a minute. I’m sorry, but I jumped to the conclusion you are a willing partner in my plan to resist these outlaws,” the old cowboy apologized.

“I don’t understand Mr. Shanks,” Ben’s face wore a questioning expression.

“I mean, as a law bidding citizen I intend to prevent this band of thieves from making off with this stolen gold and if possible to take them prisoner. It’s not fair that I get you involved without asking you first,” the old cowboy quickly blurted out.

“I’m with you all the way Mr. Shanks, you tell me what to do and I’ll do it!” Ben excitedly replied.

“Be sure of your answer son, this could get us both killed, these men are bloody criminals who are going to do whatever it takes to get their hands on that gold.” Henry Shanks statement was hard and to the point because he wanted to make sure Ben Crane understood the dangers involved in their undertaking.

Ben’s face spread into a wide smile partly because Henry Shanks had never called him son before and partly because other than his father, the man he admired most had asked him to join in a dangerous adventure. “I’m with you sir, just tell me what you want do,” the youth declared.

"We don't have time to prepare the way I'd like but we must hide the gold so you run for the buckets while I remove the well cover," the old cowboy instructed pointing towards the small red two story building. Ben returned with the two large wooden buckets before the one-handed rancher had managed to uncover the stone-lined well. He placed the pails on the ground, then began to assist Shanks in removing the heavy wooden planks that served as a covering for the open hand-dug well.

"What's next?" Crane asked as he lay the last of the oak planks on the ground.

"Lead Doc's pony over here so we can put the gold in these buckets then we will lower them to the bottom of the well," the old cowboy answered.

Ben ran to retrieve Doc Walker's exhausted mount, but the stubborn animal had other ideas causing the youth to nearly drag the pony across the farm yard. Profanity, hot black cuss words the like of which the youth had never uttered, raced through his head but he managed to keep his tongue until they reached the well. "Damn jug head!" he blurted out. "I hope Doc stole you, 'cause you ain't worth a red cent." Suddenly realizing his brazen outburst, Ben turned red faced to meet his employer's hard gaze.

"I wouldn't have paid good money for that pony either," Henry Shanks smiled, then turned back to the job at hand. The two men quickly divided the stolen gold bullion between the large wooden buckets then unloaded the outlaw's remains.

Shanks ordered the corpse to be placed on its back, parallel to the corrals board fence.

"I want his partners to see Doc's body right off, maybe if they search it and find nothing they will be satisfied and move on," the old cowboy suggested wishfully. "Now use the spy glass to see what those jay birds are up to," he instructed the youth.

Ben held the small end of the telescope to his right eye, struggled a bit to slide the brass tubes in and out until a nearly clear picture of the three desperados came into focus. "One man is walking around on the hill road, must be looking for tracks I guess," Ben reported hesitantly. "He just swung into the saddle and they seem to be headed north on the road to town," he added.

"Just as I thought, Doc could be real foxy when he wanted to," Shanks declared with a slight smile and a shake of his head. "Looks like he laid a false trail towards town, then cut back through the north pasture. That just might give us enough time to get ready," the old cowboy added in a voice, which might be considered a simple prayer.

"What do we do next?" Ben asked, tying the reins of the weary mare to the wooden hitch rail located on the opposite side of the well from Doc's body.

"Do you know how to tie a sheep shank knot?" Henry Shanks asked handing the end of a well rope to Ben.

"You mean the double loop one that you cut?" the youth inquired with a strange questioning look on his face.

"Yes, I can't tie it with this banged up hand but I'll help you," Shanks offered, kneeling down beside one of the buckets. "First make a loop in the rope, then throw a half hitch around each end of the loop. Yeah that's right, now I'll hold the long end while you tie the open end of the rope with a hard knot to the buckets bale." Shanks hurried through the instructions but the results satisfied the old cowboy who was known as a perfectionist. "Good, now lift the bucket over the well's stone wall and support it with the upper end of the rope while I cut the loop," the old cowboy ordered, as his right hand probed his wet pants pocket for the razor-sharp folding knife, which was always kept there. "There, the loop is cut, now begin lowering the bucket down until it has hit the bottom," he continued to instruct the youth.

"Must be on the bottom 'cause the rope just went slack," Ben stated trying his best to follow each step of the old cowboy's directions.

"All right, now flip the rope back and forth then give it a tug, if it doesn't come free flip it around some more," Shanks' words were quick, but calm as he worked with the inexperienced youth.

"It's free!" Ben exclaimed as he began to reel in the soggy well rope.

The two men repeated their actions as they rigged the second bucket for submersion in the bottom of the well. "I dug this well myself right after settling here, it's fifty four feet from the top of the platform to the bottom of the water," Shanks began to explain as Ben once again retrieved the rope after lowering the second treasure-laden bucket to its watery hiding place. "The water level has never fallen below ten feet in dry seasons and seldom above fifteen in wet spells like now. All we have to do is dive down ten or fifteen feet to retrieve the gold once the law arrives," Henry Shanks continued to explain his plan.

"Yes sir," Ben agreed taking a long look down the stone lined cylinder while mumbling a silent prayer that he would not be the one assigned the task of recovering the two gold filled buckets hidden below fifteen feet of cold well water. With that thought lingering in his mind, Ben began to replace the heavy oak planks , which served as a well top, but the old cowboy signaled him to stop.

"Take a look through the spy glass and tell me what those three cut throats are doing now," Shanks commanded, pointing up the road with his good right hand. The order to stop hiding the gold bullion surprised the youth, but as usual he readily complied with the old man's wishes.

"They are rounding the bend by the big rock about a mile up the road," Ben reported still holding the telescope to his eye.

"We're in luck, they have fallen for Doc's fake trail. Now be so kind as to run into the house and bring me the ink bottle, pen and paper that's laying on my desk," the old cowboy said with a smile.

Not fully understanding the old cowboy's plan, but realizing time was of the essence, Ben ran at full speed into the Rattlesnake Ranch house and returned in just seconds with the paper, pen and ink. "Here you are Mr. Shanks," the breathless youth declared as he slid to a halt beside the well.

"You are good help son, and I believe a good man, so I'm going to take you into my confidence." Henry Shanks placed his good right hand on Ben's shoulder and smiled warmly. "I don't intend to ask you to swear to never tell what you see now. I don't think it will do any good in the long run." Next, Shanks directed Ben to place the writing materials on the partially replaced planks of the well platform.

The old cowboy opened the glass ink well by using his right thumb to flip the stopper from the octagon shaped bottle. He held the sheet of paper out flat with his injured left hand before dipping the metal point of the cheap wooden pen into the ink. "Benjamin Franklin Crane; that is your full legal name isn't it?" Shanks ask as he began to scratch the pen across the top of the paper. "Yes, yes sir. At least it's what my parents say was my baptismal name, why do you ask?"

The old man failed to answer Ben's inquiry, instead he continued to rapidly work the pen on the rough paper, pausing only long enough to dip the pen in the ink bottle as the need arose. "There!" Shanks exclaimed as he blew gently on the still wet ink in an attempt to make it dry faster. "I think I have just about covered the situation." He lifted the newly drafted paper to his eye level and began to read.

CHANGING OF THE GUARD

"I, Heratio Ruby Shanks, being of sound mind and body on this twenty first day of May 1917 put pen to paper to make my last will and testament." Shanks paused for a moment to look Ben straight in the eye before saying, "don't laugh, that is my full name, that is how all my legal documents, including the deed to my ranch are made out." The old man smiled sheepishly as if he were embarrassed at the disclosure of his full name, he then began to read from the paper once more. "I do bequeath all my land, livestock, and money to Benjamin Franklin Crane." The old cowboy beamed once more, then handed the document to Ben for his approval.

The youth stood, mouth open, staring at the new will until he caught his breath, swallowed hard once, then began a stammering reply. "but, but you can't do that, Mr. Shanks. I haven't any right to your property. You must have kin who should inherit your holdings," Ben managed to mumble out.

"No, I haven't any blood kin, or distant relatives, I don't even have any close friends. But I feel after what we went through together this morning, you deserve all my holdings. Besides, if I don't make out a legal will, the state will move in and take everything I have and I sure as hell don't want to fund this Yankee government." Both men fell silent partially because of Shanks' use of the phrase, sure as hell, and because of the magnitude and suddenness of the gift.

"But I can't accept this Mr. Shanks, I wouldn't know how to run this ranch of yours like you do," Ben repeated his argument.

"I'm sure you'll do fine, and if you run into trouble your father will surely help you out," Shanks calmly rebuked all of the youth's objections then extended his hand to Ben in order to shake on the deal. Ben slowly grasped the old cowboy's callused right hand in his own and they shook hands in silence. "That handshake between two men means more to me than all of the ink on all the paper in the world," Henry Shanks stated in a loud firm voice.

"Now we must move fast 'cause those hombres will be back before long. Take the spy glass and climb part way up the windmill tower and see if you can spot them," Shanks directed as he began to write on the back of his newly minted will. "I'm going to make a quick note on the back of the will to explain how Doc drown trying to cross the river and that I expect Bates and the other two robbers to be back soon," the old cowboy's words came out in a halting fashion as he hurriedly scribbled on the back of the will.

"I can't see a thing Mr. Shanks, I think I could see all the way to the river bridge if I climbed to the top of the tower," the youth gladly offered to make the extra effort.

"We don't have time, come back down here, I have more to show you," the old cowboy called up to Ben who was already half way up the wooden windmill tower. With those curious words the youth nearly dropped from his observation perch to the well top before bounding to the ground. "Careful son, we must remain alive as long as we can," Shanks warned, then stepped to the stone well casing once more.

"Look down there and tell me what you see young man," Shanks directed pointing over the edge of the wall.

"I see lime stone blocks, a lot of water and not much more," Ben replied, looking away from the disturbing precipice.

"That's just what I want you to see, and what I hope Bates and his men will see. Now I'm going to show you a secret I have kept to myself for nearly fifty years. No one but you will ever know what I'm about to show you," the old cowboy flashed a mischievous smile.

"Here, right here, stand here, then lean over and look down the well," Shanks instructed in what one might call a playful or slightly humorous voice. "What do you see now?" he asked.

"Limestone blocks and water," Ben called over his shoulder.

"Now look at the stone blocks just below ground level. Do they look any different?" Shanks asked light heartedly.

"Yes sir, one block has a strange sign on it like a big bug is frozen in it," Ben responded with a questioning voice.

"That son, is a fossil; it's something that was trapped in the mud millions of years ago before the mud turned to solid rock. But it's not important now, just remember it and where it's located on the wall cause you'll want to find it again someday. Now force your fingers into the cracks on each side of the stone and wiggle it back and forth. Once it starts to move lift the front end up and it will come out very easily, make sure you don't drop it into the water, we don't have time to go diving for it right now." Henry Shanks' demeanor had turned serious as he instructed Ben in the procedures needed to remove the stone.

"I've got it sir!" Ben called out straightening up with the heavy fossil-bearing stone firmly grasped in both hands.

"Good work, now lay the stone on the ground and bend back over and stick both hands into the hole where you pulled that rock out. Don't be afraid, there aren't any critters in there but you will feel a chunk of metal and a chain handle. Grab the chain handle and pull straight out with one hand while you catch the box with the other," Shanks now hurried his words, each carrying more emphases than the last.

“It sure is heavy,” Ben reported causing Shanks to employ his good right hand to the task of lowering the metal box to the ground. “I know and it will be easier for you with two good hands to open the lid than for me. It’s not locked so just flip the latch and lift the lid up,” the old cowboy anxiously urged the youth.

It was obvious the box was homemade to match exactly the irregular measurements of the fossil rock which was just removed from the well’s interior wall. The dimensions of the container were roughly six inches high by twelve inches long and ten inches deep. The construction material was of heavy steel, with one handle on the front side and two crude hinges on the back edge which secured the lid in place.

Ben grasped the chain handle, then began to tug on the lid but he quickly discovered that a deposit of light rust was preventing the lid from rising. A second attempt proved a failure, just like the first until the old cowboy slammed the side of his right fist against the center of the boxes flat lid. The lid then begrudgingly gave way to the stout young man’s insistent pressure.

“I secretly made this box all by myself nearly fifty years ago, it may not be pretty but it has served its purpose gallantly ever since,” Shanks half bragged, half apologized for the less than professional appearance of the container.

“Yes sir, not only that but it would take a real man to carry it off,” Ben chuckled as he forced the box's flat lid into a ninety degree angle before moving out of the old cowboy's way.

"It's been a while since I have opened this box but I can recall everything stored in here," Shanks stated in a reassuring voice. "Here is a chunk of gold quartz I found in the river years ago. These two leather bags contain a thousand dollars each in double eagle gold coins." The old cowboy lifted each bag out of the box, handing them to Ben for examination. "This small bag holds some gold and silver coins, they have been in here for about thirty years." Shanks tossed the smaller bag to Ben before stating, "open it up and take out a half eagle and a couple dimes. Put them in your pants pocket and take care not to lose them."

"Yes sir," the youth replied upon untying the draw string and dumping the bags contents in the palm of his hand. "One five dollar gold piece and two seated liberty dimes," Ben repeated the order as he placed the three coins in the bottom of his still soggy pants pocket. "What is this money for?" he asked of the old cowboy.

"You're going to need that money before this day is over," was Henry Shanks only reply. "Now this is very important, remember this well," the old cowboy warned as he removed a quart size Ball canning jar from the box. "You'll have to open it, I can't work the wire bale that seals the lid closed," the old cowboy commanded in a serious tone as he thrust the heavy walled glass jar in Ben's direction.

The youth flipped open the wire handle which secured the glass lid to the canning jar then offered it to his employer who shook his head saying, "You open the lid and remove the contents. I want you to know exactly what that jar holds. It will be important to you very shortly," Henry Shanks directed Ben's every action now.

Ben gently removed the clear glass lid, then inserted his thumb and fingers through the mouth of the jar and removed a roll of oil cloth. A moment later the heavy semi-waterproof cloth lay on the ground as the youth began examining the folded paper documents which the glass jar and oilcloth had preserved all these years.

"This looks like some kind of legal paper," Ben reported turning the heavy-weight paper around until the top of the document came level with his eyes. "It says this is a deed. Why, it's a deed to your property Mr. Shanks," the astounded youth blurted out.

"That's right son, let me sign it over to you, don't want any legal wrangle." the old cowboy explained hurriedly. "Now fold up my new will and place it in the jar with the deed." Shanks held up his good right hand as a signal for Ben to stop, then picked up the pen and dipped it into the ink. "Let me see that will for a second, I forgot something."

Henry Shanks struggled with his will for a moment then scribbled another line on the reverse of the document. "There, I just wrote how I want to be buried in the little graveyard on the hill beside my darling Kitty Roush and baby Helen Pool. I don't suppose anyone will object. What do you think?" the old cowboy asked, handing the will back to Ben.

"No one will object Mr. Shanks, I'm certain of that," the youth assured his old friend as he folded the ranch deed and the will together, wrapped both with the oil cloth and resealed them in the fruit jar. "Would you like me to put everything back in the box for you?" he asked politely placing each item in its proper position in the steel box and closed the lid down tight.

"I want you to know I also have fifty-six thousand three hundred and thirty two dollars and seventy eight cents in my bank account in the Cattleman's Bank in Billings and I have four thousand four hundred dollars and no cents in old man Good's Bank in Big Timber. That is my business money and what's in Billings is my life savings. Both of them will be yours before this day is over," Shanks announced in a firm unpretentious but natural tone of voice.

Ben checked the closure of the heavy metal box lid and sat it on the stone well top just as Henry Shanks finished declaring his combined wealth and that Ben would inherited it all. The shock of the old cowboy's decree made the youth freeze in his tracks.

"What's wrong son, didn't you ever think about being rich?" Shanks chuckled out loud. "All you have to do is follow my orders and by this time tomorrow you will own the best ranch in the valley and you'll have enough money to do just as you and your folks please," the old cowboy laughed once more then stopped short, brought his body to attention, then placed his right index finger over his lips and said "sssh."

"The better part of the fifty six thousand in the Billings Bank came out of a glory hole I discovered almost straight across the river from here. It's been nearly forty years ago, I was chasing a wandering milk cow over there when I found the gold sticking out of a rock ledge. It was so beautiful, I just couldn't resist a few days of digging it out and toting it back to the ranch. I knew the land belonged to old Banker Good, so next time I was in town I tried to tell him what I had found, but he just cussed me and told me to stay off his land. Well he made me so mad that I took the gold to Billings and sold it, and put the money in the bank cause I didn't want to deposit it in Good's Bank, I didn't want him to make anything off of his own gold." Henry Shanks broke into a fit of laughter that brought him to lean against the well casing.

The old rancher's actions struck Ben as so completely out of character, he was driven to question his employer, "is that legal Mr. Shanks, I mean isn't it stealing?"

The old cowboy stopped his laughter, turning to stare his young accuser square in the eye. "I was the only real law around here in those days. I hung rustlers and murderers back then without any ones help or permission. Those were hard days when a man took matters into his own hands. Folks hereabouts could sleep at night, they could travel in safety and a man didn't have to worry about leaving his family alone while he was away from the house. I rode rough shod over the low life's who tried to make this valley their own personal hell on earth. I don't and won't apologize for anything I did in those years." The old cowboy hesitated a moment as his anger subsided before he spoke again, "as for Banker Good being cheated, I want you to know I never spent one red cent of the money I got for that gold. I turned the gold into hard cash, which at the time amounted to seventeen thousand three hundred dollars. It has made some interest through the years and I would add to the principle every now and then. I have kept it all these years to give to the man who rightly owned the land."

THE SOLDIER

"Who owned the land if Mr. Good didn't?" Ben inquired, trying to keep straight all of the local history he had been exposed to this day.

"I don't have the time to give you the whole story son," Shanks declared looking up the road towards the hills, fully expecting to see three mounted men racing in his direction, but the shocked look on his young friend's face changed his mind about the explanation. "Oh all right," he muttered once again glancing up the road for any sign of Bates and his men. "It was around 1876 or 77 that a big black man and his Indian wife took up land in the low hills across the river. It was just after Custer and the seventh were wiped out at the Little Big Horn. I always suspected the woman was Sioux, but she seldom spoke and as a matter of manners, I didn't ask. Well any way, I wasn't sure what to make of these two living so close but they kept on their side of the river and I on mine. Of course, every now and then I'd see one or the other along the bank of the river. At first we just eyed one another but later on we would exchange waves or hellos. This went on for a couple of years until one fall day, I was rounding up some of my stray horses when my mount stepped in a hole and threw me head over heels. The fall knocked me out and the next thing I knew I woke up in an earth lodge and the Indian woman was bending over me," Shanks paused again to look at Ben's face then scanned the hill road for any riders.

"Better get that box back in its hole son before someone blunders in here and finds out what we are up to," the old cowboy strongly suggested. "I'll tell you the rest of the story once I'm sure everything is secure."

Ben hurriedly replaced the metal box and fossil limestone rock in its hiding place in the stone well cap; he then meticulously returned each of the heavy planks that served as the well platform to their proper place. Once satisfied everything was in order the youth turned, arms fold across his chest to face Henry Shanks with an expression indicating he would settle for nothing less than the end of the story.

"All right, all right," Shanks conceded without Ben saying a word. "I'll tell you the rest of the tale if you climb up on the windmill tower part way and keep a sharp look out for Bates."

Clutching the telescope in one hand the youth quickly shinnied up the first few rungs on the wooden tower then said, "You were injured in a horse fall and the Indian woman was treating you?" This was an open ended question that demanded an answer from the old cowboy.

“Do you see anything?” Shanks asked, almost hoping for the appearance of the Bates gang, feeling it would be preferable to finishing a confession that he should never have begun.

“No sir, but you were being doctored by an unknown Indian?” It was Ben’s way of politely urging the old cowboy to finish his story.

“I can see you ain’t never going to let this go son, reckon I never saw that bull-headed side of you before,” Shanks stated before taking a seat on the well top. “Well as it turned out, I had a broken right leg, couple of cracked ribs, and a big knot on my head. The pain in my leg kept me from walking, the cracked ribs slowed down my breathing but the whack to my noggin’ made me too dizzy to walk so all I could do was lay there, nearly naked, wrapped in a buffalo skin on the floor of this earth lodge, watching a strange squaw doctoring me while all the time I was trying to keep from vomiting.”

“That must have been a terrible experience Mr. Shanks,” Ben exclaimed.

“Yeah ‘cause this was at a time when the whites and Indians were still trying to kill one another for any silly reason. I had no way of knowing just what she intended and my spinning head prevented me from doing any logical thinking. All I could do was hope the good Lord was looking out for me,” the old cowboy muttered a bit sheepishly, then paused once more to ask the status of his look out.

“Nothing yet sir, but I will call out if I see anyone,” the youth replied with a hidden smile knowing he had the old cowboy in a corner.

"You most likely never saw one of those earth lodges the redskins made but they were like a dome made of tree branches and dirt with a fire pit in the middle of the floor and a smoke hole directly above in the roof. Since I was laying on my back looking up, I could see blue sky through the smoke hole and I could tell it was getting dark when I heard a horse trot up and stop by the lodge's side opening. Now you gotta remember, I had never seen the black man or his woman up close and with my muddled brain and blurred eyesight, I didn't know for certain who this squaw was, or who just rode up. I listened real close to the footsteps approaching the lodge opening 'cause Indians and white folks don't walk the same. You may not believe it and that's all right, but you'll have to admit there is a big difference in the sound made by a pair of heavy boots clomping across the prairie and the hissing sound made by a smooth pair of leather moccasins sliding through the grass."

"Suddenly the blanket covering the earth lodge's doorway burst open and a large long haired black dog rushed inside. He was only halfway through the opening when he abruptly detected my presence. I figure the odor of the buffalo robe covered my scent, not to mention the smoke rolling out of the fire pit in the middle of the floor, but the big dog froze in place except for the curling upper lips that exposed his long white fangs and the powerful deep rolling growl , which filled every nook of the lodge. The squaw rose from where she squatted by the fire pit, spoke one word, and then pointed to the opposite side of lodge from where I lay." The old cowboy paused to look up at Ben then began again. "I don't often admit to being really scared but I will this time. That great big critter looked like a wolf with dinner on his mind and I was too beat up to fend off a sickly field mouse. The squaw spoke once again breaking the animal's fixation on me, he stopped the growling and lowered his lip over those huge white fangs. She pointed again to the other side of the lodge and the dog slunk slowly to his appointed position, however his eye's remained on me from that moment on. Foolishly I kept my befuddled attention on the threating dog, preventing my noticing the big black man as he stepped through the doorway. As I said, I was lying flat on my back looking up at the giant black man who appeared to be ten feet tall. He paused and asked the squaw a question in some strange language. Her unknown reply caused the big man to drop down onto one knee beside my head." Shanks stopped his narration long enough to look up the windmill tower and accuse Ben of falling asleep.

"No sir, I don't see a thing and I wouldn't dare fall asleep in the middle of your story 'cause I'd never get you to tell it a second time," the youth good naturedly teased, all the while knowing it to be a true statement, for once stopped his reluctant employer would never repeat this tale.

"Stay awake up there," the old cowboy admonished his lookout then said, "now where was I? Oh yeah, the big black man wore a heavily sweat stained white Cavalry hat, a faded blue army issue shirt with brighter blue marks on the sleeves where corporal stripes had recently been removed. A heavy black leather government issued pistol belt without the sword was cinched up tight around his narrow waist. A U.S. buckle served to keep tension on the belt in its struggled to hold up a pair of handmade buckskin breeches that were tucked into the top of knee-high moccasins. The soldiers hair looked close shorn under his hat and his face was clean shaven, most likely a habit acquired in the military. His facial features were strong in a manner one might call plain to common." Shanks related in detail from memory his first meeting with the black man and his squaw.

"The black corporal called me by name and asked how I was feeling. I was surprised he knew my name. His voice was deep and clear and with a wide smile, he replied that everyone knew of Henry Shanks. In fact, he was warned not to move in beside me, I'd run him off in no time. All the while the squaw kept talking from her place by the cook-fire in what sounded to me like French but it was mixed with some grunts and growls. That's when the soldier shook his head before explaining, she says you won't let her treat you. I know you are in pain and you don't trust us, but the woman has a tea that will ease the discomfort and help you sleep. I promise not to poison you Mr. Shanks and if you will do what the woman says you'll be on your feet again, fit as a fiddle in no time. He promised me with a wide white-toothed grin."

The old cowboy was now deep into his narration and suddenly seemed determined to finish the story. He took a deep breath, looked up at Ben on the windmill tower then without asking for a status report, took up the story once more.

"The squaw, now working by the fire pit, poured a dark liquid from a pottery bowl into a battered cheap tin cup then hurriedly carried it to my bedside. I must have had a sour look on my face because the soldier took the cup from her then lowered it to my lips. I don't know what's in this, he stated honestly but I guarantee it will help, he promised trying to cajole me into drinking from the foul smelling brew. I was at their mercy so I drank part of the hot liquid, choked and sputtered a couple of times in resistance but the big black kept pressing the rim of the cup to my mouth until I managed to swallow all but the last few drops in the bottom of the cup. That seemed to satisfy both the man and woman as they smiled at one another while exchanging a few words in their private language. I don't remember anything from the time I drank from the cup until being woke up by a bright shaft of sunlight coming through the smoke hole in the lodge's roof and the warming rays falling directly on my face. I had slept the night out just as the black soldier had forewarned but he was nowhere to be seen. I could hear the woman through the doorway singing some native song as she went about her work. I glanced slowly around the inside of the lodge for the big dog and I'll admit it was a great relief not to find him still watching me."

"It was near dark when I heard the soldier ride up and speak to the woman, then there was a long silence. I figure he was tending to his mount before entering the lodge for the night. The woman was first to slip silently through the doorway where she paused to look in my direction before moving wordlessly to the fire pit. The big black soldier followed close behind the woman, he walked slightly bent over with his arms around the dog's large wooly neck. He spoke one harsh word then pointed for the animal to return to the place it had laid the night before. The soldier sat down beside my sick bed, removed his hat then smiled cheerfully. He asked how I felt and if I had been able to sleep. The squaw brought bowls of thin soup to both of us before propping my head in her lap to make it easier to spoon feed me."

"The soldier and I exchanged life stories as we ate our meager evening meal. Seems he was the youngest son of a wealthy white Louisiana planter who named him Sam Houston Peters because the two men were friends. His name got somehow shortened to his initials S. H. P. so every one called him Shep Peters. After his father's sickly white wife died, his father moved him and his mother into the big house and he was raised and educated with his father's other off-spring."

"It was an old story I'd heard before except when Shep turned twenty in 1860, his father gave him his papers making him a free man. He traveled north and when the war started he joined the Union Army just as soon as the government allowed. I told him I fought for the Confederacy but Shep didn't seem to mind one bit."

"Shep apologized for being so late but he had ridden to my place to do the chores, milked the cow, fed the chickens and locked them in the henhouse. When I asked what he had done with the milk and eggs, he explained he placed them just inside the door of my house. I made it clear to him in a nice way that I appreciated the bowl of soup but I was used to eating real food and if they were going to doctor me and do my chores then I expected to pay them, but above all I wanted to share the bounty of my land, which included milk, eggs and the chickens that laid them. I made Shep promise the next evening he'd best bring back the milk, eggs and a couple of fat hens for the cooking pot. The old Cavalry man broke into a wide gin, we shook hands and we were fast friends and good neighbors from then on," Shanks declared with warmth and pride in his voice.

"Shep and I chased loose stock together, built fences, cleaned out water holes and hunted and fished together. It was while looking for a milk cow, we discovered the glory hole on his property. We dug like gophers on that hole for days until the gold pinched out. We filled in the hole in the bank then covered up all signs of our work. Right from the start Shep insisted we were partners so everything was divided fifty/fifty but we stored the gold in leather bags at his place. Then one night after the hole was closed up Shep and I were sharing a smoke outside of his lodge door when he suggested we move the gold over to my ranch."

"When I asked him why, he reasoned if a black man, free or not were to try to sell that much gold, let alone deposit it in a bank, some white man would come along and claim it, so he asked me to handle the sale and the banking, knowing he could trust me to not spend his share. Part of the fifty six thousand in the Billings Bank came from the sale of the gold.

Are you sure no one is coming from any direction?" the old cowboy demanded. "Bates ain't stupid, he must know by now that Doc tried to cross the river here."

"No sir, I ain't seen hide nor hair of those men, and I have been looking all around. I have even been watching the crossing just in case they would try to sneak in from that direction," Ben Crane stated emphatically, as he squirmed around on the tower steps from the discomfort in his feet. "At first you said the glory hole was on Banker Good's land and now you tell me it was on Shep's land, which was it?" the youth challenged.

"Well, you know how hazy those property lines are over there by the Bear Tooth's," the old cowboy said sheepishly. "Shep said it was on Good's land but when I eyeballed it, the hole was on Shep's side of the line. Besides Banker Good never worked his land, or ever saw it for that matter," the old cowboy argued in his defense.

"Then why did you go into the bank to tell Good about your strike in the first place?" Ben called down from the tower, a trace of confusion in his voice.

"Oh, we thought that up the night we were smoking in front of Shep's lodge, thought it would be real funny to get the old boy all fired up over the gold. But like I said, the old skin flint wouldn't listen to me so he never knew about the glory hole," Shanks explained trying to influence his young friend's opinion of himself.

“I guess I understand, I’m told things were different in those days, but what happened to your friends?”

SHEP'S DEMISE

"Well, the squaw died about five years later of some fever after they made a trip to town to lay in winter supplies. We figure she caught something from the whites while in town, something Shep and I couldn't doctor. It was a real shame, cause I liked the woman, Indian or not, but no matter how hard I tried, she couldn't understand me except in sign language," the old cowboy's voice saddened as he remembered the woman who had once saved his life. "As for Shep, we worked even closer together after his woman died and then one day we had agreed to meet at his place to clean out the well we had dug, but he didn't show. I started riding in a wide half circle from his place looking for signs and about two miles north I picked up the tracks of four shod horses moving in the direction of Sleeping Giant Mountain over there," the old cowboy gestured toward the large mountaintop that resembled a giant sleeping on his back. "I followed the hoof prints until they met up with another set of tracks and it appeared like they had a long talk about something. I knew the fifth horse's tracks were those of Shep's horse that had been traveling towards his lodge to meet up with me. I thought it strange that he would ride off in the opposite direction with four men. Shep didn't trust too many people nor care about spending time with others. I followed the five horsemen about two more miles until they turned up a wide brushy heavily timbered draw. A wide spot in the brush exposed the soft bare soil and the clear prints of five horses going up the trail, as well as five horses coming back down the trail. I was puzzled by the returning tracks and questioned if I should ride on up the draw or follow the fresher hoof prints. Curiosity has always been a weakness of mine, so being unable to withstand its sirens call, I rode on up the draw hoping to discover what had drawn the five horsemen to travel so far out of their way. It proved to be at the same time the right and the wrong decision, for I had ridden only a short distance when I spotted the dark shadow of a man's body dangling from the limb of a large pine tree."

The old rancher paused for a long moment trying to regain his composure knowing the next words from his mouth would require a description of what he had discovered. Shanks inhaled deeply, lifted his grey head up as if seeking guidance from above before saying, "by God in heaven, I can see it as clear today as I did all those years ago. There hanging by his neck was the body of Shep, the colored union solider who had saved my life and became my friend. That was bad enough, but lynching Shep did not satisfy those bastards, they had castrated him and from the looks of the fight signs and blood loss, it must have been done before he died." Henry Shanks paused once more before muttering softly, "I hope you will forgive my rough words but the shock of seeing an old friend murdered and mutilated in such a fashion delivered me a heavy blow."

"I crowded my spooky mount up beside Shep's body in order to cut the lynch rope, and gently lowered his body to the ground. I quickly dismounted with the wild impulse that Shep might still show some spark of life, and I might offer aid or at least some comfort, but of course, it was a foolish idea for it was clear the grim reaper had gathered in this poor soul some hours before."

"I knelt, eyes closed, head down in prayer beside Shep's body for some time; a wayward sinner trying to open the pearly gates for the soul of one more departed sinner. It was during these moments of sorrow and disbelief, as I sat beside my old friend's body, that the ghastly horror of his death really penetrated my grieving brain. Not only had Shep been lynched and his manhood butchered, I suddenly realized his eyes had been gouged out and the tips of the fingers of his right hand had been chopped off. I recalled from my youth in the south before the war, a couple of accounts of such wanton destruction being inflicted on black males, they being punished for molesting white women."

"I could not imagine Shep ever having committed such a grievous crime nor could I think of a time when such an incident could have taken place. Other than myself, the man avoided human contact and seldom left the boundaries of his ranch or mine. But then there are all too many people who see all blacks, Indians and Mexicans as killers and rapists to be set upon at will."

"The revolting condition of Shep's body drove me to cover his body with my blanket roll and to swear an oath to catch those who had inflicted these unspeakable acts on what I was certain was an innocent man. I also promised to return to give Shep a Christian burial but first I had to pick up the trail of the four killers before it was lost for all time."

"I see them Mr. Shanks!" Ben Crane exclaimed excitedly from his lookout position on the windmill tower. "They're on the other side of the river moving slowly downstream in the direction of the crossing."

The weary battered Henry Shanks bound to his feet at the youth's sudden announcement. "On the other side of the river you say?" the old cowboy asked as he shaded his eyes while trying to visually scan the far riverbank. Unable to see the riders from his lower vantage point the old cowboy asked, "can you tell what they are doing?"

"Yes sir, they are riding slowly back and forth like a dog trying to pick up a scent. They must be looking for sign," Ben attempted to describe the three outlaw's strange actions.

"That's exactly what they are doing Ben, they are trying to pick up Doc's trail. They figure he either crossed the river on the steel bridge at Grey Cliff or managed to ford the river at the crossing. It wouldn't be long before they realize Doc didn't cross at either place, then they will be headed straight back here which means trouble. You watch them real close 'cause we have to set our plans according to what they do next," Shanks warned his young friend.

"Yes sir," Ben responded, then began to deliver a blow by blow account of the men's every move. "They are getting very near the crossing now. They're riding in slow circles, eyes on the ground. Now one man is riding into the river at the ford while another man is waving his arms trying to recall the man in the water," Ben reported in a fast pace slightly nervous report.

"That man must be Clarence Bates, he lived here long enough to know the river, which means they have discovered that Doc didn't cross the river. Like I said, they will soon be on their way back here," the old cowboy concluded openly. "Keep those thugs in view Ben. I'm sure they will ride back to Grey Cliff and cross the river on the steel bridge because Bates knows the ford is running too deep."

"It looks like you're right Mr. Shanks, the man who was in the water is back on the bank and they are looking right at us," Crane reported breathlessly, "all three just turned the mounts upstream and are riding towards town."

"Come down when they have ridden out of view," Shanks instructed his youthful companion as he made one last inspection of the well area.

"They just disappeared into the trees south of Grey Cliff," Ben called out as he began to climb down from the windmill tower.

"We only have a few minutes to put our plan in place now that we know the gang is coming by way of the bridge," the old cowboy declared before Ben Crane's feet hit the ground. "If those thugs had managed to cross at the ford, I would have sent you up the road towards your house but since they are coming by way of the bridge you'll have to go through the marsh so as not to run into those killers. Remember to contact the Sheriff straight away and try to convince him that Doc and his bunch are here on my ranch."

"Yes sir, I will do as you say," Ben responded nervously as he repeatedly looked upstream in the direction of the steel bridge and the robbers approach.

"I know you're a smart young man and will do everything in your power to help catch that black hearted trash," Shanks stated with a wide smile as he placed his good right hand on the youths shoulder. "Now let's see, I told you of the money and where it's all at, we talked about my will and the ranch." Ben politely nodded his head waiting for the old rancher to continue. "I would recommend you slip off into the marsh and make your way to the river, once there, you will have to decide for yourself to move up or down stream or if everything else fails, try to cross the river. I can't tell you what to do other than to be careful. Oh, and remember, there are a lot of rattlers hiding in the marsh, move slowly and keep your eyes and ears open." Henry Shanks hesitated for a moment, his hand still on the youth's shoulder when he said, "no matter what you hear or what you might see, keep going. Men of this ilk will try anything to get their way so don't worry about me, just take care of yourself," the old man warned in a firm serious voice. "Now get going Ben while you've got a head start."

"Yes sir, but I must know who killed your friend Shep?" the youth asked in a manly fashion,which surprised the old cowboy.

"Well son, old banker Good wanted Shep's land so he spread around a story that Shep had molested some white girl, which got back to a pack of worthless rednecks. They hunted the man down and killed him. But that's enough talk, you get to moving before that trash gets here," Shanks insisted, gently pushing Ben Crane in the direction of the marsh.

"But I must know before I go, did you catch up with the four murderers?"

Henry Shanks eyes were on the road from Grey Cliff when he answered by sliding his right index finger across his throat while saying, "I dispatched them, one at a time. Now get out of here before these three cut throats see you," the old rancher insisted.

Ben Crane moved quickly past the well coming to a halt at the fence, which divided the wet cattail and the rattlesnake infested marsh from the ranch stead. He spun on his heel and extended his right hand to the old rancher and in a very mature voice said, "Good luck sir, I will see you later."

Henry Shanks' weathered right hand willing accepted the youths hand in a hardy shake as he repeated the sentiment. “Good luck to you Ben, I will see you later.” The sincere exchange brought moisture to old rancher’s eyes as he witnessed the metamorphous of a boy to a man in just one short day. The pair, their lives separated by half a century, continued to shake hands, eyes locked together for a long moment and both knew something special had passed between them. Neither man knew exactly what had happened, but accepted it as a passing of the torch of life that included respect for one another, living in a civilized manner and above all, following God’s tenants.

The men’s right hands parted with the unspoken knowledge that it would be for the last time on this earth. Ben slipped through the fence disappearing into the brush and cattails, which made the marsh an ideal hiding place or escape route.

It was with a heavy heart that Henry Shanks eyes followed Ben’s passage through the flooded swamp until he was certain the youth was safely concealed by the dense undergrowth. The old cowboy’s ears suddenly directed his attention beyond the quarter mile wide wetland to a familiar sound emanating from the direction of Grey Cliff and the steel bridge. It was the distant drumming of horse’s hooves on the hard packed dirt road leading from the steel bridge. That sound could mean only one thing, Doc’ Walkers compatriots were racing down the Grey Cliff road in the direction of the four corners.

The old cowboy's mind raced through the list of preparations already completed and those that should be finished by the time the gang of thieves arrived at his door step. Doc Walker's body was leaned against the corral fence, his horse standing nearby, both ready to be searched by the rapidly approaching bandits. The well cover was in place and all signs of activity in the area had been erased.

Henry Shanks knew there would be tuff questions asked by three very hard men about Doc - when he rode in, how he died, but most importantly the location of the stolen gold. He also knew how this encounter with three desperate men would end. He smiled slightly to himself as he thought of how frustrated the outlaws would become when he refused to tell where the stolen gold was hidden. However, his refusing to tell was an absolute goal; a goal which must be attained at all cost. Henry Shanks' eyes strained to focus on the Grey Cliff road as three horsemen emerged from the cover of a large Cottonwood tree, one of many lining the route to four corners.

The outlaw's horses were moving at a fast trot, a speed that was much too fast for tracking which indicated to Henry Shanks the trio had chosen a destination. That destination was of course, the Rattlesnake Ranch, Henry Shanks' place on the Yellowstone River. The old cowboy chuckled to himself thinking three more serpents were riding hard to join their brethren here on his ranch. The ranches nickname seemed all the more appropriate under the present circumstance.

Weary from the morning's excitement, Henry Shanks leaned against the well top as he watched the three riders move steadily along the Grey Cliff road. He tried to use the large telescope but found it unusually heavy and difficult to focus with only one good hand, but long years on the vast prairies had trained his vision for just such occasions. He sat quietly as the outlaws slowed their speed, finally coming to a complete pause at the four corners. He could see them clearly now as the riders milled slowly about the intersection, their faces turned down looking for the familiar tracks of Doc Walker's mount.

Fortunately Doc's tracks had been confused and at times obliterated by the unusually heavy traffic on the Grey Cliff to Billings Road. The question of which way Doc had traveled was due in part to Clarence Bates belief that his old partner would avoid a confrontation with Henry Shanks, something Bates also hoped to prevent. However, the few remaining tracks at the crossroads indicated Walker had indeed headed for Grey Cliff. It had become clear to the outlaws Doc had laid a false trail from the crossroads to the steel bridge. He had turned off the road at the approach to the bridge, then made his way back to Shanks lane across the softened pasture. Being a sly fox, Doc avoided the crossroads only coming out of the pasture onto Shanks lane. It wasn't until Doc Walker began to ride down the lane towards the crossing when Henry Shanks first heard his approach.

Henry Shanks sat calmly watching the bandit trio as they converged their mounts for a heated hand waving parlay. It was clear from the start, two of the bandits wanted to ride down the narrow lane that led to the Rattlesnake Ranch and face down the owner but Clarence Bates knowing his old boss's temperament continued to resist such a foolish tactic. The conference ended when the two overeager accomplices reined their horses over, heading directly down the lane to the ranch house. A reluctant Clarence Bates remained in the middle of the barren crossroads as he watched his over confident partners trot leisurely down the lane acting as if they were going to a Sunday school picnic.

In a moment of indecision Clarence Bates removed his battered hat and lacking a bandana used the worn sleeve of his checker work shirt to mop the sweat from his forehead. He replaced his hat while staring intently at his departing partners knowing the choice he had to make, either face Henry Shanks or lose his share of the stolen gold. He was reluctant to face the stubborn old rancher and Doc Walker at the same time but he had come too far to lose his share of the loot from the robbery. On the other hand, the odds were three against one. That, combined with the lure of his share of the gold totaled up to the deciding factor. Clarence Bates pulled his hat down low before spurning his exhausted mount into a dead run. He raced down the ranch house lane, easily passing his compatriots with the intention of being the first gang member to confront Henry Shanks.

THE REUNION

Clarence Bates reined his mount to a sliding stop just ten feet in front of his old employer Henry Shanks, who stood defiantly in the middle of his ranch house yard. “Good afternoon Mr. Shanks,” the bandit called out while rendering a sweeping gesture with his hat.

“Bates,” the old rancher spit back in a tone reminiscent of a pious school teacher addressing one of his mischievous students. “I see you still haven’t learned the proper way to treat a horse,” Shanks snarled.

Caught off guard Bates replaced his hat just as his two accomplishes reined to a stop beside him. “This is Red Ames and his brother Buck, they are partners of mine,” the outlaw mumbled out.

“They seemed to be faring better than your old partner,” Shanks declared in a proud firm voice as he pointed to Doc Walker’s body lying beside the corral fence.

“Is he dead?” Bates blurted out in surprise.

“Did you kill him old man?” Red Ames demanded, as he started to dismount.

“I don’t recall asking you to step down!” Henry Shanks snarled out.

Ames slowly lowered his body back into the saddle then shot a hard look at Clarence Bates. “So this is the great Mr. Shanks that you and Doc are so afraid of,” Ames laughed out loud. “He’s just a broken down old cowboy as far as I can see.”

“Keep a civil tongue in your head pup,” Shanks replied in no uncertain words.

“You two keep your mouths shut and let me handle this matter,” Clarence Bates directed his orders to both of his companions.

“It’s like this Mr. Shanks,” Bates began as he leaned forward casually in his saddle, both of his arms resting on his saddle horn, ”the three of us had planned to meet up at Reed Springs with poor old Doc there, cause he had a line on a wrangling job. But I reckon that job ain’t going to pan out with Doc being dead,” the bandit declared with a bowed head and a forlorn voice.

“Somehow I find that tale of woe hard to believe,” Shanks said with a shake of his head. “Funny thing none of you asked how Doc died.”

“I was just getting around to asking that Mr. Shanks, what did happen to old Doc, did you shoot him, or did his horse throw him? He never was too good of a rider and he was even a worse judge of horse flesh,” Bates announced looking to the Ames brothers for confirmation.

“He was even a worse judge of men.” The old cowboy’s words hit home just as he had intended causing Buck Ames to lose his temper.

“I don’t have to take guff off some skinny old no account old man. Now you tell us where the gold is old man or I’m going to put a bullet in your hide!” the younger of the Ames brothers shouted.

“Damn, now you’ve done it Buck. We might have had a chance of learning where the gold is but you had to let the cat out of the bag!” Clarence Bates bellowed out.

“Gold?” Shanks retorted. “What gold are you talking about?”

“You know damn good and well what gold, you old buzzard! The two hundred pounds of gold the four of us stole from the mine near Helena. The three of us had a shootout with a posse while Doc made off with the gold. We’ve been chasing him through hill and hollow for the last two days. Now the way I figure it, if Doc died around here then the gold must be around here somewhere,” the dirty young outlaw insisted.

“Strange, you three still haven’t asked exactly how your friend died and it just might be the answer to your search for this gold you been howling about,” the old cowboy stated with a boyish smile.

“All right old man how did Doc die?” the younger Ames snarled out, obviously a man of little patients and a hot temper.

“He drowned trying to ford the river,” Shanks replied while delivering a sharp gesture over his shoulder in the direction of the Yellowstone River. "If Doc had any gold, it may have been lost in the river," the old cowboy suggested.

"Yeah maybe and maybe you got it!" Buck Ames shouted as he urged his mount forward trying to intimidate Henry Shanks.

"Hold up there Buck," Bates ordered, just managing to grab the bridle rein on Ames horse. "That rough stuff won't get us anywhere with this man. Now do as I say and keep your mouth shut!"

"Hell," Buck Ames growled, leaning over the side of his mount and pretending to spit but nothing came out of his mouth. Habit forced Ames to wipe his tobacco stained chin with a thread-bare shirt cuff.

Brother Red Ames urged his pony abreast of Bucks then whispered, "Let Bates handle this, he knows this fella and we don't," he suggested in a stern voice.

"You say Doc drowned at the crossing?" Bates stated more than ask.

"That's right, he rode through about mid-morning, asking if he could use the crossing. He never asked about the water level or if he should go around by way of the bridge. I figured he'd been around here long enough to read the river as well as anyone. We talked for a minute, he bid me good day, then hurried down the trail to the riverbank. I walked down to the alfalfa patch to trim up some weeds and that's when I heard him call for help. I run to the water's edge in time to see Doc go down before being swept under a big Cottonwood snag. He was trapped head down against the root-ball by the current which kept pushing him below the surface. I grabbed the rope from his saddle and threw him a good loop but he never took hold making me think he was dead. I threw a second loop that caught around the root-ball then tied the other end off. I managed to climb out on the rope and retrieve Doc's body as you can see." The old cowboy gave a good lengthy explanation of the morning's event without mentioning Ben Crane's participation. He was, of course, stalling for time, time that young Crane would need to make his way through the swamp and cross the raging river.

"You trying to tell us Doc Walker rode off into that river with two hundred pounds of gold on him. I never liked the man, but I'm sure he wasn't that stupid," Buck snarled, his patients running low.

"Take a good look at Doc's mount boy. Do you really think that crow bait could carry two hundred pounds of gold plus another hundred and fifty or so pounds of man and gear all the way from Helena? I'd say you're the one that's stupid. Think about it, if Doc made off with that much loot, he must have stashed it somewhere close to where you split up, otherwise that critter would never have outrun you three." Henry Shanks' words were filled with spite which infuriated the outlaws but when the old rancher laughed out loud at their lack of intelligence Buck Ames flew into a screaming fit.

"Don't laugh at me old man!" Buck Ames' face had turned beet red as he raised to a standing position in his saddle stirrups. "I've kill men for less!"

he shrieked, as he pulled a rusty Colt Lightning from his waist band.

A loud ear splitting “No!” filled the air as Clarence Bates delivered a powerful back hand slap to Buck Ames’ face. The impact caused the irate outlaw to flinch just as the worn Colt revolver discharged, fortunately for Henry Shanks the .38 Caliber bullet plowed harmlessly into the ground at his feet.

“I’ll kill you for that!” the hostile Ames screamed, turning his weapon on Bates who anticipated just such a reaction from his pride-crazed partner. Bates, being just a bit faster had already pulled his own hand gun, a double action Smith and Wesson .45 Caliber revolver which he discharged into Buck Ames face at a distance of only three feet. The big lead bullet delivered a powerful blow to the outlaw’s skull near his temple, then being slightly deflected it dug a deep bloody trench down the left side of the bad man’s head before tearing a half circle notch out of the top of his ear.

Buck Ames screamed out in pain, dropping his Colt as he fell from his saddle. “Help me Red, I’ve been killed,” Ames cried out as he rolled around on the ground.

Red Ames jumped from his saddle to answer his brother’s plaintive call for help which caused Clarence Bates to bring his revolver to bare on both of his partners. “Don’t start anything Red,” Bates warned in a gruff threating manner.

"I just want to help Buck!" Red declared, throwing both of his hands in the air, as he hurried to his brother's side.

"You two don't have the brains of a piss ant. We need Mr. Shanks alive if we hope to find out where Doc put our gold!" Bates' voice had lost some of its sharpness but he kept his Smith and Wesson trained on the Ames brothers while turning his attention back to his old employer.

"I tried to tell them Doc couldn't carry two hundred pounds of gold," Bates shrugged, waving the barrel of his weapon at the men on the ground. "I told them not even Doc could carry that kind of weight around but they were mad and not about to listen to common sense. Now tell me the rest of the story about Doc riding through here before drowning in the river," Bates asked in his most polite polished voice.

"There ain't much more to say. Doc was caught on a snag in the river and I was too late to help him. I hurt my hand trying to wrestle him back on shore. I put him on his mount and brought him to the house so I could clean him up enough to have a presentable corpse for the funeral. There he lays, just the way I found him in the river but you're welcome to search his body and his saddle bags if you wish. In fact, since Doc was your partner you three can bury him up on the hill but not too close to the other graves," the old cowboy insisted.

Clarence Bates slowly dismounted while trying to keep his eye on the three men on the ground. He paused long enough to quickly access

Buck Ames' wound before walking to the fence where Doc Walker's body lay in state beside the corral fence, the corpse in death's repose waiting for friend or foe to pass by in review. His lifeless face was white as snow, his clothes were wet and muddy from the river dunking, both of which repulsed Clarence Bates who made only a cursory visual search of the body. "Not much of an end for a man but most folks would consider it a befitting passing for an old cowboy," Bates muttered reverently.

"Cowboy hell! Outlaw, horse thief, liar, cheat, but don't try to hang the respectable title of honest hard working cowboy on a man with his past reputation," Henry Shanks challenged Bates off the cuff eulogy. "In my book Doc met a better end than he deserved, by all rights he should have ended up on a gallows or full of lead in some chicken coup."

"That's pretty harsh talk from a man who use to be his friend," Bates charged.

"Use to be is right, and I told him so when he rode through this morning and I'll tell you the same thing Clarence Bates, you and these Ames boys will end up the same way some day. No one will mourn your deaths, no one will volunteer to bury you, and certainly no one will ever visit your graves," Shanks retorted in a hard unwavering voice.

"But when we get our gold, we will die rich!" Bates cried out in frustration as he turned to face the old cowboy. "I want that gold so you'd best tell me everything you know about it before I let Buck use his Colt on you, old man."

"I knew Doc was on the run this morning, otherwise he would never have ridden through my place or taken a chance on fording the river when it's at flood stage. I couldn't see under his duster but he didn't move like a man weighted down by a heavy load. His horse looked tired but again I didn't see any sign it was packing anything other than Doc. So you can do whatever you want to me, but I can't tell you anything more about your precious gold!" Shanks explained the events of the morning one more time.

"Can't or won't?" Bates snarled out.

Rather than reply to Bates' threatening ultimatum, Henry Shanks locked eyes with the outlaw which started a stare-down. The battle of wills continued without flinching for several minutes until Red Ames called for his partner's attention. "I think Buck will be all right, got the bleeding stopped, but some of the gun powder got in his eyes. He's having trouble seeing and hearing but that will most likely pass."

"Get him on his feet, we're going to tear this place apart until we find our gold," Bates ordered harshly.

"You can look all you want, but you know good and well Doc would never have entrusted me with any stolen goods, let alone a load of gold," the old cowboy argued still stalling for time.

"Red, look in the barn, I'll go through the house and Buck can keep an eye on Mr. Shanks," Bates commanded, like an eager young Lieutenant.

Red Ames hurried off to the barn while his brother Buck sat in the middle of the dusty yard rubbing his head and trying to make his eyes focus. Immediately a loud ruckus broke out in the barn as Red Ames began his search by breaking everything that came to hand, each crash was followed by a howl of glee to illustrate how much he enjoyed his work. With the barn in ruins, the outlaw continued to run amuck as he raced from out building to out building inflicting as much damage as possible on each, until he came to the little white two-holer privy. Ames kicked the door off its hinges before setting the small wooden outhouse on fire. Its jumping flames unleashed a demon in the man as he danced around the burning building like a wild savage might dance around a campfire.

Clarence Bates emerged quietly from the small ranch house, paused in the middle of the yard to access the situation, then walked slowly to where Henry Shanks stood in silent disgust. “That,” Bates said softly, “is the reason I searched your house, the man is crazy when it comes to burning or destroying anything.”

“Thank you for that at least, but how in the world did you and Doc get tangled up with a couple of feeble minded fools like these Ames Brothers?” Henry asked with a negative shake of his head.

“They had the inside track on this gold robbery and two hundred pounds of gold will buy a lot of forgiveness,” Bates answered, before approaching the still gyrating Red Ames.

"Why in the hell did you burn the privy?" he demanded.

"I remember our pa use to hide guns, moonshine, even money down the outhouse hole. I couldn't see down there so I lit her up for a better look-see," Red explained joyously.

"Why didn't you just tip the privy over, then you could have seen down the hole. You can't see anything down there now cause of the smoke and flames. Besides that smoke can be seen for miles, it might draw people and the last thing we want is people nosing around!" Bates scolded his dimwitted accomplice, raising his hand as if he would strike Red.

"I'm sorry, it seemed like a good idea at the time," Ames pleaded, as he covered his head and quickly ducked away from any forthcoming blows.

"Get over there and see to your brother!" Bates growled knowing he had just established the command order of the small group. Once again Clarence Bates stopped in his tracks to take in the trail of destruction his partner had inflicted on the Rattlesnake Ranch and wondered what the overzealous fool might have overlooked in his eagerness to destroy. His eye's examined each battered building, fence post and tree on the place but nothing appeared out of ordinary until he remember the old man's well.

"Come over here Red, I nearly forgot how proud the old man is of his hand dug well. Let's pull this cover off and see what might be hidden from our sight," Bates announced, as he closely scrutinized

Henry Shanks face for any sign of fear. But the old cowboy remained calm, and confident knowing his hiding place would go undetected by the three lazy outlaws. His aloof mannerism distracted Bates enough that the bandit leader merely opened the door of the heavy well platform before Red Ames thrust his shaggy head into the opening and quickly announced there was nothing unusual secreted in the well.

"Except for this here rope," Ames bellowed out after realizing his initial inspection had been faulty. His excitement was uncontrollable as he began reeling in handfuls of the small rope. "Whatever is on the end of this lariat don't weigh no two hundred pounds though," the slow witted outlaw's voice revealed his disappointment. "Hell, it's just a bucket of milk," Ames snarled.

"It's the old man's cooler," Bates declared. "He hangs his milk and cheese down there where it's cooler, haven't you ever seen that before?" the gang leader inquired of his underling.

"We never had a well on our place, Pa made us tote water from the spring down the hill but it was always warm by the time we got back to the house," Red explained, as he lifted the pail of milk over the edge of the well ring. "I reckon you are right, nothing here but cow juice." With that, Red smiled before pulling a belt knife to cut the rope then slowly poured the bucket of milk on the ground. He smiled once more, then spit down the open well cover.

"What a piece of trash you are," Henry Shanks growled out loud enough for everyone to hear.

“Trash huh?” Red Ames snarled at the old man.

Henry Shanks didn’t take Ames’ threat seriously but watched as the man wiped the rim of the milk pail with his scurvy sweat-stained shirt sleeve before positioning it carefully on the ground against the well base. These meticulous preparations were followed by an odd hopping, twirling dance that Red preformed while humming some unknown tune. Suddenly Red let out a blood curdling howl just to attract everyone’s attention he then dropped his filthy grease smeared leather pants and squatted over the milk pail. He emitted a loud grunt then evacuated the entire contents of his bowels into the milk bucket. Red rose with a smile, pulled up his pants, then turned around like an old hen inspecting a freshly laid egg to admire his deposit.

“Now old man, if you think that was trashy, watch this!” Ames screamed out as he grasped the bucket with both hands and slowly poured its stinking putrid contents down the well opening. Once the filth could be heard splashing in the water some fifty feet below, Red Ames unceremoniously dropped the bucket down the well. “I didn’t think you’d want that bucket anymore ‘cause you ain’t got any clean water to wash it out,” he laughed hysterically.

“You damn fool!” Clarence Bates exclaimed. “That was the best drinking water around and we needed to fill our canteens.”

“I wouldn’t have done it ‘cept the old man ain’t got a proper privy for company anymore.”

"I did have until you burned it down, you scum!" Henry Shanks countered Ames' silly excuse for his behavior.

"Scum you say?" Red Ames screamed. "No one calls an Ames scum," he added while pulling his belt knife.

"Cut the old bastard Red!" Brother Buck, still having difficulty regaining his senses bellowed out his loyal encouragement. Those words drove Red to run at full speed to where Henry Shanks bravely waited the knife-wielding maniac's attack. Ames raised the long thick bladed weapon high over his head then with a high pitched scream delivered a downward blow to the old cowboy's body.

Henry Shanks, using his battered left hand managed to block Red Ames' crashing overhead attack but the impact drove him to the ground. Sensing a weakened victim, Ames jumped astraddle Shanks' body then using a two-handed grip drove the blade into the old man's chest. A loud metallic snap filled the air indicating the inferior steel blade had failed in its mission when it came in contact with Henry Shanks rib cage.

Red Ames lifted the bloody knife up to his eye level where he bewilderingly studied the blade, now missing a good two inches from its tip. The outlaw turned the knife slowly around in his hand, a look of complete disbelief on his face realizing his once trusted weapon had betrayed him at a most inopportune time.

A loud thud accompanied Clarence Bates' rifle butt striking the side of Red Ames' unprotected head.

The blow forcefully drove Ames from his perch atop the old cowboy's body to a prone face-down position in the middle of the ranch house driveway. The stunned outlaw rolled around in the dirt, holding his head, cussing Bates and the world in general. Once his head stopped buzzing, Ames rose to his knees and with a loud snarled demanded, "why in the hell did you hit me?"

"Because, you damn fool, I need that old man to tell me where the gold is hidden, I don't need you or your empty headed brother!" Bates retorted.

"But he called us trash and scum!" Red shouted in defense of his action.

"You and your brother are stupid scum and with Doc and Shanks both dead you're poor scum. They were the only ones who knew where the gold might be and for my part I'll let anyone call me scum for two hundred pounds of gold!" Clarence Bates' voice was filled with rage at the action of his unthinking partners.

"Maybe the old man is still alive," Red said in a sudden hopeful voice as he crawled close to Shanks body. "There's the tip of my knife," he declared pulling the pointed piece of bloody steel from the old man's chest wound. "That damn traveling peddler swore up and down this blade was unbreakable. I paid two dollars of my hard earned money for this piece of junk and look at it now, wouldn't make a good fish sinker," he cursed while throwing both pieces of the weapon into the weeds.

"You ain't never made any money the hard way Red, all you've ever known is stealing someone else's hard earned money," Buck Ames stated before trying to laugh but the pain from his movements stopped his attempted humor.

"Never mind all that, if Shanks ain't dead he soon will be, so he won't be telling us anything about that hard earned gold we worked so hard to steal and cut up," Clarence Bates' words were full of pain and dejection.

"Does the old man have a hired man?" still on his hands and knees, Red Ames asked in a strange far off way.

"I don't know, reckon he hires seasonal help. Why do you ask?" Bates demanded of his halfwit partner.

"I see another set of foot prints that don't match ours, or Doc's or the old man's boots. You don't reckon someone else was here this morning and made off with our two hundred pounds of gold do you?" Red asked dryly, still unable to fathom how difficult it would be for one man to transport two hundred pounds of gold.

ON THE TRAIL

Clarence Bates, head down, began to slowly move around the ranch house yard scouting for more boot tracks like the ones Red Ames had discovered. He found boot prints near the house, beside the well, and strangely enough a trail of the unknown boot prints heading into the wetland north of the well. “Whoever it was making these tracks walked all over the place,” Bates complained bitterly.

“Do you think this fella was here when Doc rode through?” Red Ames asked of his partners.

“Could be, but we probably will never know, cause you just had to kill the only man who could answer that question!” Bates snarled, pointing to Henry Shanks body.

“All right, all right, I should have used my head.” Ames gave a halfhearted apology for his actions as he also wandered about the ranch yard looking for boot tracks. “We didn’t see anyone on the road coming in so either he’s hiding here somewhere, or he left by way of this here slough,” Ames argued, pointing to the tracks leading off into the wetlands.

"No one who knows this area would ever walk into that marsh 'cause it full of poisonous snakes. Why, there's more rattlesnakes in that swamp than there are on the rest of this whole ranch."

"Still," Bates continued, "with Doc and old man Shanks both dead, and we ain't able to find the gold around here, our only chance is to find this fella and make him talk." The gang leader stopped to think a minute, then announced his plan, "We'll do this just like you hunt birds," he began. "Red, you move down the far side of the marsh and I'll go down this side while Buck plays like a bird dog and follows this fella right to the riverbank. Now this ain't no prairie chicken we're after, so don't lose your head and shoot him when he flushes from cover."

"Now wait just a damn minute, I ain't no bird dog and I hate snakes so if you want this bird run out of the swamp, you're going to have to do it yourself," Buck Ames growled out in no uncertain terms.

"If you want your share of the gold you'll crawl on your belly through that slough if need be. If you're not going to help catch this fella, I'm going to mount up and ride out then you two can figure out how to get the gold all by your lonesome," Clarence Bates threatened in a deep harsh voice.

"Don't get your tail in a twist," Buck Ames blurted out. "We gotta stay together, the three of us," he warned, hoping one of his partners would volunteer to play the role of hound dog. But when neither one spoke up, the outlaw cursed a blue streak then said, "you're a couple of cowards, ain't either one man enough to take a chance for a pot of gold. Well hell, I'm man enough to track this fella through hell, if it will get me my gold!" Ames bellowed out his belittling challenge, curst once more, then walked reluctantly to the point where the mysterious foot prints disappeared into the wetlands beyond the fence.

"Let's go!" Bates called out, leading his horse down the dirt track which lay between the hayfield and the swamp. His coercing the Ames brothers into doing his bidding brought a grin to the gang leader's face. He knew winning this standoff was just one more step towards having total control of his partners.

Ben Crane moved low and slow as he neared the confluence of the marsh and the Yellowstone River. His progress had been delayed by several sudden encounters with large rattlesnakes, not to mention the gunshot report, which originated from Mr. Shanks ranch house. The sound of that shot had stuck fear in the youth's heart causing him to disobey Henry Shanks orders to ignore any sounds coming from his place.

Crane remained hidden in the marsh's tall cattails for several valuable minutes until sounds of arguing voices told him the men at the Shanks ranch hadn't discovered their lost loot. The youth found solace in the tall sharp blades of the cattail grasses, but guilt and fear for the safety of his old friend Henry Shanks twice brought him to abandon cover to retrace his trail. Each time however the promise he had made to find the Sheriff drove him back into hiding among the gnarly cattail roots. Ben's course was clear, his duty lay in reporting to the law while his heart would ache for his old friend's safety. Ben's keen hearing easily detected the sound of muted arguments coming from Henry Shanks place, but strain as he might, he could not understand what was being discussed. Then suddenly the voices went silent, the disagreement had been settled and Ben wondered who won the debate until he detected movement in the swamp behind him. A horse whined to his right and a man to the left cussed as he slapped at a swarm of biting flies, which rose up out of the tall grass to attack both the man and his horse. It was only then that the inexperienced Ben Crane realized he had waited too long to make his escape to the river.

Somewhere down his back trail the whirring buzz of a rattlesnake's tail filled the still morning air as did a long string of profanity from an unseen man who had been surprised by the inhospitable serpent. "Are you all right Buck?" came a voice from the north side of the wetlands.

"Yeah, the damn thing just missed my hand, scared the living hell out of me," a man's voice called out from somewhere in the swamp lands directly behind Ben.

"Shut up you two," Bates ordered in a sharp tone. "Kill that snake and get moving," he added.

Young Ben Crane was now absolutely certain Doc Walker's three partners were on his trail just as Henry Shanks had warned. He took a deep breath then using all the stealth and woodsmen skills he possessed, began to crawl in the direction of the Yellowstone River. Normally Crane would be better than two hundred yards from the riverbank at this point, however since the water level was above flood stage it had backed up into the marsh reducing the distance to less than half or about 70 yards. The closer the youth moved, the deeper the water became until he realized it was easier to swim than crawl.

"I think I see him," someone called out. "Yeah I can see his head in the water," the voice stated excitedly.

"Yeah I see him too," another man cried out just before the report of a gunshot ripped the dry Montana air. The lead slug from the Colt revolver smacked into the water a good four feet behind Crane's head, but it was enough of a warning that the youth immediately dove below the surface of the water. A second and a third shot impacted with the shallow water before Clarence Bates began to scream at his companions.

"What in the hell is wrong with you two?" the gang leader cried out. "I just said not to shoot at this man, I hope neither one of you fools hit him!"

"From here it looked like Buck might have winged him," Red Ames called out from his position on the north side of the slough.

"Damn you Buck, if that fella's dead I'm going to kill both of you idiots! Now keep your eyes open, if he's alive, he'll have to come up for air shortly."

Ben Crane's lungs burned and his brain screamed out for air but the splashing of bullets around his head was enough of an incentive to remain submerged a little longer. His right hand struck a solid object which turned out to be a rough bark covered log that had been washed into the reeds by the flood waters. One end of the log was securely grounded on the rock bank while the opposite end floated peacefully in the two foot deep brackish water. The floating end of the log provided just enough bottom clearance for Ben Crane to slip between its course bark and the sloughs muddy bottom. Young Crane slid the palms of his hands around the logs rough exterior feeling for any limbs which might prevent his swimming under the floating obstacle. Ben's head pounded and his muscles began to fail him as he swam underneath the log, finally popping to the surface on the opposite side, where he began gulping massive amounts of moldy decayed smelling air.

The floating log gave Ben's movement positive concealment from the three pursing outlaw's sharp eyes. His fingertips dug into the irregular tree bark as he fought to keep his head above water, his eyes were filled with the sloughs dirty grime which impaired his vision, preventing him from detecting the large rattlesnake that had taken sanctuary from the floodwaters atop the very same floating log. The whirring buss of the big reptiles vibrating tail filled Ben's ears with horror, triggering an automatic fear response in his brain. The water and dirt in the youth's eyes prevented his visualizing the life threatening serpent's exact location but his hearing indicated the sound originated from on top of the log and just a bit to his right. Instinct drove the youth to jump backwards and down into the sloughs dark smelly water. This was the only defensive action that mother nature's instinct to survive had ingrained in Ben's brain, however the stark terror many people experience when in the close proximity to a snake of any kind immediately overcame his normal common sense causing him to rise up out of his cover in an attempt to walk on top of the water. All of Ben's splashing and commotion drew the three outlaw's attention and they quickly rushed toward him.

Trying to run through waist deep water is a very difficult proposition so after a few feet of this effort, exhaustion combined with a quieting of the nerves brought Ben Crane to his senses. He realized the pursuing outlaws were just as much a threat to life as the poisonous rattlesnake had been. Still unable to run, the youth dove head first once again into the shallow water and began to swim under the surface as fast as possible in the direction of the raging river.

Ben's lungs were beginning to ache once more as he swam under water struggling to remain close to the sloughs rough bottom. The need to surface for air became stronger by the second and the youth began to surrender to his body's urgent requirement for oxygen when the Yellowstone Rivers powerful current assumed command of his body. He had unknowingly exited the mouth of the slough and was now in the grasp of the flood waters powerful current. The raging torrents sucked Ben farther into the river channel, while it's whirling eddies drove his body to the river bottom where he banged against large boulders and submerged logs. Young Crane, with arms and legs flailing, struggled to the surface several times only to be drug down without inhaling a single breath of life giving air. Locked in the invisible arms of the furious flood waters, Ben Crane said a short prayer as he bounced and scraped against the river's rocky bottom. He had given up the desperate struggle for life and accepted the fact that he was powerless to prevent the grim reaper from shortly harvesting his soul. "Thank you God for my life now at its end and I pray you will console my family when I'm gone. I am ready Lord." The thought had barely cleared Ben's oxygen deprived brain when his body slammed into what felt like a large flat wall.

Ben Crane found himself spread-eagled, arms and legs wrapped around a hard immovable object with the full force of the raging Yellowstone River pushing against his back. The water's pressure prevented the youth from moving his body away from the flat surface, but even through the fog of oxygen deprivation, his brain realized the rushing current was trying to lift him up toward the surface. He instantly dug his fingers into the surface of the entrapping obstacle and pushed up with all his remaining strength. The sense of rising up spurred the youth to repeat the movement again and again until suddenly his head broke through the water's surface. Ben had never experience a sweeter taste than the clear cool Montana air which filled his lungs at that moment of true deliverance. He coughed and choked repeatedly while instinct drove him to spit out the water, drawing in one gulp after another of precious life giving air. It was a natural impulse to cling tightly to his perch while recovering from a near drowning experience, but it took a few minutes of rest before the youth came to the conclusion he was saved by the grace of God and by Monitor Rock, which was normally used to gage the depth of the river at Shanks Crossing.

"The river level must be dropping," Ben thought as he clung to the top of the rock which earlier that day had been completely submerged. "Not only am I on top of Monitor Rock, I'm half way across the river," his foggy brain concluded. "Thank you dear Lord for my salvation."

The youth surveyed the river from bank to bank before turning his attention to the robbers, who were just moments before in hot pursuit. In the trees about fifty yards up stream he could see a rider leading another horse, break into the clear. A moment later a second man climbed up out of the marsh to join the rider.

"They've caught up with me already," Crane whispered to himself as he carefully moved around to the right side of the huge rock. It was his intent to hide behind Monitor Rock but the powerful current tried to rip his arms and legs from their tenuous hold. Strong young muscles and sheer determination can often times overcome negative luck and bad breaks, as was the case this time, as Ben worked his way to the downstream side of the rock. Here he found relief from the incessant pressure of the raging current in the form of a narrow wake produced by the undefeatable presence of the huge boulder. Crane watched from the wet security of Monitor Rock as the two men walked slowly up and down the riverbank trying to decipher the many tracks laid down during Doc Walkers drowning and the attempted rescue. After a few minutes, a third man joined the first two, which started a lengthy conversation that was animated with a lot of pointing and arm waving. After a meeting of the minds, all three bandits began to walk down the riverbank and once again they struggled to sort out the different signs.

This was Ben Crane's first close look at Doc Walker's gang members but as much as he yearned to stare at the bad men, he feared they might discover his position so he stayed low in the water. However, for some reason the robbers kept their eyes to the ground, only occasionally looking at the rushing water. Clarence Bates paid a good deal of attention to the large tree where Doc had lost his life, so much so that he ordered his companions to wade about in the shallow water between the trunk and the bank. He may have hoped to find the lost gold his late partner was carrying. But nothing was gained from the search except wet feet and a pair of irritated brothers.

The bandit trio widened their search to include Henry Shanks alfalfa field, which was bordered by the riverbank. They rode back and forth making every effort to retrieve the gold they had helped steal. But they found only prairie dogs and rattlesnakes that were hunting the hairy little varmints who called the hayfield home. The Ames brothers had a deeply ingrained dislike for both the burrowing prairie dogs and the noisy slithering serpents that pursued them so they made repeated excuses to abandon the search through the nearly knee high foliage.

Ben watched with great interest from his hiding place behind Monitor Rock as Bates tried in vain to keep the Ames brothers involved in the search. He saw this farcical search as a unique distraction, which might allow him to escape by crossing the other half of the river.

CROSSING THE RIVER

Looking far up the river, the youth spotted a small tree with several leaf covered branches being swept along with the racing current. Two of the tree's larger branches rose a foot or so above the water before arching back to the rolling surface.

Ben peered cautiously around Monitor Rock's edge and to his estimation the approaching tree would pass very near to his location. He glanced over his shoulder to find the three highwaymen were moving farther and farther away from the riverbank. The passing tree could prove to be the youth's best chance to escape unseen across the river, he knew it was a slim chance but one that he was willing to take.

Ben knew his timing would have to be nearly perfect if he hoped to use the passing tree for concealment from his pursuers. He also knew the dangers of jumping in front of the root-ball which could be washed over his body or he could become snared by the tangle of exposed roots. The trailing limbs would present the same hazards but if he were lucky enough to grab one of the smaller leaf covered branches it might be possible to hand over hand his way around to the far side of the tree, which would provide adequate concealment from his tormenters.

Just as Mr. Shanks had said, as the river drops the trash will move toward the center of the river. River currents are highly unpredictable at best and as the tree closed on Ben's position, he realized the muddy root-ball would shortly collide with Monitor Rock. Crane feared a collision would throw all of his plans for escape into a cocked hat. The tree's new path seemed to be aligned with the rocks north and west side so instinct told the youth to move around to the south and east side of his granite shield.

At the last possible moment the tangle of mud and roots only scraped the edge of the massive boulder but the top branches hissed and groaned as they slithered across the stones peak. A few of the leaf covered branches the size of switches slapped Ben's face and hands hard enough to produce a burning sting.

He released his desperate hold on the rock as he lunged out into the writhing water, his hands flailing in a desperate attempt to grab hold of one of the rapidly passing tree branches. Ben Crane's extended body landed in the top willowy branches of the passing tree and being limber they could not support his weight. He immediately sank, not only through the flood water but through the myriad of small leafy branches where he quickly became entangled. The youth struggled in vain to free himself from the trap but each time he neared escape, the powerful water current swept him back into the snarled limbs. He fought valiantly to keep his head above the dark water, each and every gulp of air was one more victory that encouraged the exhausted youth to fight on.

The battle raged on for several minutes more but as the youths strength waned desperation filled his brain, washing away the power of rational thinking. Ben's hands began without plan to tear instinctively at the imprisoning foliage which only burned up oxygen and muscle strength.

The match between man and nature was drawing to a quick conclusion as Crane's body grew limp; he sank downward through the tree's slender non-supportive branches until he struck the river bottom. The harsh impact with the hard rock strewn river bed shocked Ben's senses just enough for him to realize he was free of the trees bark covered tentacles, but life would continue only if he could swim to the surface immediately.

The roaring of the river left Ben's ears and was quickly followed by the world turning black. His sense of balance rapidly diminished to the point that up and down were the same direction and yet the stubborn youth struggled on. His legs kicked and his arms flailed but they were not coordinated efforts leading in any one specific direction.

Young Crane's body moved up, then to the left, then to the right until his movements ceased entirely. The powerful waters of the raging Yellowstone River were on the cusps of extinguishing the flame of life from one more unfortunate soul. But the natural buoyancy of the human body combined with the rivers ever present turbulence eventually lifted Crane to the sunlit surface.

Ben lay spread eagled, unmoving face down, and dirty water lapping against the upstream side of his body. The power of life ebbed away with each wave that splashed into his chest and over his body. All the dreams and plans for Benjamin Franklin Crane's future accomplishments were silently dissolving in the rolling waters of the Yellowstone River.

Chance, coincidence, fate, or divine intervention, the name varies but the outcome is often the same from case to case but without such unplanned interference, the history of man would indeed be irreverently altered. Ben Crane's life was saved not by a miracle from above, there wasn't any explosions or great flashes of light, but was brought about by a ten foot long 2x12 plank, which had washed away far up stream. The wide flat board had been water logged just long enough that it now floated just below the rivers choppy surface.

The unpredictable meeting of the plank's squared off downstream end and the side of Ben Cranes head might be classed as a miracle, but plain dumb luck would be a more fitting term. The dull rap against his skull stirred a primitive response deep within the youth's brain, a second, then a third strike stirred an automatic defense reaction, which caused Ben to throw his right arm up and out in a self-defense move. Fortunately for the unconscious youth his misdirected arm landed on top of the great plank which forced his face above the water line.

It was of course, that indomitable instinct to survive, which triggered the nearly drowned Ben Crane to take that first deep sweet inhalation, but it was quickly followed by an intermittent series of choking, retching and more gulps of air. This drill lasted for several minutes with the outcome in serious doubt but each round of gagging expelled more muddy water from Ben's airways which induced his lungs to suck in more and more oxygen.

The narrow 2x12 had become a long slender life raft, which drifted closer and closer to the south bank of the Yellowstone River. The strong current carried the plank and its human cargo downstream until it ran aground at the mouth of what was known as Deer Creek. The sudden impact threw Ben forward, causing his body to roll onto its back then off the end of the plank onto the rock strewn riverbank.

The sharp rocks dug into Ben's flesh and the stinging pain further stimulated the youth to rally his consciousness. The wonder of the human brain began to sense and think, it began to reason and relay messages to the living machinery that would conduct lifesaving motions. He began to pull with his arms in an attempt to clear the banks high water mark but his oxygen starved muscles immediately cramped into hard knots. Some corner of Ben Crane's befuddled mind kept warning all the other corners of his brain, it was imperative that the entirety of his wet battered body be retrieved from the clutches of the powerful waterway. Acting under heavy pressure from his overly stressed brain, the youth began to roll over and over while trying to push against the river bottom with his feet and legs. This rudimentary movement was slow and painful at best but he finally managed to wriggle beyond the grasp of the rolling current.

Escaping the rivers watery grave was a herculean effort, but now that it was accomplished every second of life was even sweeter for the doing. Now it was time to rest among the leaves and grass which lined the riverbank while whispering a prayer that the three outlaws on the opposite bank did not discover his presence. Ben's breathing became easier, his painful muscle cramps subsided enough to allow minor movement, but it was abundantly clear he would need more time to recuperate from the effects of this day. Still somewhere hidden deep in the back of his subconscious brain a little spark, not unlike the clattering of a telegraph key, continually urged the youth forward. The very thought of leaving this resting place, now that life was in regeneration, seemed an insane option at best. And just why would he wish to give up the new found comfort of a weed infested rocky riverbank without an urgent call to duty?

Unfortunately that call to arms was quick in coming. A single gunshot, a shocking sound, which had started many a battle was the bugle call that snapped the physically drained Ben Crane from a near comatose state to one raw ragged nerve. Suddenly every sense in the youth's body was on edge trying to access the level of his personal danger.

It was natural curiosity more than self-protection that lifted Ben's head off the ground for a quick peek at the far side of the river, which logic told him should be the source of any threat. But to his surprise there wasn't a single sign of the three outlaws or any other movement on the opposite side of the river.

ESCAPING THE RIVER

"My God, are you all right?" A voice exclaimed from far up on the riverbank. That excited call was immediately followed by the sound of someone or something rushing through the brush lined riverbank. Ben remained still, following the tenants he had often heard repeated by the old-time Indian fighters, keep to your cover or play possum they often warned. But the sounds of movement grew ever nearer stirring a natural wild desire in the youth to jump up and flee in the opposite direction from whomever was approaching. Ben struggled to his hands and knees just as the voice called out once more. "Hold on there fella, I don't mean you any harm. It's me, Amos, Amos Moody. I don't mean you any harm," the quickly approaching voice called out.

"Mr. Moody?" Ben Crane inquired raising his head off the ground sufficiently high enough to look in the old man's direction. "Mr. Moody, what in the world are you doing over here?" the youth asked, totally surprised at finding the recluse on the west side of the river.

“Oh,” Amos Moody exclaimed, showing a shortness of breath as he neared Ben’s hiding place. The short slim built old man groaned slightly then dropped to his knees beside Ben’s head. He held up his boney right hand to indicate a moment’s rest would be required before any words were forth coming.

“You look tired Mr. Moody,” Ben managed to say as politely as possible. “I wish I could offer you some food or drink but I just swam across the river ‘cause three hard cases are chasing me. I think they have killed Mr. Shanks,” the youth half whispered while looking across the river.

“What?” Moody managed to blurt out as if questioning Ben’s statement.

“It’s true,” the youth began to speak rapidly as he was eager to relate the day’s events to anyone who might listen to his story. “Doc Walker, you know who he is, well, he rode into Mr. Shanks’ place while we were doing the morning chores. They talked for a couple of minutes before Walker tried to cross the river but he drowned by that big Cottonwood tree on the other bank,” Ben explained pointing to the position of the tree just up the river. “Then three of Doc’s gang rode in, Clarence Bates and the Ames brothers, Red and Buck was their names and they were demanding to find Walker or the gold he had on him. It seems the four of them robbed some mine of two hundred pounds of gold only Doc beat these three partners out of their share then took off for the high lonesome,” the youth rattled out in a nonstop recounting as if the faster the tales was repeated the more truthful it would sound.

"Easy there son, I believe you, 'cause I knew Doc Walker and Bates too. But what are you doing here?" Moody inquired hoarsely, still showing signs of exhaustion.

"Mr. Shanks made me promise I would sneak down the swamp to the river then make my way to the Sheriff's office. He told me not to look back nor to stop for any reason 'cause he didn't want me to get hurt. But those three did some shooting after I left then they tracked me into the swamp. They shot at me a couple of times but I managed to get in the river and float to this side. I believe they think I drown," Ben continued to explain his situation. "I'm sorry Mr. Moody I was so wound up in my story I didn't give you a chance to tell me why you're on this side of the river," the youth apologized for his rudeness.

"Some scoundrel butchered my yearling calf and I tracked him over the steel bridge and down this side of the river. I thought I had found him when I spotted you laying here in the creek bottom, but that ain't important now. We've got to get you to the law somehow," the old man stated in a firm no-nonsense declaration.

"Mr. Shanks wanted me to get to Grey Cliff and phone the Sheriff over in Big Timber from the general store, in fact he gave me money to pay for the call." Ben tried to reach in his pocket to retrieve the coins Henry Shanks had allotted for the phone call but his muscle cramps returned, preventing such an action.

"Hold on there son, you ain't in any shape to be moving around, in fact I think we should get you to Billings to see Dr. Bacon," Moody decreed unsure of what to do for a near drowning victim.

"I'll be all right Mr. Moody, besides I doubt if the men on the other side of the river will allow me to get up and walk away," Ben explained his situation once more.

"What men are you talking about son?" Moody inquired quizzically.

"Why the three men who were part of Doc Walker's gang, the three men who may have shot Mr. Shanks and the same three men who shot at me and chased me to the river," the exhausted youth growled out. Ben's disrespectful reply caught Amos Moody so off guard, he unthinkingly emitted a low groan before rising to his feet.

"I don't see anyone across the river," he declared in a loud voice just as a rifle bullet slammed into the ground beside the old man's feet. Moody remained standing for a second until the report of the rifle shot echoed across the churning river water and fell on the old man's ears.

"Get down Mr. Moody, those men mean business!" Ben called out, as he struggled to pull his old friend down to the ground.

"What the hell is going on?" Amos Moody demanded.

"I've been telling you, I think those three killed Mr. Shanks and they tried to kill me. They are members of Doc Walker's gang who stole a chunk of gold from some mine up north," the youth tried to explain once more but was quickly interrupted by a voice hailing them from across the river.

"You there, on the other bank, who in the hell are you?" the voice growled threateningly.

"That's Clarence Bates," Ben whispered. "He seems to be the head of the gang now that Doc Walker is dead."

"You on the other bank, declare yourself or we will start shooting," Bates roared out.

"I'm Amos Moody, I own a small place on the other side of the river. I been tracking some scoundrel who stole my calf and butchered it," Moody called back without showing himself to the outlaws.

"You mean miser Moody?" Bates' voice was tinged with humor in an effort to show off for his half-witted partners.

"That's what some folk call me," the old man responded quickly. "But why are you shooting at me?"

"We are hot on the trail of a fella who killed Henry Shanks. Have you seen any strangers around here?" the outlaw leader asked.

"No, but tell me what he looks like," Moody challenged.

"Well, to tell the truth we ain't seen him up close but I'd say he is youngish, on the thin side and on foot," the outlaw leader offered the best description he could.

"You say Henry Shanks is dead?" Moody pretended to be shocked.

"That's right, some pole cat knifed him in the chest," Bates hesitated a moment, then called out, "stand up Mr. Moody so we can talk easier," he added hoping to draw the man into the open.

"I'm old and tuckered out and I have been on that thief's trail all night so I'd rather just lay here and rest," Amos Mood countered. "Besides if there has been a killing it's your duty to report it to the Sheriff."

"Ain't got the time, my friends and I are working on a big deal so we got to move along," Bates lied smoothly as he clearly had no intentions of speaking to any lawman.

"I wish you fellas would wait around a while, you see I called the Sheriff's office from the general store in Grey Cliff and they promised to have a deputy down here this afternoon to investigate my stolen calf. So if you hang around a bit you can tell the law your account of Mr. Shanks' death."

"Like I said we gotta keep moving, but you can tell the Sheriff what we said," came Clarence Bates' weak excuse. "We'll be moving on now and I hope you find that cattle rustler." Ben and Amos Moody could hear the three hard cases laughing among themselves as they mounted their horses and rode away.

"That was real quick thinking Mr. Moody, those fella's weren't about to wait around if the law's coming," Ben praised his elder.

"I did call the Sheriff but they couldn't get a man down here for a couple days but I didn't think Bates needed to know just how long it would take the law to get here." The old man chuckled as he slowly rose to his knees in order to peek over the creek bank at the outlaw's position. "I can see three riders moving slowly towards Mr. Shanks' house," he reported to Ben who still lay exhausted on the creek bottom. "Now we need to find you some help son," Moody stated in a fatherly manner as he moved close to where the youth lay.

"Molly, my mule is tied to a bush by the railroad tracks, I'll bring her down here and we will load you up and head for town. Now you stay put and I'll be back in minute," the old man promised as he slowly rose to his feet, he groaned slightly as he placed both hands on his back as if trying to work a kink out of his spine.

Ben watched closely as the aged Amos Moody shuffled slowly up the creek bottom in the direction of the railroad tracks. The railroad right-of-way lay some half a mile west of the riverbank which led Crane to think it would be some time before the stoved-up man could make the round trip, but only a few minutes elapsed before Moody and his mule Molly broke into view.

“That didn’t take long Mr. Moody,” Ben stated in a complementary way.

“Molly untied herself and was headed this way when I run into her. Dern fool mule follows me everywhere I go but sometimes just like now it’s a blessing,” the old man explained as he led Molly beside where Ben lay. “I have a canvas tarp here, which I intend to wrap around you so if those three see us they might think I have wrapped up the calf carcass,” the old man explained as he spread the worn canvas on the ground beside Ben. “Now Young Ben, if you will roll onto this canvas, I’ll load you on Molly’s back and we can get a-going,” Moody directed softly.

Crane knew he must make every effort to cooperate with Amos Moody, still the thought of rolling on the canvas seemed impossible but he gathered up all his strength and gritted his teeth against the pain. Ben emitted one low grunt before pushing sideways to start his body rolling in the direction of the tarpaulin; to his surprise the exercise proved much easier than expected. One more exertion and the young man’s body landed center of the ragged canvas sheet.

“Your muscles must be loosening up a bit,” Moody declared as he began to fold the rough material around Ben’s body. “First I’ll stand you on your feet, then you’ll have to help a bit ‘cause I don’t think I can load you on Molly’s back all by myself,” the old man instructed.

“I’ll do all I can to help Mr. Moody,” Crane promised while doing his best to keep his balance.

"One, two, three," Amos Moody counted in a hushed tone. The combined effort of the old man and the youth propelled Ben's body on the razor sharp back of the mule. "It's a good thing Molly ain't tall," the old man chuckled as he made sure the load was situated just right.

"I think we're ready if you are?" Moody whispered into the end of the rolled up tarp.

"Ready," Ben whispered in reply.

With that signal, Amos Moody grabbed the mule's halter rope and led her up the creek bottom towards the railroad right-of-way. Both men, young and old were surprised they did not receive a challenge from Clarence Bates or his partners. Instead Mr. Moody walked slowly up the creek bottom carefully picking the best path to prevent his load of human cargo from sliding off Molly's boney back. The little mule moved cautiously along the trail as if she understood her cargo on this trip was not tools or construction materials but instead the heavy weight hanging over her back was a fragile human being. "We're almost to the little railroad trestle," Moody whispered. "I'll go around to the other side before I unload you," he added softly.

Good to his word, Amos Moody struggled through the pile of driftwood and brush which had been trapped by the bridge piling during this most recent run off. Once they had cleared the brush pile, Moody turned to the right moving up a slope, out of the view of the three outlaws on the opposite side of the river. The old man halted on a small flat spot before gently pulling Ben from Molly's back. He groaned through the whole strenuous process of laying him on the ground. The canvas flaps slid down Ben's sides, exposing his face to the world once more; he took a deep breath then began trying to move his still cramped limbs.

"Sometimes moving a cramped up muscle will help, so if you want to stand up I'll be glad to give you a hand," the old man offered, still whispering although they were hidden by the railroad bed from the outlaws view. Amos Moody extended his right arm allowing Ben to grasp onto the old man's surprisingly muscled forearm. The youth pulled with all his might, finally managing to stand erect on both feet though his leg's trembled violently. "You're doing just fine," Moody encouraged, while using both hands to steady his young friend.

"Thank you Mr. Moody, I don't know what I'd have done if you hadn't come along," Ben stated as he worked to regain control of his body. "I have to get to Grey Cliff and contact the Sheriff to explain what has happened, but I don't know how I will get there," the youth lamented.

"I reckon Molly and I can get you to Grey Cliff and you can send a message from there but it will be slow going," Moody offered in his slow soft way of speaking. "But let's try walking around a might, it could help work the knots out of your legs," the old man suggested, leading off without waiting for Ben to reply. As the man and boy moved slowly around the flat area, it soon became clear to both that the exercise was indeed improving Ben's mobility.

"Do you hear something?" Amos Moody asked as the pair halted beside Molly. "It's too early for the west bound flyer and the number seven freight passed by before I found you in the creek."

"Yes sir, I do hear something, sounds like it's coming from the east. It could be a handcar, maybe the section crew is out repairing the track," Ben proposed, turning to look down the shiny steel rails, which eventually disappeared around a long sweeping bend to the east.

"Hang on to Molly while I climb up the bank and have a look," Amos Moody instructed as he began to claw his way up the railroad right-of-way's steep slope. He was clearly short of breath and some exhausted when he gained the flat rail bed but the game old man rose to an upright stance in order to get a better view of the tracks. Suddenly Moody ripped the battered grey felt hat from the top of his head and began waving his arms wildly in the air.

"You're right Ben, it's a handcar coming this way," Amos called down the slope while still waving his hat in the air. "It's Emer Plank and he's stopping," Amos Moody added excitedly.

HITCHING A RIDE

The railroad handcars were small flat topped vehicles with four small steel wheels, and a lever that pivots like a see-saw. They were propelled by a person pushing up and down on a "T" handle lever, which turned the four wheels, moving the handcar along the railway. The manually driven handcar began to slow as the man operating the big T handle fought against the wheels forward motion. "What's the trouble?" he called out as he drug his feet through the rail bed cinders behind the handcar, finally bringing its momentum to a stop beside Amos Moody.

"Am I glad to see you, Emer! I got some real trouble and I was hoping you would be able to help," the old man began to explain. "That's Ben Crane standing down there by Molly, you know he's been working for Henry Shanks. Well he say's Doc Walker and his gang rode into the Rattlesnake Ranch this morning and killed Mr. Shanks. Somehow Doc also got killed and now Clarence Bates is leading two other gang members in hot pursuit of young Ben here." Moody quickly rattled off the story as best he could remember, then took a deep breath before taking a seat on the handcar deck.

"Are you hurt kid?" Plank asked as he began to slide down the rail bed embankment to where Ben and Molly stood.

"Not really hurt, but I'm all cramped up and can't walk very well. Still I must get to town and contact Sheriff Mayhew before Bates and the Ames brothers get away."

"Ames brothers?" Plank demanded sharply. "Red and Buck, are they tangled up in this?"

"Yes sir, they are riding with Clarence Bates and I think they killed Mr. Shanks after he made me leave to find the law. Do you know those men Mr. Plank?" Ben inquired, unsure of the railroad man's connection with the outlaws.

"I knew Doc and Bates when they lived in these parts, but I only know the Ames brothers by reputation and by the fact that the railroad would pay a pretty penny to get hold of those two scoundrels."

"Now who did you say killed Doc Walker?" Plank asked, his facial expression showing his confusion.

"No one killed him, he drowned trying to cross the river early this morning. He knew Bates and the Ames brothers were hot on his trail. We pulled his body from the river just before the three outlaws rode into the ranch. Mr. Shanks made me leave just before they rode in but I was hiding in the weeds when I heard gunshots coming from the house, then

Bates and the Ames brothers picked up my trail and followed me to the river," Ben explained still struggling to stay on his feet.

"Did you see any of this Amos?" the big railroad man called up to Moody.

"No sir, but right after I found Ben laying in the creek, three men on the other side of the river shot at me. They never gave their names but I reckon they were Bates and the Ames boy's. They claimed to be in pursuit of a young fella who had just killed Henry Shanks," the old man added to his narrative.

"You didn't shoot Mr. Shanks did you boy?" The six foot four inch tall Plank's imposing figure towered over and intimidated Ben Crane's slender body. The Union Pacific's well known section boss, Emer Plank had a reputation for controlling the fight prone, hard drinking gandy dancers who performed the back-breaking repairs on the tracks and bridges which kept the train traffic moving across the vast northern American prairies. His form of labor relations was often metered out by a closed fist or a hickory pick handle, fear of any man was not in the makeup of such indestructible men.

"No sir, Mr. Shanks is my friend. I don't know how my family would have gotten along without his help these last couple of years," Ben, a bit nervous of the huge man answered quickly.

"Good, I didn't think so. Now, we have to get you to town as soon as possible. The best way to do that is on my work car, if you can make it to the top of the grade. If you can't I'll have to carry you up there," Plank stated flatly.

“Oh sir, I don’t think you can carry me up that steep of grade,” Ben protested the idea of the big man transporting his body up the long steep incline.

“Hell son, I can tote you and two more just like you up this little hill,” Plank bragged in a loud bass voice as he thumped his chest with his massive right hand. “Now let go of that mule ‘cause I don’t want to carry her up there too,” Emer Plank ordered, as he placed his right shoulder in Ben’s midsection before standing erect which caused the youth to fold over, the upper part of his torso behind the big man’s back while his legs hung down in front. “Are you ready son?” Plank asked as he turned to start the difficult climb to the rail bed above.

Emer Plank had set a herculean task for himself, but he was half way up the slope before Amos Moody realized what was happening. He rose from the handcar, calling out an offer to help but his assistance was summarily refused by the section boss whose powerful long legs drove both himself and his burden smoothly up the hill. The old man watched in disbelief as Plank took one more long bounding step which cleared the rail bed shoulder, which brought the section boss to a standing position beside his work car.

“Here we are son,” Plank declared in a boisterous voice. “Like I said, wasn’t much of a chore,” he laughed out loud before laying his cargo on the front of the cart. “I’ll have Ben in town before he knows it,” the big man announced stepping up to his position behind the pump handles. Surprisingly

Moody failed to display any ill effect from the task. Plank was neither winded nor weak.

"It's midafternoon so I'll gather up Molly and head for home," Amos Moody stated softly as the rail cart began to move.

"Thank you Mr. Moody, I owe you a great deal for helping me today. I hope you don't run into Bates and his partners again but if you do tell them the truth. I don't want you to get hurt on my account," Ben called out over the hissing sound of the carts steel wheels rubbing on the steel tracks.

"You two be careful," the old man shouted out at the quickly disappearing cart.

Ben raised his head high enough to look back at Amos Moody who was standing straddle of one steel rail, his hand raised over head to wave good bye. "I sure hope Mr. Moody doesn't run into those men on his way home," Ben yelled back to Emer Plank as they continued down the railway.

"I've known Moody for a long time, he's an old Indian fighter, smart and tuff, I reckon he'll get along better than we would roaming around out on the prairie." Plank's powerful voice called forward in an effort to reassure his passenger.

Ben Crane lay still as his already sore body absorbed shock after shock that jolted with each rail splice and was immediately relayed through the handcar's rigid undercarriage into the hardwood deck where he lay. He quickly accepted the rhythmic pounding of the rails, so much so his youthful exuberance began to enjoy looking forward as the handcar raced down the polished steel rails. Emer Plank pumped the carts handle at a furious pace causing the steel wheels to sing a high pitched whine bringing Ben Crane to realize his powerful rescuer was doing his upmost to reach civilization as fast as possible.

As the small settlement of Greycliff, Montana came into view Emer Plank called out in his loud foghorn voice. "Whereabouts in town do you want to go?"

"Mr. Shanks thought it would be faster if I telephoned the Sheriff from Mr. Ballard's store," Ben responded feeling the handcar beginning to slow down.

"I hope the phone line is still open, 'cause the last I knew the telegraph line to Big Timber got washed out by the rainstorm," Plank explained as he fought to retard the car's forward momentum. "I'll let you off right out front of the general store if you want," the big man promised and true to his word Emer Plank stopped the little work car right on top of the wooden crosswalk which extended from the front of the store to the other side of the railroad right-of-way.

"Thank you Mr. Plank, you have been very helpful and I shall always be in your debt," Ben declared while trying to rise to his feet.

"Are you going to be able to make it to the store?" Plank inquired, as he witnessed the youth's difficulty gaining his feet. "I can park this rig off the rails and help you to the front door," he offered, moving to assist Ben up right.

“You’ve done too much already Mr. Plank,” the youth politely refused the big man’s offer. “I believe I can make my way to the store on my own,” he added with a broad smile.

“Let me know if there is anything else I can do son,” Plank called out as he watched Ben struggle to walk to the covered front porch of Jim Ballard’s General Store.

BALLARD'S STORE

Realizing Emer Plank was watching his progress, Young Crane turned and waved as he strained to open the General Store's heavy wooden front door. Plank smiled and nodded his head before moving the work car back down the track to the section crew work shed. Ben watched with a bit of envy as the big muscular track boss easily propelled the heavy work car to its assigned place just off the busy right-of-way.

Returning to the business at hand, Ben once again leaned his shoulder against the iron bound oak door, which triggered a small brass bell attached to a coil spring located at the top of the door. This was a device designed to signal all the building occupants that someone was either entering or exiting the dwelling. The sudden raucous tinkling of the bell combined with the buildings dimly lighted interior brought Ben to a complete halt facing towards the counter located near the back wall at the opposite end of the store. The building had few windows and even fewer light fixtures due to Jim Ballard's miserly nature, but many of his customers thought the dim light was intended to hide the shoddy quality of the store's merchandise. That may be true, but Ben usually paused just inside of entrance of any local store to savor the scents and sounds emanating from the wide array of goods that general stores were required to stock. Two time pieces, one a softly ticking mantle clock sat on a shelf above the rear counter and a loud clanking animated cuckoo type clock hung high up on the side wall out of reach of busy little fingers. Both instruments were priced for sale but they had been in the same locations as long as Ben could remember. Still it was the smells, which really brought Ben up short, aaaah, the delicious mingling of scents of smoke cured hams hanging by a string from ceiling rafters, the fifty gallon wooden barrelful of large pickles floating in vinegar, another barrel filled to the brim with large white soda crackers, and a third barrel contained apples in various states of ripeness. All of these aromas blended with the pungent odor of coal oil, lye soap, and clean bolts of cloth, not to mention the draw of sweet molasses and twists of tobacco hanging from pegs on the rear wall.

As Young Crane's eyes slowly adjusted to the low light of the store's interior, he became cognizant of only two other people inside the building. One, a small built older woman who Ben didn't recognize stood near the counter examining the construction of a ten foot long braided leather buggy whip. She was remarkable for her attire more than her face, which was shaded by the long bill of her old fashioned cloth bonnet, which was tied firmly by a thin ribbon around her neck. The old woman's high collared, long sleeved dress was made of blue sun-faded cotton which exactly matched her head gear.

Ben pulled his eyes from the old woman only after Jim Ballard, who was standing behind the counter adding up the bill for the elderly woman's meager purchases bellowed out, "You boy! What the hell do you think you are doing tracking up my clean floors with all that mud on your feet?"

"I'm sorry Mr. Ballard, but I must use your telephone to call the Sheriff's office," Ben answered apologetically thrusting his hand into his soggy pants pocket to retrieve the three coins Henry Shanks had ordered him to take. "I have a dime to pay for the use of your telephone," the youth explained, holding one of the seated liberty dimes up for Ballard to see.

"You can't use the telephone, now get out of my store and take your mess along with you!" Ballard snarled.

"I can pay you more Mr. Ballard and I will gladly clean up my mess but I must call the Sheriff, it's a matter of great urgency," Ben declared holding up a second dime.

"I'll not tell you again," the bad natured proprietor growled out as he rushed around the end of the wooden counter and began to walk briskly towards Ben. "You can't use the telephone, or telegraph either because the lines are down but even if they weren't, I wouldn't let you walk around in my store in the condition you're in! But I will take whatever money you have in your procession and apply it against the bill your family owes me!" Ballard shouted out as he grabbed Ben by the hand while trying to wrestle the coins from his hand.

"This money is not mine, Mr. Ballard it belongs to Mr. Shanks. But even if it was my money we don't have a charge account with you, 'cause my father says credit will be the ruination of this country," Ben declared, as he struggled to prevent the store owner from taking the money Henry Shanks had entrusted him with earlier that day.

"I'm sick and tired of you hill trash moving in here, trying to make farms out of that scrubby land down south, all the while thinking the rest of the world should finance your pipe dreams," the store owner shrieked even louder when he saw the five dollar gold piece that glowed through Ben Cranes fingers. The greedy merchant grabbed Ben's hand in an attempt to pry loose the shiny gold coin.

The fight over the money caused the man and boy to fall against the store's front door with a loud thud, which was followed by powerful high pitched words, "Unhand that boy Mr. Ballard!" The store keeper, realizing the words of warning must have originated from the old woman and having no fear of her intervention, pressed the struggle onward. The next sound that fell on the trio's ears was a swish, and a sharp snap, accompanied by a near shattering scream.

"What in the Sam hell do you think you are doing woman?" Mr. Ballard hotly demanded as he held his profusely bleeding right ear in both hands. "This young hellion is Tom Conner, he's one of those trashy Conner's that live in the hills about ten miles south of town. They owe me a lot of money and refuse to pay, so I feel it's within my rights to confiscate any and all money in their procession when on my property!" the irate merchant cried out in his defense.

"This young man is Ben Crane from down by Pool Draw, he works for Henry Shanks so I'm sure the funds in his procession are those of Henry Shanks. The Conner boy is a head shorter and darker complexioned than Ben," the old women stated in a stern voice that made Ballard forget his wounded ear for a moment while he looked closely a Ben's face.

"All this southern trash look the same to me," he added as he turned his attention to stemming the blood flow from his ear.

"I know both families Mr. Ballard, and neither are of southern extraction. However, I'm from Georgia and I take particular offense with those who besmirch my home and heritage," the old woman informed both men in a calm even voice.

"I don't give a good God damn where you hail from, you old bitch, 'cause you nearly tore my right ear off!" Ballard growled out.

"Not without good reason sir, but that last remark will cost you your left ear too and if you don't apologize, it might cost one of your eyes." That said, the old women took one step back before applying the buggy whip to Ballard's left ear. The powerful whip stroke was quickly followed by lash after lash to the offensive proprietors head and neck.

“Get the hell out of my way boy!” Jim Ballard screamed as he threw Ben to one side while ripping the store’s front door open. He ran screaming through the door and down the front boardwalk, his arms flailing over his head as if fending off a swarm of stinging bees.

The whip wielding elderly lady matched the storekeeper stride for stride and with each hurried step she lay another stroke of the buggy whip on Jim Ballard’s head and back. Ben Crane, still a bit impaired by leg cramps fought his way through the door and onto the board sidewalk to watch.

“What the hell is that all about?” Emer Plank, his voice filled with humor called out from his position on the opposite side of the railroad tracks.

“It’s kinda complicated, but it seems Mr. Ballard tried to bully the wrong person this time,” Ben replied, as he watched the well-known belligerent merchant receive his rightful come-unpins at the business end of one of his own whips.

“I didn’t know Jim was that fast on his feet,” Plank cried out as he slapped his hand on his leg in an expression of his delight. Every citizen on Main Street of the little town of Grey Cliff, Montana witnessed the flogging, but no one intervened nor spoke out in his defense. Ballard, with his store apron pulled over his head for protection ran blindly across the railroad tracks in an attempt to out distance his antagonist by running down the road toward the new steel bridge which spanned the Yellowstone River. Upon reaching the bridge, Ballard made a flying jump onto the steel railing and began to climb the metal overhead structure like some demented squirrel. By the time his attacker gained the bridge, Ballard had scurried to the upper most limits of the steel bridge beams, a position which provided some semblance of safety and security.

"Did you get to use the telephone?" Plank inquired, but his eyes remained fixed on the action at the bridge.

"No sir," Ben replied beginning to walk in the direction of the railroad man, "Mr. Ballard said the line was down," the youth explained as he came face to face with Emer Plank.

"Do you still need to speak to the Sheriff?" Plank asked with a questioning smirk on his face.

"Well yes sir, that's what Mr. Shanks told me to do and since I work for him I'd better follow his orders," Ben lamented.

"If Henry Shanks thinks you need to see the Sheriff, then that's good enough for me," Plank began to explain his idea for assistance. "The west bound flyer will be along in exactly eleven minutes," the section boss declared after pulling a large heavy crystal faced watch from his pocket. "It doesn't usually stop here, but I will flag her for you if you want," the big man offered with a smile.

"I don't know, I only have five dollars and twenty cents Mr. Shanks gave me in case I had trouble. Will that cover the price of a ticket to Big Timber?" the uncertain youth asked.

"You won't need any money son, you'll ride as a friend of the railroad. Besides the engineer and the

Conductor are old friends of mine, they'll haul you along as a favor to me." Emer Plank's face was one big smile as he derived great pleasure from helping the inexperienced youth along on his quest.

"Oh, I don't know sir, I'm afraid it would be a great deal of trouble for you and the railroad. Besides I've never ridden on a train," Ben confessed a bit unsure of what the ride might entail.

"Ain't afraid are you son?" Plank's devilish smile and twinkling eye caught Ben completely off guard.

"Why no sir, if that's what's required to obey Mr. Shanks' orders I'll do it," Ben stammered out, his voice showing grave doubt.

"Good man, duty first," the section boss praised. "I'll get the white flag from my handcar and be right back," the big man promised, hurrying to retrieve the signal flag. With a small flag in hand Emer Plank ran gracefully down the edge of the rail bed for a distance of some three hundred yards before sticking the sharp metal point of the flag staff into the end of the wooden tie. He paused, still facing down the track as if listening for the on-rushing train while at the same time drawing out his big silver pocket watch to glance at the time.

"I can hear her coming," Plank called out as he began to run back to where Ben waited. The youth watched in amazement at the heavily muscled man's speed and agility as he stepped on the exposed end of the wooden ties to avoid losing his footing in the loose gravel that made up the rail bed. "Do you hear her?" Plank asked slowing to a walk as he neared Ben.

"Yeah, there she is coming around the bend at the Carr Ranch." Not only could Ben hear the approaching steam engine, he could see a trail of white smoke rising into the clear blue sky just around the Carr Ranch curve. Suddenly the smoke stack of the large black engine raced into view, causing Ben to remark out loud about its excessive speed.

"It's the flyer son, you know the west bound express. People are in a hurry these days, they want to get somewhere fast or have something shipped fast. All this hurry is a real quandary to me, rush, rush, hurry, hurry as fast as you can but for what reason?" Emer Plank moaned with a shake of his massive head.

"But they're going so fast, do you think the engineer will see your flag and be able to stop in time?" Young Crane asked in disbelief.

"He damn well better see my signal and stop in time. He ain't on no sightseeing trip, it's his job to watch far down the track for any problems and stop short of hitting anything," Plank explained.

THE TRAIN RIDE

A high pitched scream from the engines steam powered whistle filled the Yellowstone River valley and echoed off the surrounding hillsides. “That’s my old friend Francis Michael O’Toole at the throttle and he’s signaling that he has seen our flag and will stop with the cow catcher right here at the crosswalk,” Plank declared, drawing an imaginary line across the top of the shiny steel rail with the toe of his work boot. “Now let’s you and me step off to the side and give Mr. O’Toole room to work,” the big man suggested with a firm tug on Ben’s arm.

The train was made up of a large black engine, a tender, a mail car, a freight car, two passenger cars and a bright yellow caboose. The engineer smoothly reduced the massive machines forward momentum until finally coming to a complete halt with the cow catcher just covering the mark Emer Plank had drawn on the steel rail.

“Come on,” Plank yelled out so he could be heard over the huffing and puffing, not to mention the hissing steam of the engines boiler. “These boys are on a tight schedule but I want you to meet Mr. O' Toole," the powerful section boss announced in a loud voice as he drug Ben down the rail bed past the engine's four huge steel drive wheels. They came to an abrupt halt just below the engine cab's open side window. Ben craned his neck to look up at the upper torso of a huge man hanging half way out of the cab window. "This is my good friend Francis O' Toole," Plank announced, gesturing up to the engineer who was dressed in clean pin-striped bibbed overalls, a perfectly ironed long sleeved blue work shirt, gauntlet leather gloves and a pin-striped work cap. "Mr. O'Toole, this is my friend Benjamin Crane who works for Henry Shanks. He's on orders from Mr. Shanks to contact the sheriff. The telegraph and telephone lines are out so I told him we could take him to Big Timber as a friend of the railroad," Emer Plank bellowed out with a wide knowing smile.

"Glad to meet you Ben," O'Toole called down, while leaning farther out of the cab's window to shake hands with the youth. "I'd be proud to give any friend of Henry Shanks a ride," he declared in a strong base voice. "Better get him back to the caboose and introduce him to Mr. Mills, I'm already behind schedule," the huge Irish engineer directed with a smile.

Plank wrapped his huge right hand around Ben's upper left arm, partially to aid the still weak youth and partially to direct him to the caboose without trying to be heard above the engine noise. The added support proved welcome to the youth who tripped over the rail tie ends and staggered through the loose footing of the gravel rail bed. Emer Plank on the other hand found the difficult terrain of the track bed as familiar as walking across his parlor floor. The pair hurried down the length of the train and each time Ben faltered the section boss's mighty arm set them both back on the straight and upright path.

Ben could see an older dignified looking gentleman standing, red flag in hand beside the steel steps which led to the rear of the caboose. He was dressed in a dark blue uniform and wore a round black leather billed hat. "Good afternoon Mr. Mills," Plank called out while waving his left hand over his head.

"What is the delay Emer?" the uniformed man cried out in a strong voice that reflected his natural authority.

"It's my fault Mr. Mills," Plank apologized as they approached the important man.

"This is Ben Crane, he works for Henry Shanks who has entrusted him with taking an urgent message to the sheriff. The telephone and telegraph lines are out, so I told him we could see him safely to Big Timber," Emer Plank announced with a song in his voice and a wide smile.

"Hmm, Mr. Shanks you say?" Mills responded as if thinking seriously about the request. "Henry Shanks. Yes, yes, climb on board we are running late now," the Conductor urged, raising the red flag to signal the engineer to start the train moving. "All aboard!" Mills cried out in a loud voice that over-powered all the noise of the Grey Cliff railyard.

Engineer O'Toole blew the steam whistle and rang the bell to warn any nearby persons or animals the train was going to move. Conductor Mills grabbed the handrail and with a practiced hop landed on the caboose's lower step. "Now Mr. Plank, let's hear the story that brought this young fellow to high jacking my train," the Conductor said pleasantly as he ushered both Emer and Ben into the caboose.

"It's a long story Mr. Mills, in fact I don't know the whole tale but Amos Moody and I will vouch for this young fella," Emer tried to explain.

"Amos Moody? Is that old hermit still alive and how did he get mixed up with Mr. Shanks and this young pup?" the Conductor asked with a shake of his head while offering the two men to take a seat on the caboose's side bench seat.

All three men found a comfortable place to sit and even more important, a good hand hold as the caboose bounced and swayed along the uneven track which led up the Yellowstone River Valley to Big Timber, Montana. Ben related his story from the time he arrived at Henry Shanks' ranch early that morning to the appearance of Doc Walker. He gave a detailed account of the outlaw's drowning and his being pursued by Bates and the Ames brothers. Ben told of the robbery, but wisely neglected to report the gold found on Walker or the money Mr. Shanks had hidden in his well. Ben continued his narrative by telling how the outlaws had chased him down the slough to the river and the difficulty he had in crossing the raging rain-swollen river.

It wasn't until Ben mentioned Amos Moody's name again that anyone interrupted his factual report. "Old Amos Moody," the Conductor lamented softly looking away from the other two men's faces. "That old man took me in nearly twenty years ago when I first come to this country. I was an orphaned kid from New York City headed west trying to make my fortune," Mills stated in a plaintive expression. "I worked on his place for several years until he helped me get a job on the railroad. I've been here ever since, but I have been very lax in visiting the old man or trying to repay his generosity," Mills reminisced in a plaintive demeanor.

Emer and Ben remained silent for a long minute to allow Mills to regain his composure at which time the Conductor straightened his uniform coat and hat before returning his attention to Ben's account. "Sorry son, what happened next?" Mills inquired hesitantly.

"Well, Mr. Moody put me on his mule, Molly and we headed to town, we ran across Mr. Plank as we passed under the railroad track. Mr. Plank carried me up the rail embankment and brought me to town on his handcar."

"And you say both the telegraph and telephone are out of service?" the Conductor asked as if he had anticipated such an occurrence.

"That is what Mr. Ballard said when I asked to use his telephone. In fact, when Mr. Shanks realized Bates and his men would be riding in, he gave me money to pay for the use of the telephone,"

Ben explained while secretly catching glimpses of the passing scenery through the caboose side window.

"He's never ridden on a train before, Mr. Mills," Plank blurted out in a humorous voice.

"Oh, well then, I wouldn't want you to miss the thrill of your first ride son, so let's step on the forward platform, we can talk there," the Conductor suggested.

"Yes sir," Ben exclaimed rising to make his way to the door.

"We are running about forty five miles an hour because Mr. O'Toole is trying to make up our lost time. Look around all you want son, but don't stare down at the track or you'll get dizzy, maybe even sick to your stomach," the Conductor warned.

"So you think Mr. Shanks is dead?" Mills asked in a raised voice so he could be heard clearly over the noise of the train.

"Well, I didn't see him die, but I heard Bates and the Ames brothers shooting near the ranch house. To think back now, I believe Mr. Shanks expected those men to harm him, that's why he told me to run away and not to look back," Ben replied turning his eyes from the scenery to look both of the older men straight in the eye.

"All right," Mills called out, hoping to change the subject. "Tell me what in the blue blazes was going on down at the new steel bridge? I could see a crowd on the bridge as we topped the grade at mile hill. Looked like a lynching from up there," the Conductor stated firmly.

“It nearly was,” Plank laughed out loud, “but let Ben explain.

“When I stopped in the store to use the telephone, Mr. Ballard tried to take my money and accused me of owing him money, which I don’t,” Ben began to explain. “When I told him neither I nor my family charged at his store, he became irate and began to rough me up. It was then that some elderly woman began to use a buggy whip on Ballard. He let go of me to defend himself, but finally Mr. Ballard ran out the door and down the street with the woman right behind. They ended up at the steel bridge where Mr. Ballard climbed up the metal overhead, hoping he could stay out of reach of that whip,” the youth humorously reported the story.

“But who was the women?” Mills inquired, looking back and forth from Ben to Emer Plank in hopes of learning the identity of the old woman.

“I don’t know Mr. Mills, I have never seen the woman before,” Ben declared shifting his gaze to Plank’s eyes.

“I could be wrong but I thought it was Mrs. Dimmitt,” Emer Plank responded with a shrug of his massive shoulders.

“You mean Mary Isabel De Ross, Day, Dimmitt?” the Conductor asked in a high pitch voice as he threw this arms in the air to emphases his disbelief.

“I said I thought it was her but, I ain’t seen the woman in eight or ten years,” Plank shook his head.

“Who is this Mrs. Dimmitt?” Young Crane asked in a questioning voice.

“It’s a long story son, but I suspect you have as much right to know as anyone,” the Conductor began.

“Well as I understand the story, Mrs. Dimmitt’s, er Mary’s parents, the DeRoss’s emigrated from France before the Civil War. Mary’s father, a banker finally landed in Georgia. Mary’s parents died during the war and her four brothers never returned from the war so she assumed they had been killed. The carpet baggers stole everything the family owned and she was declared an orphan by the courts. It seems some family friends put Mary on an immigrant wagon train headed for Oregon but she became ill somewhere in western Iowa where some folks who ran a hotel and restaurant took her in and raised her. After school she married a man named Day and they had five children, all but one little girl died during an epidemic. Mary’s first husband Charles Day blamed himself for the loss of the children and eventually drank himself to death. With one child left to support, Mary wed a cattle buyer named Dimmitt. They moved out here to buy animals to be shipped east for slaughter or to be fattened.”

“But I don’t recall such a family living around here,” Ben stated questioning Mills story.

“Maybe not, you see Dimmitt died about ten years back and is buried at Reed Springs. Her only child, Gertrude insisted Mary return to Iowa and live with her family. So you can see why you probably never met Mrs. Dimmitt, but your parents know her.

If it is Mary Dimmitt, I can vouch for the fact that several other men in this area sport a shredded ear or scarred back at the woman's hands, and I might add they were just desserts," Mills ended his tale with a smile and a pat on Ben's back.

"There you are son, Big Timber, Montana," Emer Plank exclaimed pointing to a group of buildings a couple of miles further down the track. "Have you ever met our sheriff?" Plank inquired as if everyone should be a personal friend of the lawman.

"No sir, can't say I've had the pleasure," the youth responded openly.

"Not everyone would call meeting Tom Mayhew a pleasure," Plank stated in a matter of fact way. "But I'll be glad to go along with you and make the introductions if you like," the big man offered with a wide smile.

"That would be very kind of you sir," Ben agreed.

"I'd go along but I must stay with the train, but you have the right man in Emer Plank to introduce you to Whispering Tom," Mills reassured Ben with a big smile. "We make a regular five minute stop here in Big Timber but Mr. O'Toole's still behind time so we may not be here that long. I suggest you two get ready to step down just as soon as the caboose comes to a halt," the Conductor warned as he made his way to the bottom step on the caboose.

Engineer O'Toole let loose a long scream from the steam whistle as the speeding train approached the first road crossing one mile south of town.

It was at this point the rail bed drew close to the raging Yellowstone Riverbank. This close proximity of the river and the railroad was due to the narrowing of the valley by two mountain ranges that pinched into the valley from the north and south. The native citizens of Big Timber claimed the close proximity of the two ranges turned back winter storms, giving the town much milder weather than what the surrounding area experienced.

A second powerful blast from the steam-powered whistle coincided with an application of the brakes on the engine's eight massive drive wheels; the sudden stop threw Ben and Emer forward causing them to impact the caboose's metal hand rail.

"We'd best get down the steps where we can jump off easier," Emer Plank, the big experienced railroad worker suggested, pointing to the bottom step of the cabooses ladder.

The able not to mention very confident engineer brought the tons of steel and wood train to an abrupt stop with the passenger car exactly in front of the depot doors. "Big Timber, Big Timber, Montana," Conductor Mills called out as he hurried from one passenger car to the next. "Last call for Big Timber," Mills bellowed out as he stepped down to the rail bed between the passenger car and the baggage car, he then turned to look at Ben and Emer who were safely on the ground. "All aboard, all aboard for...." But the Conductor's words were lost in the screech of the steam whistle as Mr. O'Toole started the big steel wheels turning once more.

“Those folks are in a hurry,” Ben yelled to his companion not being familiar with the railroad time schedule.

Conductor Mills stood his ground until the caboose’s front hand rail zoomed by then he deftly grabbed hold of the rear handrail and gracefully swung on board. He waved to Ben and Emer as the youth yelled good bye and thank you to the man who had made it possible for a naïve youth to make good his pledge to an old friend.

MEETING SHERIFF MAYHEW

"The sheriff is most likely in his office at the jail this time a day. If not, it's a good place to start our search for him," Plank stated leading the way down the brick sidewalk that led from the railroad depot to the town's main street.

"I'll give you a couple words of advice," Plank began as the pair walked with a hurried gait. "I know your folks, so I know you've had a proper upbringing, be polite and avoid profanity, which will go a long way when you meet Whispering Tom."

"Whispering Tom?" Ben asked. He had never heard the Sheriff referred to by that name.

"The man is very soft spoken, some folks claim he had his throat cut down on the Rio Grande, others say he was kicked in the Adam's apple by a horse. But whatever really happened, it's best not to bring the subject up around Tom. Just call him Sheriff or even better, sir. He kinda likes being called sir," Emer Plank grinned.

"Yes sir, I'll remember to show him respect and say sir," Ben promised knowing he was getting sound advice from his big companion.

"Now, Tom has a deputy named Burl Trimmer, he is big and mean as a sunburned rattler. The man doesn't like anyone, including himself. He may try to fluster you 'cause the man is a natural bully and is lazy to boot. He will try to find a flaw in your story so he doesn't have to ride down to Mr. Shanks' ranch to investigate. Just keep your head and don't let Burl get under your skin," Plank warned the youth of what trials might lie ahead.

"Thank you Mr. Plank for your help and guidance and I will try to follow your lead," the youth stated, trying to reassure his new friend. "Sheriff's office and jail," the youth announced nervously reading the white letters that were professionally painted on the door.

"Don't be nervous," Plank calmly instructed. "We ain't done nothing wrong," he added turning the knob on the jailhouse's windowless solid oak front door. Emer held the heavy door open while motioning for Ben to enter first. The Sheriff's office occupied the first floor of an oblong two story brick building, the second floor held four small iron bar cells. A small area in front of the cells was designed for foul weather exercise but its main function was to hold a large steel wood-fired heating stove.

Ben Crane took two step into the jailhouse then one step back as the pungent odors assailed his tender young sense of smell. A haze filled the air of the main floor like a valley fog, it carried the aroma of cigar and pipe smoke, not to mention an overpowering mingling of old rank sweat from years of incarcerated unwashed bodies and the lack of bathing facilities. Of course, the air also swirled with a sweet scent of gun cleaning oil, cheap whiskey, stale vomit and old leather from the lawmen's gun belts and leather chaps.

Ben was of course familiar with all of these substances but not when confined to one small unventilated dark room. The scene came as a shock to a clean-cut youth who lacked experience with smoky bar rooms or local sporting houses.

Ben and Emer stopped just inside the front door to allow their senses to adjust, especially their vision, which had to suddenly compensate for the semi-darkness of the buildings poorly lit interior. Just inside the front door lay two narrow wooden steps which were difficult to see on the best day, but this was not even a poor day where lighting was concern. The dark steps tripped Ben as he advanced blindly towards the center of the room.

"Damn, you are a clumsy kid," a raspy voice from an unseen speaker ridiculed Ben for falling down on the small steps.

"Yes sir," Ben replied as Emer lifted him from the floor to a standing position.

"What brings you to my office?" a soft, almost feminine voice inquired from the deep reaches of the Sheriff's office.

"I am Ben Crane," the youth stated in a cordial even tone. "Henry Shanks sent me here to report a crime, possibly several crimes, one of which may be murder," Ben explained while gently feeling the floor with his toe in an effort to find that first perilous step once again.

"What are you doing here Emer?" the soft voice inquired.

"As I understand it, Amos Moody fished this young buck out of the river and carried him to Trestle Number Three where I run onto them. I transported him to Grey Cliff on my work car. Ben had hoped to call you on the telephone from Ballard's store but the line is out so we jumped on the flyer, hoping to deliver the message to you as soon as possible," came the big railroad man's confused story.

"You two come up here and take a seat by my desk so we don't have to yell back and forth to each other," the soft voice seemed weaker with each verbal exchange, causing Ben to assume it was the Sheriff speaking to him. But in any case, he hurried up the steps to the main floor where it was easier to see the office lay out. One of the great advantages of youth, a young person's body operates at the peak of perfection so Ben's eyes quickly adjusted to the near twilight of the jailhouse. However Emer Plank, being a bit older became disoriented by the dim light of the little entryway. Standing flat footed with his left hand planted firmly on the hallway wall, he refused to move.

"Are you two coming up here or not?" Deputy Trimmer growled out.

"I can see now," Ben whispered to his big companion, "let me help you up these steps," the youth offered, grasping Plank by his massive right arm. Emer, a powerful prideful man was not accustomed to accepting assistance from anyone, especially a youth. He hesitated for a second to the point he began to pull away from Ben's hold. "Please let me help you Mr. Plank," Ben explained quietly once more as he felt Plank's huge bicep relax, an unspoken acknowledgement he would accept the youths guidance.

"What's the matter Plank, you getting old and feeble?" the deputy taunted in his loud over-bearing way.

"Not at all!" Ben snapped back. "Mr. Plank is helping me up the stairs and that's after he carried me up the grade at Trestle Number Three, then pumped his handcar like a mad man to get me to Grey Cliff as fast as possible."

"What's the matter with you boy?" Trimmer demanded with a scowl in his voice.

"Well, to tell the truth, I'm pretty well stoved up from swimming across the flooded Yellowstone River at Shanks Crossing," Ben replied. "Thank you for helping me up those stairs," the youth added trying to further his cover up of Emer Plank's inability to see in the dark entryway.

"You're a damn liar. There ain't nobody who could swim that river at flood stage, not even at Shanks Crossing!" Trimmer bellowed, as he shot to his feet from where he sat near the Sheriff's large roll top desk.

Ben and Emer stood at the top of the steps trying to take in the jails layout. They could visualize Sheriff Mayhew sitting at his roll top desk, and the rack of long guns on the wall behind him. Just beyond that was a small cell made of horizontal flat steel strips which measured four inches by two inches. Each of these metal strips was riveted to another vertical 2x2 wide strip that was woven through the horizontal strips. This small homemade cell had a solid steel door with a large brass padlock to keep things secure. There was a crude unkempt bed in the corner near the cell, next to that sat a large dinged and battered oak armoire. A cheap washstand in the corner held a dented metal pitcher and wash basin which was topped off by a small cracked mirror.

Ben could easily make out a large wood burning stove; its four legs sat on a square pad of red brick in the center of the floor. A large black tin stove pipe ran from the top of the wood stove to a hole in the wall just above the homemade cell.

“No reason to call anyone a liar,” Emer Plank said in a hard voice challenging Deputy Trimmer’s insult.

“That’s right,” Sheriff Mayhew agreed in his firmest yet weak voice.

Ben Crane realized they must move forward or be exposed for their vision problems. He moved slowly forward without saying a word to Emer Plank but he kept a steady pressure on the big man’s right arm. “Here’s a couple of chairs Mr. Plank,” the youth stated in a pleasant tone as he lined his friend up with the larger of the two straight back wooden chairs.

"Thank you Ben, but I can see fine now," Plank said with a warm smile. "Tell me Tom, why do you keep that entryway so dark?" the big railroad man inquired.

"You see how much trouble you two had coming in from the bright sunshine into this black hole. Well sir, not many men can barge in here with their guns drawn and be able to see their targets. We keep several lamps burning down there at night so any shooter who comes in out of the dark with evil on his mind will have the reverse experience. But it don't make much difference if its day or night, nearly everyone trips on those stairs," the old lawman chuckled.

"Reckon that makes good sense," Plank agreed. "Now as to what brought us here, I'll let Ben tell you the story from the beginning," he added warmly.

"Well sir," Ben began, "as I said, I work for Henry Shanks on his ranch and this morning we were getting ready to cut the hay in his west forty when a man rode in wanting to use Mr. Shanks' crossing. The man turned out to be the outlaw Doc Walker who I did not know, but Mr. Shanks recognized him right off," the youth continued to relate the morning events until he was rescued by Emer Plank.

The big railroad man took up the tale at this point, explaining the confrontation in Ballard's store and the proprietors resulting whipping by an old woman. He told of flagging down the western flyer, finally ending with a humorous remark about the Sheriff's trick entry way.

"That old woman sounds like Mary Dimmitt, but the last I knew of her, she was living in Iowa," the Sheriff stated.

"Bull Shit!" Trimmer bellowed out. "Can't you tell when someone is stringing you along Tom?" the irate deputy shouted out as he leaped to his feet. "This here snot nosed kid is trying to pull a fast one on you Sheriff. Besides Doc Walker hasn't been around here for years, he was last reported across the border in Canada."

"That may be, but he said he was Doc Walker, Mr. Shanks recognized him as Doc Walker, not only that, but his men said he was Doc Walker," Ben argued.

"We have been friends for a long time Emer, do you believe the boy's story?" Tom Mayhew asked in his most powerful whisper.

"Yes Tom, I do. I say that not having seen any evidence of a crime. But I do know Ben's family and I know Henry Shanks well enough to know he would never have a liar work for him nor start a rumor like this," Plank said verifying Ben's report.

"I don't believe a word either of you say," Trimmer declared, charging across the Sheriff's office hard wood floor stopping just short of the Sheriff's desk. "If you did meet up with Walker and his gang, they would have killed a young pup like you in a heartbeat!" the deputy added in a loud antagonizing voice.

"That may be true but the outlaw seemed to feel obligated to Mr. Shanks for some reason, besides, like I said, he drown in the river before his partners rode in."

"You're a God Damn bold face liar, you piece of trash. You're just trying to get us out of town so some of your hoodlum friends can ride in here and raise hell with everyone."

"There ain't no need for that kinda talk, or name calling Mr. Trimmer and I'll have to ask you to refrain from the use of profanity," Plank scolded the bad tempered lawman.

"Just what are you going to do about it if I don't?" Trimmer demanded, pulling himself up to his tallest five foot eight inch height.

"Well sir, I'm most willing to step outside with you at any time, lawman or not," the big railroad worker stated in a calm voice as he rose to meet the deputy's threat. Plank towered above the unusually short Trimmer and outweighed the lawman by at least forty pounds. Ben, being a young farm boy, had no idea of Emer Plank's reputation as the boss of the rough necks who the railroad employed as gandy-dancers. He was often called upon as a trouble shooter who settled labor problems with whatever manner the situation required.

"That's all right Mr. Plank, let the man talk, he's not hurting me. I came here at Mr. Shanks' direction to report what has taken place. If these men don't believe me it's their loss, so I will ask you one time Sheriff Mayhew, what, if anything, do you propose to do about these crimes that were committed in your county?" Ben Crane asked in a polite yet firm voice.

"He's not going to do a thing on your word, you hill trash," Deputy Trimmer screamed out, his face red with anger.

"Settle down Burl!" Sheriff Mayhew commanded in his loudest tone. "I'm still in charge here and I will make all and any decisions concerning this office." The two men had a short staring match which Whispering Tom won without the blink of an eye. Finally Deputy Trimmer spun on his heel and marched off to a wooden chair which sat near the homemade cell.

"Now, you say Walker and his men stole a large block of gold, which they cut up before lighting out?" Mayhew asked but didn't wait for an answer before posing another question. "You also say that all four men passed through Henry Shanks ranch this morning?"

"Yes sir, and I believe the three gang members may have killed Mr. Shanks. I do wish you'd make up your mind to either investigate or allow me to return to the ranch so I might look to Mr. Shanks' welfare," Ben strongly suggested hoping to urge the lawman to make a move.

"Hmm," Sheriff Mayhew responded, rubbing his large boney hand against his long narrow chin.

“If it will help, I can get us on the next east bound train for Grey Cliff and I can supply us with enough horses to ride to Mr. Shanks’ ranch,” Emer Plank offered in his normal heavy booming voice.

“Well, Emer, I reckon if you’re willing to gamble on the boy’s story, the least I can do is travel to the Rattlesnake Ranch and have a look see. Burl can stay here and keep a lid on the town while we’re gone,” the Sheriff quickly decided, rising to his feet behind the big roll top desk.

“No siree!” Deputy Trimmer’s voice exploded out to indicate he disagreed with his boss’s orders. “I ain’t staying here while you three are out searching for a couple hundred pounds of gold. Besides the kid said Doc Walker is dead he didn’t say his men are.”

“I bet after that hold-up there’s a pretty sizable reward for those pole cat’s, not to mention for the return of the gold,” the Deputy’s voice had returned to normal and it was clear to all, he was doing some fast math calculation in his head. “No siree Sheriff, I can’t in all good conscious let you face those three killers alone,” Trimmer added with a sly look on his face.

“I won’t be alone, Emer and Ben will be with me if there’s any trouble,” Mayhew protested.

“Don’t matter what you say Sheriff, I’m going with or without your permission,” Trimmer growled out in no uncertain terms.

“All right but where the gold’s concerned, don’t become part of the problem because I’ll shoot you just the same as I would any other thief,”

Whispering Tom's soft voice became hard as he looked Burl Trimmer straight in the eye. The deputy didn't respond to his boss's warning; he found it less nerve racking to turn away and begin gathering his gear.

"The next east bound must be the 6:10, is that right Emer?" Mayhew asked trying to fish his well-worn watch from his pants pocket.

"So that means we will have to hurry a might," the railroad man answered looking at his own well cared for time piece. "Better gather up whatever you think you might need and we'll be off."

"The sun will be setting by the time we reach Grey Cliff, Deputy Trimmer hissed. "On second thought maybe we should wait till morning," he added hopefully.

"You three can wait until sunrise if you want, but I'm going back to see about Mr. Shanks even if I have to walk!" Ben blurted out his challenge to the older men.

"But we'll miss supper and breakfast if we leave now, not to mention, it will be full dark by the time we can get to Shanks' Rattlesnake Ranch," the deputy Trimmer insisted.

"Ben and I are headed back right now, if you two come along, I'll feed you supper at my house or I know we can find a meal at Mr. Shanks or one of the neighbors," Plank offered in a stern manner before adding, "either way we two are going back to Grey Cliff."

“I thought you were interested in a reward?” Whispering Tom teased. “The longer we wait around the more time the holdup men have to get away with the gold,” the sly old lawman knew Trimmer’s greed would outweigh his reluctance over missing few meals.

“I'll be ready in just a moment,” the scheming deputy announced as he grabbed up his coat and hat.

All four men headed for the tricky stairs and the heavy door just beyond, however with everyone’s senses familiar with the jails interior no one stumbled or fell. Sheriff Mayhew hung out a ‘back soon’ sign and locked the front door then hurried to catch up with his posse.

“I can hear old 98 chugging up blue grass grade,” Plank announced looking to the west. “We should have plenty of time to reach the station before she arrives.”

Whispering Tom Mayhew led the small procession down the middle of East Street, while Ben struggled along just behind the Sheriff and to the right of Emer Plank. Deputy Burl Trimmer tagged along behind purposely keeping some twenty yards between his position and that of the Sheriff’s.

A powerful scream from Locomotive 98’s whistle announced the train had topped the blue grass grade and would be rolling downhill the remainder of the run to the Big Timber station. “We’ve got about 8 minutes before the train arrives,” Emer Plank declared picking up the pace a bit. “If you don’t mind I will hurry on ahead so I can speak to the train crew about our passage," the big man added as he moved by Sheriff Mayhew and broke in to a long fast stride. Ben watched as the long legged Plank quickly out distanced the little group easily reaching the railyard before they came to the end of the block.

"'That man sure can cover ground," Mayhew declared, turning to face Ben hoping to make his weak voice heard over the noise of the railyard.

"Yes sir," Ben replied with a smile. "He's pretty strong too," the youth added, thinking back to earlier in the day when the big railroader had easily carried him up the railroad right-of-way to the handcar.

Locomotive 98's whistle blew a warning blast as it approached the Upper River Road bend, the high pitched shriek reverberated down the valley irritating every animal in town. Ben suddenly realized many dogs howled at the sound and several of the work and carriage horses near the station moved about nervously. "Old 98 sure has a powerful whistle," Sheriff Mayhew, who had dropped back to walk beside Ben, stated with a shake of his head. "Ain't no doubt when that critter comes to town," he added with a wide smile.

"Yes sir, I'd hate to stand beside that monster when it goes off," Ben quickly agreed. "Looks like the engineers slowing to stop," he added pointing to the big black steam engine as it braked to a halt.

"I see Mr. Plank walking beside the engine, must be speaking to the engineer about giving us a ride," Ben indicated by pointing in the direction of the large white sand stone station. "I wonder if Mr.

Plank knows this engineer and Conductor like he did on the train that brought us here?" the youth added not realizing how well his new friend was known in the area.

"I'm sure Emer knowns everyone connected with railroading in Montana. In fact, your friend Emer Plank is well known for quite some distance around. The man is a real scrapper in a fight, what's more, the railroad owners call him in to break strikes or settle any other such problems. He has been known to take on three or four tuff men at a time and as far as I know he's never been whipped. Ain't that right Burl?" the Sheriff asked over his shoulder but the deputy failed to reply. "I should tell you, your new friend is an unusual man for his line of work, he don't drink nor visit low places except in the line of duty," the Sheriff stated. "It was about a year ago now, we got a call to break up a fight at the Gold Spike Bar, just down the street from the depot. Deputy Trimmer and I rushed down there and barged in to find Emer standing in the middle of the barroom with several tuff cases unconscious at his feet. He had two big rough necks, one in each hand, cracking their heads together, sounded like thumping ripe watermelons. I feared Emer might accidently kill one so Burl and I grabbed Plank by the arms, which caused him to drop his unconscious opponents but didn't stop him from fighting us. We struggled all over that saloon floor, I holding onto Emer's right arm, Burl there had the left and we were hanging on for dear life 'cause we knew what would happen if one of us lost our hold. Old Emer was flopping us around like rag dolls, so I yelled at Burl to hit Emer in the head with the lead sap he always carries," Whispering Tom paused to chuckle before continuing his tale. "Deputy Trimmer yelled back, I already have hit him with my sap twice but he didn't seem to notice," the Sheriff laughed out loud.

"What did you do?" Ben asked in astonished excitement. "Well son, we held on until Mr. Plank got wore out and short of breath. I yelled to Burl on the count of three to head for the front door or any other exit he could find, so on three we pushed Emer backwards and we ran like hell thru the swinging doors, then up the street to the jail where we locked ourselves in until the next morning. Remember earlier at the jail when Emer scolded my deputy for his language and Burl didn't take him to task, now you know why," the Sheriff chuckled once more.

MEETING THE CREW OF OLD 98

"We'd better hurry up, Mr. Plank is waving his arm for us to come up to the station." Ben picked up his pace which caused the Sheriff and his deputy to follow suit. The three men moved at a fast walk until they came to the tracks whose loose cinders and crossties required slower movement and more concentration of their footing.

"Ben, I want you to meet an old friend of mine," Emer Plank called in his loudest voice in attempt to be heard over the steam engine's noise. "This is Jiggs Powers, the best engineer to ever pull a throttle handle," Plank announced, pointing to a big ruddy-faced man that was hanging half way out of the side cab window. "Jiggs, this is my friend Ben Crane," he added as the two men stretched to shake hands.

"I understand you're going to ride a ways with me," Powers replied with a wide white toothy greeting. "Any friend of Emer Planks is a friend of mine and I'm honored to haul you on my train," the big engineer declared.

“Who’s the Conductor on this run?” Emer asked the engineer.

“None other than Elbert Driver, if he gives you any trouble tell him I said to let your boys ride,” Jiggs Powers declared with a shake of his huge right glove covered fist. Plank waved in response to the big engineer’s gesture, then began herding everyone in the direction of the caboose.

“Is there something wrong with this Mr. Driver?” Ben inquired, being a perceptive young man he caught the engineer’s inference. “No, Mr. Driver is a good Conductor, it’s just that he’s a company man, he’s mighty cautious about making money for the railroad and who rides on his train. Mr. Driver is pretty rough on hobos and bums who try to hitch a free ride on his train. But I don’t think we’ll have any problem, especially with old Jiggs on our side.”

“I hope you’re right, I feel like I have caused a great deal of trouble for a lot of folks, but I’m only doing what Mr. Shanks told me to do,” the youth apologized.

Ahead in the lengthening shadows, Ben and Emer could see a large rotund man dressed very nattily in a dark blue military cut coat and round billed cap holding a red flag in his right hand. The large man stepped down from the caboose and stood ramrod straight as he awaited the four men to approach him. “Mr. Driver!” Emer called out as they neared the Conductor. “I want you to meet my friend Ben Crane.”

“Crane,” Elbert Driver huffed out in an acknowledgement of the introduction. “I see Sheriff

Mayhew and his no account deputy are right behind you. So let me guess, you four want a free ride to some place down the line?" the Conductor growled, then spit on the ground at his feet.

"As a matter of fact, we believe the Doc Walker gang murdered Henry Shanks and Ben here is the nearest thing we have to an eye witness," Plank declared pointing to young Crane.

"I don't suppose this has anything to do with the gold that Walker's gang stole?" Driver's face was flushed with anger believing he was being duped. "The telegraph line is still working as far as Livingston, so we got the word about the robbery as we came through."

"We know all about the gold heist, Ben told us the story as he knows it. What we need is a ride to Grey Cliff because we believe the Walker gang murdered Ben's boss, Henry Shanks and those killers are getting away," Plank explained firmly standing his ground in the face of the hard case Conductor.

"Sounds like a treasure hunt to me," Conductor Driver scoffed in response. "Tell me what makes you think Shanks has been killed?" he demanded, while giving young Crane an evil eye.

"Mr. Shanks ordered me to hide in the slough until Clarence Bates and the Ames brothers were gone then to tell the Sheriff as quickly as possible," Ben explained completely unaffected by the Conductors intimidating look.

"So you ran for cover while your friend was being attacked, eh pup?" Driver's accusation of cowardice stung Ben like a slap in the face, causing his temper to flair.

"That was Mr. Shanks' orders, I didn't hear any shots until I was in the slough. Mr. Shanks knew Doc Walker and Clarence Bates, and didn't think they would hurt him but I feared he was wrong. The Ames brothers shot at me several times when I tried to sneak back to the ranch house, they chased me down the slough to the river crossing. I followed Mr. Shanks' advice on how to swim the river at flood stage and finally managed to reach the west side where Mr. Moody found me hiding in a washout. Mr. Moody took me to the railroad bridge where we ran into Mr. Plank, who graciously brought me to the Sheriff," Ben stated in a firm declaration while looking squarely in the doubting Conductors eye.

"I don't believe a damn thing you say kid, especially the part about swimming the river during high water," Elbert Driver shook his head in disbelieve just before he spit on the ground once more.

"No disrespect Mr. Driver, but I don't give a damn what you believe. If I can't ride your train, I'll find a horse. And if I can't find a horse, I'll walk back, but no matter what, I must get back to The Rattlesnake Ranch and try to help Mr. Shanks!" Ben had reached the limit of his youthful patience with so many adults calling him a liar and coward.

Sheriff Mayhew stepped closer intending to join in the argument but Conductor Driver's upraised hand brought him to a stop. “No one rides my train for free, I mean no one! If you men want to reach Grey Cliff today, I suggest you buy a ticket.” With that said, he spun around and headed for the caboose. But the domineering railroad Conductor hadn’t seen the huge engineer, Jiggs Powers had walked up and stop right behind Driver. The two big men collided with a loud thud but both men managed to keep their footing.

“What the hell is the problem?” Powers bellowed out right in Driver’s face.

“These men want a free ride to Grey Cliff and you know my rules, everyone pays, no exceptions!” the Conductor declared in a loud voice for all to hear.

“Well by God, I told them they could ride because they are on official business,” Jiggs Powers stated, his arms folded across his massive chest. “You find room for these men in the caboose or that engine ain’t moving one foot.” The engineer’s demeanor was that of a hard confident man who expected his wishes to be obeyed.

“I’m the Conductor of this train and as such I’m the boss, now I’m ordering you to get back in your cab and be ready to move in two minutes!” Driver commanded as he glanced at his gleaming gold pocket watch.

“Can’t move, we have a leak in a steam line. We’ll have to replace the valve packing before we pull out,” Powers argued as he tried to hide the grin on his large ruddy face.

Elbert Driver raised his right hand in a threatening manner but Ben Crane stepped between the two railroaders yelling at the top of his lungs. "I've seen enough fighting for one day, so you can have your precious train Mr. Driver!" the youth warned trying to make the Conductor hear what he said. "I never rode on a train before today mostly walked wherever I was going so I figure I can get home without a ride on your old train. But I will never forget the generosity of Mr. Plank, Mr. Mills and Mr. O'Toole for being so helpful. Now if you don't mind I've got a fair piece to walk tonight, so I'll take my leave!" Ben shouted as he turned walking away from the Big Timber railyard. Mad and unaccustomed as he was to carrying money, Ben had forgotten about Mr. Shank's five dollars and twenty cents he still carried in his pants pocket.

"I understood the owners of this railroad ordered us to work with the local law, who they expect to help protect railroad property," Jiggs Power's growled out leaning towards the Conductor in an attempt to intimidate the man.

"That was the order, but I have reported damage and theft of railroad property all the way up and down this line and never got a single response!" Driver shouted back in an angry roar.

"Maybe its times like these that keep us from helping the railroad," Sheriff Mayhew interjected in his most powerful whisper. "But it doesn't mean a thing now cause we just lost our guide and star witness," the tuff old lawman added. His statement caused all five men to look around the railyard and suddenly realize Ben Crane had disappeared into Big Timber's gathering dusk.

"That settles that," Driver exclaimed. "You get back in your engine and let's get this train rolling," he commanded Jiggs Powers.

"That doesn't settle a thing, as duly elected Sheriff of Sweet Grass County, I am obligated to investigate all crimes that are reported to my office," Sheriff Mayhew stated calmly. "So I must make my way to Grey Cliff and look into a reported murder. Now if you can't see your way clear to assist in my official business, then we will find other transportation but be assured, I will report this to your superiors," the wily old lawman promised with a partial smile on his weathered face.

"That's neither here nor there gentlemen, as I said before we can't move the train until that bad steam valve has been repaired," Engineer Powers protested violently.

"All right, all right, I know when I'm beat. You three get in the caboose and you Mr. Powers make your repair as fast as possible. We have a lot of time to make up," the Conductor shouted out waving both of his hands in the air.

"I'll try tightening the packing nut and wrapping a rag around the valve, maybe we can make do until we get to Billings," the Engineer suggested with a smirk.

"I wish we could find Ben before we leave," Emer Plank's voice reflected his concern of his young friend's welfare.

“Either get on the train or walk, whichever you chose, but this train is departing just as soon as possible,” Conductor Driver warned.

Emer Plank, Sheriff Tom Mayhew, and Deputy Trimmer followed along in the wake of Conductor Driver as the ill-tempered man rushed to his duty station on the caboose. Engineer Powers blew a long and a short blast on his steam whistle to indicate all repairs had been completed and that he was prepared to get underway.

The small posse quickly found seats within the caboose as the Conductor stood, red flag in hand on the bottom step of the yellow caboose. Elbert Driver waved the red flag up and down instructing the Engineer to proceed, which drew a slow pealing of the small brass bell just forward of the engines cab, a signal to the train crew that they were getting under way.

The train lurched and jolted as the slack in the coupling between the cars was quickly taken up when the train began to move, Conductor Driver quickly rolled the red cloth flag around its wooden handle and turned to climb the steel steps to the caboose platform when he heard a dull thud coming from the top of the railcar just to his front. The thick black smoke from the engines tall stack made visibility difficult at best, but the dense smoke began to dissipate as the train picked up speed, allowing the Conductor to see the thudding noise was being made by the train’s huge brake man, Bruno Claus. He had been trying to get Driver’s attention by striking a large wooden pick handle on the top break wheel. Many of the brakemen carried just such a handle to assist in turning the brake wheel, which was employed to set or release the car's brakes as needed. Claus was making wild gestures toward the front of the train, which usually indicated that some ill-advised tramp was trying to steal a ride on Elbert Driver's train, something neither the Conductor nor Brakeman would ever allow. Driver stuck the rolled up red flag in his back pocket as he reached just inside the caboose's rear door to retrieve a five foot long length of three-eighths inch chain. The rattle of the steel links caught Plank's attention and he spun around to get a glimpse of what was causing the sound. But the burly Conductor disappeared up the ladder to the top of the caboose before Plank realized what was happening.

THE STOWAWAY

The occupants of the caboose studied the cars yellow ceiling as they listened to Driver's steps progress across the roof top walk way.

"What the hell is he up to?" Sheriff Mayhew inquired of Emer Plank, but it took a second for the big section hand to comprehend just what was taking place.

"There must be a tramp trying to sneak a ride and I'll bet you it's our boy Ben Crane," Plank announced as he rose from his seat and hurried to look out the caboose's front door. "If Driver catches Ben trying to steal a ride he'll beat the boy senseless," Plank continued as he swung his massive frame around the front ladder, which led to the caboose's rooftop.

"Where you going?" Trimmer asked, shocked that a railroad employee would help anyone to stowaway on a train.

Emer Plank, who was out of hearing range failed to respond to Deputy Trimmer's question but Sheriff Mayhew replied in his raspy whisper, "I don't know where Emer's going, but I'm going along just in case."

Trimmer shook his head in disbelief, then called to his boss, "I don't like heights so if you don't mind I'll just stay right here and guard the caboose." But once again the deputy spoke too late as he watched the Sheriff's boots disappear up the caboose's ladder. "Damn fools," Trimmer muttered to himself as he looked about the car's interior for the most comfortable place to sit.

Emer Plank cautiously poked his head above the top of the railcar but was surprised to find the catwalk empty. There wasn't any sign of Driver or anyone else for that matter. He was certain the Conductor hadn't fallen from the train, but a natural curiosity forced the big man to look back down the tracks before climbing to the rooftop. It was only after the section boss had gained his footing and balance on the top of the rolling railcar that he discovered Sheriff Mayhew at his heels. Plank extended his beefy right hand to the Sheriff and all but lifted the smaller lawman to the top of the railcar. "What's going on?" The Sheriff tried to be heard over the train noise and while Emer Plank wasn't able to hear the question, he knew what had been said.

"I don't know, but I think our Conductor is up to something," the muscular section foreman bellowed out as he pointed toward the engine. No further conversation was needed as both men began to make their way forward atop the rocking railcars. The diminishing daylight cast irregular shadows across their swaying pathway, but the inexperienced men became a team and assisted each other like a pair of staggering drunks, until they reached the end of the first car. At the front end of the car they confronted a flexing gap between the car ends which would require a bit of timing to navigate, because when the first car swayed to the right, the next car moved to the left. The two men looked down the opening that separated the two cars to discover the dizzying sight of railroad ties whizzing by, a blurring reminder of their fate if the proposed jump from rooftop to rooftop failed. Sheriff Mayhew extended his left hand and quickly took Emer's hand in his, then holding up three fingers with his other hand, indicated they would make the jump on the count of three. Emer nodded his head in agreement then turned back to face the perilous jump. Sheriff Mayhew swung his free hand in the air and extended one finger, he then repeated the movement counting two, and on the count of three both men jumped the opening. Tom Mayhew landed like a cat on the narrow raised walkway, but Emer Plank landed off balance on the sharply sloping metal roof of the baggage car. Plank's body weight being much greater than Mayhew's, caused an awkward landing that nearly rolled both men off the unstable car's roof. The Sheriff made a cat-like movement by grasping the railcar's horizontal braking wheel with his right hand, while at the same time, retaining his grip on Emer Plank's hand, thus managing to prevent the big man from falling off the slippery metal roof.

"That was too close!" Plank exclaimed to the lawman. "Thank you Tom," he added quickly. The lack of a powerful voice prevented Mayhew from preforming any acknowledgement other than nodding his head and smiling. But the smile quickly waned as the Sheriff's left index finger came to his lips to indicate silence before he pointed to the other end of the car.

"What is it?" Plank whispered in the lawman's ear. His simple unspoken reply came in the form of a hand cupped around his ear. "Someone on the flatcar?"

Again Mayhew merely nodded his head to the affirmative as both men turned to face the opposite end of the car. Crouched low, they began the precarious transfer from one end of the unstable car to the other. They stooped lower and lower until both men were on their hands and knees by the time they reached the end of the catwalk. Carefully the pair peeked over the car's end in order to observe the wooden bed of the flatcar some five feet below their position. There in the faded light of day, the pair could make out three people as they scuffled about the flatcar's edge. The center of the flatcar held a large stack of new lumber which left some two feet for walkway around the perimeter of the rough wooden railcar floor. The diminished light allowed enough illumination to recognize two of the men on the platform, one was Conductor Driver, while the other appeared to be the large brakeman Bruno Claus. The identification of the third person was difficult, because he was trapped between the two larger men as they fought over him like two dogs fighting over a bone.

Sheriff Mayhew dropped to his stomach, Emer Plank followed the lawman's example as they observed the three men tussling on the narrow edge of the car. Suddenly the big brakeman, Bruno Claus's huge right arm shot skyward exposing a large wooden pick handle which he was known to always carry. Tom Mayhew rolled to his left side then back flat again as he maneuvered to retrieve his holstered Colt 1873 44-40 caliber revolver and bring it into action. The lawman attempted to give a vocal warning to the men on the railcar but it was obvious, either Whispering Tom's shout was too weak to be heard over the noise of the train or if heard, the men chose to ignore the signal. But the clever lawman quickly resorted to his back up identifier as he placed the thumb and forefinger of his left hand in his mouth and blew. The resulting whistle could only be compared to the screeching steam whistle on this very train. The Sheriff's one long powerful shrill whistle caused Emer Plank to cover his ear in pain, while the three men on the flatcar froze in place.

"What in the hell was that?" Driver called out to his companion.

"It's Sheriff Mayhew!" Plank shouted out in his booming voice. "He's got the drop on you men so I'd suggest you stand still until he gets down there."

The Sheriff and Emer Plank carefully rose to their knees then to a crouched position before the lawman leaned near to his partner and stated something. "The Sheriff said to release whoever you two are holding then lay down on the flatcar floor, you've got to the count of three before he lets loose with his revolver!" Plank bellowed out.

Bruno Claus shot a defiant look toward the lawman but when Plank bellowed out the number one in his powerful commanding voice, the big brakeman released his hold on the third man before sinking face down on the flatcar floor. Driver on the other hand watched in disgust as his compatriot bent to the Sheriff's will then shouted out, "this is my train and I'm in charge here Mayhew, now either you drop that weapon or I'll be forced to do my duty and throw this bum off my train."

"Two!" Plank cried out. But the power-hungry Conductor held his ground and began shaking the still unidentified third man before pushing him to the edge of the flatcar. "Three!" Plank screamed out as he jumped from the top of the baggage car across the open three feet of coupling space to land several feet below. The big man landed like an agile cat solidly with both feet on the top of the stack of lumber then leaped to the narrow walkway on the flatcar's edge. Plank had, in a matter of seconds, and at great danger to himself, gone from the defense to the offense. Now from his new position, he grasped the third man by the arm and swung back towards the lumber pile which ripped the smaller third person from the surprised Conductor's control.

The two men charged each other like two bull elks. The resulting violent collision with Emer Plank threw the Conductor off balance, causing him to flail his arms about to prevent falling over the side of the moving flatcar. Driver struggled on making one exaggerated move after another to regain his balance but it was a losing fight and in a final lifesaving desperate act the Conductor threw himself face down on the flatcar floor. However, the maneuver came nearly too late, as he landed with his upper torso on the car, but his legs hung over the side very near the heavy steel truck wheels that was the dread of every railroad man.

The sight of a fellow human being in danger triggered a sympathetic reaction in Emer Plank who sprang from his place by the lumber pile, hoping to save the train's Conductor. His diving catch connected with Driver and the two powerful men's hands locked together like the positive steel couplings that kept the two moving railroad cars linked as one.

Emer Plank pulled with all his strength; he braced his knees against the flatcar's rough-cut wooden floor then reared back with all of his might but his efforts were in vain. A sudden scream of pain from the endangered man brought additional force in the form of a second, then a third person seizing the Conductors upper torso. Once the men were anchored in place, Plank yelled out a coordinating command. "All together now, ready, pull!" The big man's years of experience in directing men in the task of preforming heavy physical labor quickly shown through as their unified effort accomplished what one or two men alone could not.

All three men fell backwards onto the railcar floor as Conductor Driver was yanked on board like a fresh caught fish. It took nearly a minute to untangle the four exhausted bodies, but it was easy to see by the copious amount of blood pumping from Driver's leg as to the severity of the man's injuries.

"Go tell the engineer," Mayhew shouted as he leaned close to Planks ear. "I'll try to stop the blood."

Plank now charged with an urgent task, turned sharply, causing a collision with the third person who was involved in the altercation. Emer had just assumed this person was Ben Crane trying to sneak on the train but it suddenly became clear even in the gathering darkness, the third person was someone other than young Crane. Shocked by his misidentification, Plank reeled back, recovered then shouted to the third person. "Stay here and help the Sheriff!"

"Yes sir," came the soft almost inaudible reply. Plank gave the unknown person a hard glare then jumped to the top of the lumber pile to begin his race to the engineer.

Sheriff Mayhew, assisted by the mysterious third person, quickly applied a tourniquet to Conductor Driver's lower leg before checking his pulse and respiration. "Give us a hand," the Sheriff ordered with a wave of his hand to Bruno Claus who still lay face down on the flatcar floor. "Let's move him away from the edge."

The huge brakeman rose slowly to his hands and knees then crawled to the injured Conductor's side. It took a combined effort but they finally managed to drag the unconscious Driver closer to the pile of lumber before they stood upright and exchanged long questioning glances.

The sudden impact of Emer Planks big feet landing on the top of the lumber pile broke their stunned trances and they turned in unison to hear the engineer's advice. "Jiggs says Driver's only chance is for us to high ball to Billings. He says there's no doctor close behind us and with the telephone and telegraph wires down he can't wire ahead for help. He will slow down as we pass through Grey Cliff if we want to jump off," Plank reported in a clear concise manner.

"I wouldn't feel right getting off in Grey Cliff and leaving Driver to fend for himself," Sheriff Mayhew declared with a shake of his head. "Besides without Crane we don't know who we are looking for anyway."

"I haven't had a chance to tell you, but Ben Crane caught a ride with Jiggs, he is riding up on the coal car ready to get off at Grey Cliff."

"I'll see your man through to the doctor in Billings," the unknown person announced as everyone turned to look at the dark slender figure. "I, well, I figure not much can be done for him until we reach Billings and I'm sure with some help from the brakeman, he will get medical treatment," the soft spoken but reassuring voice continued.

"I reckon you're right about that," Plank agreed before turning to face the dark figure. "Just who the hell are you anyway?" Emer demanded as he shoved his right index finger into the faintly outlined face.

"I'd rather not say and I know you caught me stealing a ride on this train but I promise to get off at Billings if you let me go," the words came with a slight tremble that the men took as sincerity.

"Won't do, I'm the Sweet Grass County Sheriff on a lawful pursuit and I must have your name," Mayhew hissed as he leaned close to the unknown person. "If you don't identify yourself, I'll be forced to arrest you," the Sheriff added seeking to enforce his authority.

"I'm Boston," the weak voice trailed off. "I'm Boston Corbit," came the full reply but even in the darkness, Plank could see Tom Mayhew wordlessly mouthing the name Boston Corbit as if it were someone he should know. "Where are you from and where are you headed?" the lawman countered.

However, three quick blasts on the steam engine whistle stopped the interrogation as Emer Plank called out. "That's Jiggs' signal we are coming into Grey Cliff, he'll give one long whistle when he has slowed down and is ready for us to jump."

"I ain't taking orders from no scrawny bum like this, he ain't even railroad," Bruno Clause announced for everyone to hear.

"I'm in charge here and you will help get this man to the Doctor or face an arrest warrant," Tom Mayhew threatened Brakeman Clause in his fiercest raspy tone.

"The hell you say!" Clause bellowed out as he raised his trusted pick handle and charged the lawman like a wild bull. Emer Plank stepped between the two men while pushing the pick handle aside landing a hard right to the brakeman's jaw. Plank's hard right fist only stunned Clause but a second, then third blow to the head put the attacking bully face down on the flatcar floor.

"Thank you Emer," Sheriff Mayhew announced as he kneeled down beside Bruno Clause in order to place hand cuffs on the big man's wrists. "You are now under arrest for assaulting a lawman in the performance of his duty!" the lawman declared to the still unconscious brakeman. "I have to go back to the caboose to retrieve my deputy and our gear," Mayhew stated while speaking directly to Plank. "I would greatly appreciate it if you will drag this man off the train when we stop at Grey Cliff." The big section hand merely nodded his head to the affirmative as the lawman began making his way to the rear of the train.

In preparation for departing the train Emer Plank rolled the huge brakeman's limp body nearer to the flatcar's edge, then turned to face the stranger. "The Sheriff and I appreciate your help and I'll tell you this, Tom Mayhew makes a better friend than an enemy," Plank said with a smile.

DINNER AT MRS. PLANK'S HOUSE

Grey Cliff, Montana, with a population of some hundred and fifty citizen, has most of the dwellings laying on the Yellowstone river bottom to the north of the railroad tracks. However, a few homes lay to the southwest on the higher grass-covered ground that gently rises up into the foot hills of the Bear Tooth Mountains. Several of the buildings glowed with yellow lamp lights, trying to drive away the gathering darkness.

The mighty Number 98 Steam Engine whistle roared one long blast, signaling it was slowing down and it was time for the little posse to jump off. Ben Crane, who had stolen a ride with the engineer was the first man off the still moving train. He landed running down the rail bed slope but quickly recovered and turned around in time to see the flatcar approaching. In the dim lights of the railyard Ben witnessed Emer Plank lift Bruno Clause's limp, handcuffed body from the edge of the flatcar and lay it gently on the gravel rail bed. That fleeting moment provided young Crane's first and only glimpse of the mysterious small dark figure on the flatcar. The train began to pick up speed again and as the caboose flashed by Sheriff Mayhew and Deputy Trimmer stepped down, one each from the car's front and rear steps.

"Is everyone accounted for?" Mayhew asked, looking around at his companions, then at the disappearing red lantern that hung on the end of nearly every railroad caboose then in use. "Is there some place where we can lock up our prisoner?" the Sheriff asked without waiting for an answer to his first question.

"He should be safe in the coal shed for the night at least," Plank responded from out of the gloom. "But he doesn't seem willing to walk so I reckon we will have to drag him. It ain't far so if everyone grabs an arm or leg we can get this job done without hurting anyone." Sheriff Mayhew and Deputy Trimmer each lifted one of the man's tree trunk-like leg's while Ben and Emer Plank tugged on the brutes massive arms until only a little of the brakeman's backside drug the ground as they walked.

The four men struggled to move their captive a short distance off the right-of-way, finally stopping in front of a large square dark building constructed of two inch thick vertical planks. "This is our coal bunker," Plank declared. "We only fuel out of it in an emergency, so it's not often opened up. I've got a key for the lock on my ring so I'll have it opened in just a second." Plank fumbled in the darkness for a moment before hearing the brass padlock snap open with a loud click. "Here we are," the big man announced, swinging the heavy door wide open so Clause could be easily drug inside.

"That should hold him," the Sheriff decreed, as Plank shut and padlocked the coal bin's door.

"There, that's done," the big section boss stated cheerfully, his demeanor quickly changing with the thought of home and a meal. "Now if you men will follow me, it's only a short walk to my house," he added. Emer Plank then stepped out smartly, leading the way from the railyard. The four men climbed a sandy slope, which led to a bordering dirt street that paralleled the rail bed. At the road Plank turned left, walking at a quick pace until he approached a dark house located on a T intersection. "We turn here," Emer announced. "Tom?" Plank asked as he turned the corner in front of the dark foreboding house. "Do you remember the stories of Aunt Elsie Ford?" the big man asked.

"You mean the Ford who killed a couple of boarders, the one who hid fugitive outlaws and turned out to be a man in disguise?" Tom Mayhew replied.

"That's the one. Well sir, that's the house she or he lived in at the time of the murders," Emer chuckled as he pointed at the dilapidated two story house. "Everyone says it's haunted; that's the reason we're the only family living over here now. I only brought it up because there's another empty house before we get to my place and I want to warn you, there is a huge wild dog living under that house. He is as big as a pony, black as night, with big white fangs and a growl that makes your blood curdle.

Folks say he only comes out at night and he is the ghost of one of the murdered boarders seeking revenge. So I'll warn you to walk softly and keep your ears open because he usually doesn't give any warning before he strikes," the big man explained in a hushed tone which made a chill run up Ben Crane's spine. After telling the story of the ghost dog, Emer silently ushered everyone to the side of the road opposite the abandoned house.

"I don't believe I've ever heard of a ghost dog in Grey Cliff," Ben's voice reflected his doubts about Plank's story, but he had been so helpful, it was difficult for the young man to make a stronger rebuttal.

"That's cause you ain't in town much at night and that's the only time this critter moves around. All right now, we're getting very close so you fella's walk soft and listen real close. If you do hear this ghost dog, your only chance is to high tail it for the light on my front porch," Emer instructed in near whispered voice.

"What was that?" Deputy Trimmer whispered, before repeating the question in a louder, high pitched voice.

"Yeah, I hear something moving through the grass in the yard," Ben added and then said, Deputy Trimmer dropped his rifle and other belongings and exploded into a run. He screamed like a girl who had stepped on a snake. Deputy Trimmer continued to sprint all the way to the Plank house where he vaulted over the picket fence, finally coming to rest face down on the front porch floor.

"Here killer," Emer Plank said softly, as he knelt down in the middle of the dark street. "Come killer. Come here," he repeated, as a small thud rolled up from the big man's mid-section.

"What the hell was that?" Tom Mayhew demanded, still standing his ground beside Ben.

"Oh this," Plank roared with laughter. "This is killer, my daughter's dog. He greets me this way every time I come walking up this hill," Emer explained rising to his feet, while holding a small shaggy dog above his head.

"That's your ghost dog!" Sheriff Mayhew shouted in his loudest raspy voice, "the one that's out to revenge its murderer, the one that attacks without warning?" the lawman howled in a high pitched reprimanding voice.

"He has killed several rattlers in our yard and we know whenever there's a stranger, or varmint around," Plank explained as he tucked the wiggling licking fur-ball under his arm and headed for the house.

Ben Crane chuckled nervously then fell into line behind his host. "You really had me going for a moment there Mr. Plank," the youth freely admitted but Sheriff Mayhew, not finding the joke as entertaining, stood his ground in the middle of the dirt road.

Suddenly the front door to the Plank house swung opened and a small framed woman stepped into the light of the kerosene lamp hanging on the wall nearby. "What in the world is going on out here?” the woman called out, while looking around the house yard and down the dark road. “Is that you Mr. Plank?” the woman called out while holding her right hand over her eyebrows in an attempt to shield her vision from the yellow glow of the porch light.

“Yes Mrs. Plank, it’s your loving husband, home from a hard day’s work and it’s hungry that I am,” Emer Plank replied with what Ben took as an Irish accent. “Oh, and I invited some friends home for one of your famous home cooked meals,” he quickly added.

“Is this drunk laying on my porch one of those friends?” she demanded in a firm voice.

“No my love, that man is Deputy Trimmer from the sheriff's office and he isn’t drunk, he’s just resting.” Emer Plank chuckled as he neared the gate to his front yard. “Sheriff Mayhew and Ben Crane are with me too. I promised them one of your elegant suppers Mrs. Plank.

“I already fed the little ones and put them to bed an hour ago, but I’ll do the best I can,” Mrs. Plank tried to sound aggravated at her husband for springing dinner guests on her, but she had become accustomed to her spouse’s irregular hours and inconvenient meal times. “Bring your friends to the house while I fetch some hot water to wash your face and hands.” The woman turned back to the open door and began giving directions to someone inside. “Stir up the fire in the cook stove, get a ham from the smoke house and some eggs from the pantry,” the woman gave orders like a military man, orders which she expected to be followed without question.

Emer swung open the wooden gate and directed Ben to pass on through, he then called back down the road to the Sheriff. “Come on Tom, Mrs. Plank has a firm rule that no one eats with a dirty face and hands and you don’t want to miss this meal,” the big man encouraged the stubborn lawman to get in line for the wash basin. “You too Deputy Trimmer,” Emer Plank said in a pleasant voice as he walked across the yard to the front porch where the deputy was still lying face down.

“You stay away from me Plank, that was a damn fool stunt you played on us and I for one don’t have to take such childish treatment. I’m going home!” Trimmer announced as he sprung to his feet, hurdled the yard fence and raced full speed down the hard packed dirt road.

“That man sure can run,” Plank said with a chuckle to Killer, the little dog who started the whole affair.

“Father!” a scolding young female voice rolled out the front door, obviously catching Emer Plank off guard. “Have you been using Killer in your practical jokes again?” the young woman inquired as she stepped through the front door into the revealing porch light.

Upon reaching midpoint of the yard, Ben Crane frozen in mid-stride when his eyes fell on the beautiful girl standing on Emer Planks front porch. “I, er, Ben, I want you to meet my oldest daughter, Ann. Ann, this is my good friend Ben Crane who ranches beside Henry Shanks’ place,” Plank announced in his booming voice, in a desperate attempt to divert his daughter's wrath.

The young woman turned her face to the lantern light and Ben suddenly realized he had seen Ann occasionally about town. The youngsters had never spoken to one another, lacking a proper introduction. Ben had completed all eight years at the local country school while Ann was just graduating from high school in Grey Cliff.

"We don't have time to waste daughter, we are on a manhunt," Plank continued, still trying to avoid a confrontation over his practical joke. "Please send Coe out here, I have several chores for him to do," Emer ordered in his fatherly voice.

"Mother just sent him to the smoke house for ham and to bring in more wood and I can't help because she needs my help in preparing the meal," the young woman replied.

"All right, I'll saddle the horses myself. Oh Ann, I hope you don't mind if Ben rides your horse, he's the lightest of the three of us and I know he will treat her well," Plank asked his daughter in a cajoling tone.

"I don't have much choice since there's only three horses in the barn because the rest are in the north pasture and it's too dark to find them. But what manhunt are you talking about and where are you taking my Penny?" Ann shot back finally realizing the seriousness of her father's statement.

"We have wasted enough time, so I think it best if we all saddle our own mounts and do without supper for that matter," Tom Mayhew declared, speaking for the first time since Killer's attack.

"Oh please don't leave without supper, I'll have ham and eggs and bread and gravy ready for you before you have saddled your horses and loaded your gear," Ann promised turning to hurry back through the front door.

Emer Plank quietly sat Killer, the family's small dog down on the porch which instituted a sudden burst of energy in the furry beast. Tiny toenails could be heard trying to get traction on the smooth wooden porch floor as the excited canine raced through the door in hot pursuit of his loving mistress.

Helen Plank and her two oldest children Ann and Coe scurried about preparing a late supper that was just being placed on the large wooden table situated in the middle of the front yard as the three men tied their horse's to the front yard fence.

"Both of our parents were homesteaders," Helen Plank explained as the men approached the table, hats in hand. "Because the cabins were so small in those years it became a custom to eat outdoors even on nice winter days." Her words were warm and winning about the dining arrangements but became stern as she added, "there are pans of warm water on the wash bench," the lady of the house stated in a manner which was clearly a direction not an offer. The three men quickly lathered up both face and hands, then rinsed and toweled off without a word of resistance. Hospitality was the standard of these people, but the lady of the house was in charge of all things domestic. If she said wash or comb your hair or scrap your boots before you eat, everyone complied. Going hungry was the only alternative and meals came few and far between in this still unsettled country.

"Please be seated, Mr. Plank at the head of the table, you gentlemen down either side," Helen Plank instructed while placing a kerosene lantern near her husband's place at the table. "There's ham and eggs, fried potatoes, fresh bread and milk gravy."

"You fellas are in for a real treat 'cause Ann makes the best gravy in the area, bar none." Emer Plank praised as he took his seat at the head of the table.

"Please father," Blushing, Ann half-heartedly reprimanded her father as she shot Ben a quick glance, "let me fill your coffee cups," the pretty young woman offered, as she poured the hot black liquid from the spout of a large blue enameled pot into the Sheriff's cup.

"Did I hear something about fresh bread and milk gravy?" Ben Crane asked, as he took his seat at the table. "I could live on bread and gravy," he added, as he glanced at Ann with a joyfully smile.

The three men's plates were quickly filled and they began to eat with a gusto that pleased Helen Plank, but her smile disappeared as she began to ask questions about the manhunt. "I heard there was some trouble at the store today, is that what this manhunt is all about?" she asked hoping to be given the details of this posse.

“Go ahead Ben, tell them about what happened today and don’t leave out the trouble at the store,” Plank urged with a masculine smile as he took another long sip of coffee.

“Yes Mr. Crane, please do tell us the whole story,” Helen Plank’s voice was filled with doubt as if she had caught three little boys up to some mischief.

Mother, son and daughter quietly took a seat at the long table, their attention fixed on Ben Crane like children waiting for a bedtime story. Realizing he had become the center of attention, Ben drew a long sip from his coffee cup, cleared his throat and began retelling the events of the day. He found relating what he believed had happened to Henry Shanks very difficult, but the remainder of the story flowed out quite freely.

The group sat in silence for a long minute, each trying to digest what they had just heard, then Emer Plank pushed his dinner plate toward the center of the table and said, “I think it’s only right Tom, that I apologize for running off your deputy,” he began earnestly.

“That’s all right Emer,” Tom Mayhew accepted his friend’s apology graciously. “I’ll admit I was a bit peeved at first, but the longer I thought about how Trimmer broke and run from a kid’s fairy tale, I knew we are better off without him in this posse.”

“I’ll confess you had me shaking in my boots Mr. Plank,” Ben Crane readily, if not a bit sheepishly, confessed; a difficult task for any young man.

"Yes, but you didn't run off and hide, and you weren't even armed," Tom Mayhew praised. "It's not how scared you are son, it's how you handle that fear that's important." The lawman hesitated a second then stated, "I believe Deputy Trimmer dropped his rifle down the road a piece and I would greatly appreciate it Ben, if you'd take care of it until we are through with this ride."

"Yes sir, I'd be pleased to," the youth announced feeling it a great honor to be armed by the County Sheriff.

"If I may be excused Mrs. Plank? I have an errand to run," Ben asked as he began to rise from the table.

"Yes certainly young man, and I do hope you got your fill of our meager repass," the lady of the house replied as if they were seated at some elegant dining room table feasting on an expensive banquet.

"Oh yes, thank you ma'am, it was a fine meal and I don't believe I have ever tasted better milk gravy than Miss Ann prepared for us," Crane directed a warm smile at the young lady then hurried to retrieve Deputy Trimmer's abandon belongings from the middle of the road.

"Good boy that one," Emer Plank declared, once Ben was out of hearing range.

"Yeah seems to be," Whispering Tom managed to second, stopping short of any more comments.

"Is there something on your mind Tom?" Emer Plank asked directly before he drained the last drops of coffee from his cup.

"Not really, it's just that fella on the train said his name was Boston Corbit, that name sounds so familiar but yet I can't place just where I know it from."

"Boston Corbit is the name of the Union Army Sgt. who killed President Lincoln's assassin John Wilkes Booth," Ann Plank announced in a firm voice as if she were giving a recitation in school.

"Say you're right!" Emer Plank declared. "Leave it to Ann to remember that, she's a real corker when it comes to history," the proud father added with some gusto.

"Yes, yes Boston Corbit shot Booth in a tobacco barn, you'd think I would remember that. Thank you Miss Ann," the Sheriff said earnestly. "That name would have been stuck in my mind for days, if you hadn't recalled the fact."

"Glad to be of service Sheriff," Ann Plank responded in a pleasant, if not a bit proud voice.

"Got Trimmer's rifle and canteen Sheriff!" Ben Crane called out from the fence where the horses where tied. He hesitated a moment before adding, "I don't want to be pushy but I would like to see Mr. Shanks as soon as possible."

"Yes of course, you're right, we'd better ride, Mr. Shanks may be in need of help," Mayhew agreed, rising from the table to tip his hat to Mrs. Plank and Ann. "Thank you ladies, it was an excellent meal with very congenial company, something I rarely have the opportunity to enjoy," the lawman whispered out in all sincerity.

"Thank you kindly Mr. Mayhew; we take great pleasure in your visits and remember our door is always open to you sir," Mrs. Plank announced for all to hear.

"I wish more of the citizens of this county were as generous and understanding as you folks," the lawman declared as he turned to walk away. "Good night to you folks," he added, hurrying to where Ben waited impatiently by the horses.

Emer Plank tenderly kissed his wife goodbye then joined his companions at the fence. "No need for you and the children to wait up for me, I don't expect to be back before sunrise at the earliest," the railroad man instructed his loving family, as he guided his horse to the middle of the road.

"You take care of yourself Mr. Plank!" Helen Plank called from the darkness of her yard as she recalled the untold number of times this scene had been played out in the twenty years of the Plank's marriage. She had watched her husband ride off time and time again on railroad business, or on posse's, or just to mediate some local dispute because he was big and fearless and everyone listened when Emer Plank spoke. Now she stood once again in the cool dark Montana night air wishing her man good luck with full knowledge she could not nor would not prevent his doing the right thing as he saw it.

VIGILANTE'S

"What's your plan Tom?" Emer Plank asked, as the three men rode side by side down the middle of the dark dirt road.

"Well, I figured on getting to Mr. Shanks' place by way of the new steel bridge," Sheriff Mayhew stated. "That is unless either one of you have a better idea."

"Sounds good to me, how about you Ben?" Plank inquired of young Crane not wishing to leave him out of the decision making.

"I'm new at this so I'll go along with you fellas who know what you're doing," Ben answered in an easy polite tone. With that unanimous vote Mayhew urged his mount into a slow trot causing his companions to equal his gate. They moved past several houses with golden lamp light pouring from their open windows and doorways until they reached the main street. Of the town's half dozen businesses, the saloon was the only commercial building still showing any signs of life. One lone dark figure stood half way through the swinging doors as if he couldn't decide if he wanted to enter. Four tired saddle horses were tied to the hitch rail patiently waiting for their owners to emerge with the hope of returning to the barn soon.

The little three-man posse moved quickly down the dark street, crossed the railroad tracks, then headed for the new metal bridge which spanned the Yellowstone River on the south east edge of town. The new all steel structure provided a solid link and safe crossing between the town of Grey Cliff and the railroad, with all the ranches on the north side of the river valley.

The horses trotting hooves thudded and echoed as the animals steel shoes impacted with the thick wooden planks that served as deck flooring, then all too quickly the steel framework started to bounce and sway from the horse's movement. Tom Mayhew reined his mount back to a walk then shook his head and said, "I don't know what it is about a horse's gait but they just shake a bridge like this to pieces; I saw it when I was back east last year. The only thing a fella can do is slow down to a walk and hope the horses don't spook," Mayhew stated matter of factly.

"We shouldn't have trouble with these three animals, the very first thing my kids did when this bridge opened was to ride every animal we own across to the other side. I don't know if they were trying to get the horses used to the bridge or because they thought it was fun," Plank chuckled.

"Well, either way it was good thinking, nothing I distrust more than a skittish mount," Mayhew declared with a shake of his head. "By the way just in case push comes to shove, how do these critters handle gun fire?" the Sheriff inquired.

"All three have been around gun fire, train whistles, and yelling drunks, they'll stand ground tied in a stampede or under you if need be," Plank promised with an exaggerated statement of trust for his well-trained mounts.

"I hope we don't have to put them to a test," Mayhew muttered in his low raspy voice.

Tom Mayhew urged his mount into a trot the instant its hooves cleared the end of the bridge and began to emit a loud thud from impacting the hard packed dirt road. The trio had advanced about three hundred yards when an explosion of sound coming from behind them filled their ears. It was obviously running animals crossing the new bridge. Instantly recognizing the noise, all three reined in their mounts while turning in a half circle to face whatever late night traveler might be crossing the new river bridge.

The little posse waited in a wary anticipation, their eye's straining to focus on the blackness of the east end of the new river bridge, all the while expecting at any second to visualize some known figure come bursting out of the darkness. The running hoof beats echoing from the bridge reached a powerful crescendo just as two men riding abreast followed by two more men erupted out of the blackness and raced at full speed down the dirt road towards the trio's position.

Plank's three mounts stood their ground as predicted in the face of the four hard charging horses from the new bridge. "Halt who goes there!" one of the oncoming riders demanded as he reined up facing Sheriff Mayhew.

"Identify yourself!" the same man cried out. "We have four double barrel shotguns pointed at you men so I'd advise you to speak up," he hurried to take up a position of strength on each of the posse's corners, thus virtually surrounding the lawmen.

"And just who the hell are you to make such a demand?" Tom Mayhew growled out in a slow confident voice.

The first man looked around the gathering, hesitated a moment before taking a deep breath as he realized this was turning into a standoff. "All right," he began, "I'm Lowell Jackson and I'm in charge of the vigilance committee in search of the men who murdered Henry Shanks today."

"All right," Mayhew said, copying the other man's opening, "I'm Tom Mayhew, Sheriff of Sweet Grass County, and I'm here looking into the death of Mr. Henry Shanks. Now as an illegally formed group, I'm disbanding you this very minute from any and all law enforcement activities."

"We need more identification than just your word saying you are the Sheriff and have the power to disband us," Jackson argued in a firm hard tone.

"I know its dark and I can't see the man's face but I'd recognize that voice anywhere," one of the four riders declared. "That is the voice of Whispering

Tom Mayhew, I'd know it anywhere and he is the County Sheriff," the man assured his leader.

"If that's who you are, and I ain't saying you are the law without seeing a badge, who are these other two men?" the leader of the vigilante's continued to flaunt his presumed authority.

"The big man to my right is Emer Plank, lives in Grey Cliff and is boss of the railroad section gang."

"Jackson knows me, in fact he has worked for me on the section crew," Emer's loud masculine voice filled the darkness with disgust at Lowell Jackson's attitude. "The man beside me is Ben Crane, Mr. Shanks' hired man and neighbor. Doc Walker's gang tried to kill him but he managed to get away and report to the law."

"Did you say Ben Crane?" Jackson blurted out in an indignant rage. "The last words Shanks said before he died was Ben Crane and three men who attacked him. Now you can understand why we chased you down after you three rode by the saloon. We'll just take Crane with us and save you anymore trouble Sheriff," Jackson announced in a loud snarl.

"Ben Crane is in my protective custody as a material witness and no one is going to take him from me without one hell of a fight and I don't give a damn how many shotguns you have trained on me," Tom Mayhew stated in his usually soft calm voice.

Lowell Jackson cleared his throat in a very audible manner then sat quietly on his mount, obviously planning his next move. "We are law abiding citizens," he stated in a proud voice for all to hear. “We have no desire to interfere with your official investigation; however since I found the bodies, I rode to Grey Cliff and formed up a vigilance committee and I feel it is our duty to accompany you to the Shanks ranch,” Jackson argued.

“Only if you four place yourself under my authority,” Whispering Tom declared.

“We so agree Sheriff Mayhew,” Jackson stipulated to the lawman’s offer.

“Agreed,” Sheriff Mayhew countered. “Now because it’s dark, one of you more familiar with this road should take the lead. How about you Emer?” the cautious lawman asked.

“Whatever you say Tom, but I would like Ben to join me. I’m sure he’s been up and down this road many times recently.”

“Good, you two up front, our vigilantes can be next, while I’ll bring up the rear. Oh, and stay spaced out a bit, hate to ride into trouble all clustered up like a covey of quail,” the wise old lawman advised.

Quickly implementing the plan, Emer Plank and Ben Crane turned their mounts around taking up a gait just below a trot that most would consider a fast, yet smooth walk. Jackson and his vigilantes fell in a few yards behind reserving the rear guard position for Whispering Tom Mayhew.

“Your daughter’s horse has a very easy stride Mr. Plank,” Ben Crane reported to his companion after covering only a short distance.

The older man chuckled slightly then in a soft voice replied, “Yeah, anyone who can walk can ride Penny but let me warn you, she has very fast reactions so if she decides to move or run then hang on with everything you’ve got,” Plank warned.

“Yes sir, I will remember that,” the youth acknowledged what he considered a solid piece of advice.

“We should be nearing Mr. Shanks’ turn off,” Planks words were part question, part statement.

“Yes sir,” Ben agreed. “His lane is just beyond the signpost on the left side of the main road,” the youth whispered, pointing at a large native cedar post that had several sign boards nailed to its trunk. The signs were hand carved or painted to inform travelers which direction to proceed to find a town, ranch or homestead. A large board nailed at the very top of the cedar post read ‘Henry Shanks Rattlesnake Ranch’ and pointed directly across the main road down the narrow lane that would lead a stranger to the old pioneer’s ranch house.

THE AMBUSH

"Let's pull up here for a minute," Sheriff Mayhew called softly from his position at the rear of the small procession. The lawman's words had not cleared his mouth when a gunshot exploded from the direction of Shanks' lane. The first shot was followed by a second and third volley of bright yellow flame ripping the calm night air blinding every eye that focused in the direction of the three muzzle blasts.

Lowell Jackson expelled a loud groan then toppled from his saddle, landing with a loud thud on the main road. The suddenness of the ambush caught the little posse completely off guard. One long moment passed before Tom Mayhew called out for his men to take cover. That urgent command induced Emer Plank and Ben Crane to dismount and run to cover behind the large cedar signpost. Sheriff Mayhew's experience told him to return the attackers fire even if he couldn't see any targets. He deftly drew his revolver, throwing three quick shots down the lane in the direction of the hidden adversaries before dismounting and hurrying to the protection of a fallen log. The three uninjured vigilantes remained mounted in an effort to control their nervous, skittish horses that were moving erratically around Lowell Jackson's prone body.

Three more gunshots ripped open the silence, filling the air with flame, gun smoke and lead that struck another vigilante. The wounded man's body rose straight up in his saddle stirrups then without a sound, he melted like butter on a hot griddle, then without any resistance he poured out of the saddle. The noise and commotion drove his mount into a frenzy, causing the disturbed animal to race off up the road towards Grey Cliff.

"Get the hell out of those saddles!" Tom Mayhew screeched out in his most powerful voice; however the last two men were slow in taking the Sheriff's sound advice. Only one cartridge was expended this time but its path was unerring even in the darkness and a third posse member rolled off his mount's right flank to plop face down on the shoulder of the road.

"What's the matters with those men?" Mayhew asked in disbelief.

On seeing his companions shot from their saddles, the fourth vigilante vaulted from his mount before breaking into a dead run. He had become so disorientated by the noise, so much so that he moved at full speed in the direction of Shanks lane and ultimately into the gun sights of the unseen assailants. Three nearly simultaneous gunshots caught the fourth man, as he reached the west side of the road where he slumped to the ground in an irregular pile of arms and legs.

"Lot of good those four accomplished," Sheriff Mayhew growled. "Now listen here, you men on the other side of the road, I am Tom Mayhew, the duly elected Sheriff of this county. You have just killed four innocent men. I suggest you surrender to me or face my wrath, for I have every intention of taking you into custody!" the lawman warned in his most powerful yet gravelly voice.

A deathly silence fell over the ambush site, which was broken only by the sounds of an occasional nocturnal insect going about its life's work without any awareness of the four human deaths. "You men are under arrest! Give yourselves up now and I promise you a fair trial. I make no promises if you resist!" Sheriff Mayhew called out in slow, even words. The ultimatum delivered, silence reined once more until far down Shanks lane came the sounds of horses being mounted, followed by the pounding of running hooves on the entry to the Rattlesnake Ranch yard.

As the sound of racing horses faded down the lane, Ben Crane stepped from behind the cover of the large cedar post only to immediately jump back when Tom Mayhew scolded his premature move. "Stay under cover!" he warned with a growl. "We don't know how many shooters are over there and more importantly we don't know how many rode away. I thought there were at least three different guns firing but it's so hard to tell in a situation like this. How many guns did you two count?" Mayhew asked, his eye's concentrated on the cover across thc road.

“I’ve a mind there were three shooters,” Emer Plank readily stated. “What do you think Ben?” the big railroader asked.

“I had trouble sorting out the shots, but I think three and that would be right since that’s how many of Walker’s gang were riding around here and chased me to the river,” Ben stated thinking their assailants would prove to be the remnants of Doc Walker’s gang, Clarence Bates and brothers, Red and Buck Ames.

“Trouble is, I couldn’t tell how many rode away just from listening to the hoof beats, one of those snakes could still be lying in wait hoping to pick us off.” Years of experience tracking criminals had taught Tom Mayhew caution and patience above all else. “We ain’t in no hurry, it’s still dark so I think it best if we stay put for a while,” the Sheriff declared not expecting any disagreement from his men.

“Sounds reasonable to me,” Plank acknowledged softly. “Where do you suppose those riders went to?” he asked more for Ben’s benefit than for the Sheriff’s.

“That lane leads to Mr. Shanks’ house, then a hayfield which runs down to the river and the crossing,” the youth explained politely, thinking the older men should have known where the lane led. “I reckon they are trying to make a getaway by crossing the river,” Ben suggested.

“Yes or maybe they want us to think they are trying to get away,” Sheriff Mayhew warned. “Maybe they are setting up another ambush by the ranch house or down by the hayfield," Mayhew added quietly.

A dim red glow began to slowly form over the hills behind the lawmen, its light spread by a mere fraction of an inch at a time like cold molasses spilled on a dirty wooden floor. Little by little the deep shadows lightened, exposing the Yellowstone River Valley to the sun's miraculous illuminating powers.

"My folks are just getting breakfast ready," Ben said softly, exposing the thoughts of his weary mind. "Come to think of it, they don't know where I am or what happened yesterday. Wish I could get word to them that I'm safe."

"I wish I could let you go home son, but you are my best witness and I must keep you close by," Tom Mayhew apologized earnestly.

"I understand Sheriff, I promised Mr. Shanks to see this thing through no matter the outcome and I intend to keep my word," Ben stated in an adult manner that somehow made Emer Plank proud.

"I know Ben's father and I'm sure he would take my word for what's happened if you want me to ride up that way and explain," Plank offered, then hesitated for the Sheriff's decision, but when he didn't answer the railroad man added, "I just might rustle up some more posse members while I'm at it."

"All right Emer, you ride up to the Crane's cabin and tell them the story and bring back any help you may find. But first we'll have a look at the four posse men and take a look at where the shooters were hiding. I don't have to warn you to be careful ‘cause we have no idea where this Walker gang may be now,” the lawman stated in a worried voice.

“You two keep a sharp eye out while I take a look around,” Mayhew ordered as he began to wearily abandon his cover and move silently towards the road. With all his senses on high alert, Tom Mayhew knelt beside Lowell Jackson’s body then announced, “Dead.” He moved carefully to the second then the third posse men’s bodies giving the same declaration after examining each. The fourth and final man lay face down near the side of the road, a testament to the effects of fear and panic of a normal man. The lawman’s examination of this body was noticeably longer and more thorough than those of his vigilante comrades, but this time Tom called out in surprise, “By God this one is still alive. Ben you stay on look out and Emer you ride to the Crane’s and get some help and a wagon to haul this fella.”

“Be back as soon as possible,” Emer Plank sang out as he ran to his waiting mount.

“Ask mother for some food,” Ben Crane called out as the big man urged his mount in to a run as they passed Ben’s hiding place.

“Lend me a hand Ben, we’d best move this fella out of the middle of the road before some damn fool comes racing along here and runs over him,” Tom Mayhew suggested, then after a moment’s thought added, “Might be best to gather up all the horses first, but you keep your eyes open and don’t take any chances.”

Once the horses were collected and tied off the two men gently moved the surviving posse member to a safe place near the signpost. Now the waiting began, but idleness plus natural curiosity can drive even the most cautious of men to tread where brave men would refrain. An hour after Emer Plank rode off in search of help, Tom Mayhew gave in to an over powering urge to investigate the bush whackers position as well as their horse's tracks.

"Stay here Ben, I'm going to have a look across the road. Maybe I can tell how many shooters there were and get a look at their tracks," Mayhew announced in a near whisper, surmising he did not believe after the passing of so much time, anyone could be hiding in the cover across the road. The determined lawman inspected his weapons as to load and readiness before stepping out in the road once more. His eyes took in every shadow, every blade of grass and twig but his well-trained mind failed to detect any signs of danger. Whispering Tom took several tip-toeing steps then paused as if he were stalking deer; he looked all about the area, then moved on again. His second stop was just beyond the center of the road where Mayhew took his eyes off the west side of the road long enough to turn his head around and shoot Ben Crane a questioning look. The youth replied with a shrug of his shoulders which drew a mimicked shoulder movement from the lawman.

The threat from the ambush site seemed negligible; no sound or movement could be detected by the sharp-sensed men, but just as Sheriff Mayhew's foot contacted the rocky road, an explosion of fire and shot belched from behind a small tree on the west side of the road.

The lawman's legs crumpled like a rag doll, allowing his body to pitch forward landing face down near the west edge of the road bed. There wasn't any question in Ben's mind the Sheriff had been hard hit by what sounded like a shotgun blast. Then thinking only of aiding the Sheriff, Young Crane jumped out from behind his wooden signpost cover just as a second blast from the attacker drove him back to its protection.

"It was a scattergun," Ben said aloud confirming his original thought that the assailant's weapon was a shotgun. He had seen and felt tiny pieces of wood had been stripped from the signpost by the small lead spheres and his body began to register a burning sensation in several locations. A trickle of blood ran in his left eye as other dark red spots began to ooze through the fabric of his shirt and pants. As shock swept over the wounded youth, he inspected and counted each bleeding hole in his body. Ben knew full well the only thing that saved him from being seriously wounded or killed could be attributed to the greater distance the buckshot had to travel. He estimated the Sheriff was at least forty feet closer than he to the shotgun's muzzle when struck and the greater distance allowed the small buckshot to decline in velocity and for the pattern to lose its density. His life was possibly saved by the shooter's lack of firearms knowledge and eagerness to quickly dispose of both men.

A quick examination of his wounds reassured Ben that, while painful, none of his injuries were life threatening and could wait until later to receive attention. He realized now was the time to assess the situation, should he advance or retreat? He experienced some discomfort while trying to extend his head around the signpost only to discover it was a futile effort. Sheriff Tom Mayhew lay where he had fallen and the youth found it particularly discouraging that the lawman showed no signs of life. His attention moved to the place where he was certain both shotgun blasts had originated, but no matter how hard he strained his eyes, they failed to record anything ominous.

The youth's mind began to take stock of his options, he could try one more time to reach the Sheriff's body, or he could crawl to the road leading to his home and wait there to warn Emer Plank on his return trip. The latter was probably the safest but neither choice appealed to Ben, his not quite mature brain kept presenting images of improbable heroic actions. He wondered how Teddy Roosevelt or Daniel Boone might have handled such an encounter; surely they would stand up and fight it out with the killer. This being Crane's first gunfight, his minor wounds filled him with romantic pride and he dreamed more impossible feats of daring do.

A sudden sound of brush cracking from across the road interrupted Ben's daydreams of greatness and settled the question of what response would be proper. His eyes became riveted on the opposite side of the road where they easily detected the frantic movement amidst the tall grass and sapling tree limbs.

A combination of foolishness and the movement across the road drew Young Crane to extend his head beyond the safety of the signpost, causing another shot to echo up and down the roadway. The numerous lead pellets blasted pieces of wood and bark from Ben's cover, some of which penetrated his face and neck. Whether it was dumb luck, poor aim, or sheer chance, not a single lead shot entered the youth's skin. But this last shot helped to erase some of those visions of glory as Ben come to realize someone across the road was bent on taking his life.

As the shock and bravado wore off, Ben found great solace in the protection the signpost provided. Still the question of what action to take next stirred Ben's brain into a disturbing quandary. The embattled youth's brain had run the full gamut of feelings from fear, pity, courage, power and many in between but suddenly rage filled his brain and directed his body. It was at that moment when Ben realized the killers had shot five men without receiving any serious fire in return. Those killings were bad enough, but whoever was hiding across the road had a hand in killing Henry Shanks, a man the youth respected above all others, except of course his own father. Ben's temper began to flare as he remembered the two shots fired at him, one of which drew blood that was a hard pill to swallow.

"Well," Ben thought as he pressed the rifles steel butt plate to his shoulder. He thumbed the hammer back, took careful aim at the middle of the brush pile then whispered, "Let's see how you like it?"

A loud explosion filled the morning air as the Winchester 32-20 caliber rifle's steel butt plate slammed against Ben's shoulder but the youth didn't hesitate for a second as he quickly worked the lever to load another round in the chamber. The second bullet was followed by a third, all three lead slugs tearing pieces of wood from the attackers cover. Once more Ben moved the metal lever loop of his rifle forward and back, but this time he held his fire, his sharp eyes detecting a slight movement in the brush. That slight movement suddenly exploded into a large dark figure sprinting from cover, before turning west to run full speed in the direction of Henry Shanks ranch house. Ben Crane took a fine bead on the fast moving dark target as he squeezed the rifles trigger, only to hear the disappointing sound of a metallic click of the weapon's external hammer falling on an empty chamber. In total disbelief, the youth racked the rifles lever back and forth repeatedly until he realized that he had fired the only three cartridges that had been in the tubular magazine. "Damn worthless deputy, didn't even load his rifle." A long string of profane oaths filled the air as Ben condemned Deputy Trimmer for being a coward and lazy for not loading the Winchester with a full complement of cartridges. The seldom used profanity continued to flow from his lips as he helplessly watched the large dark figure disappear down the narrow lane leading to Shanks Ranch.

Overcome by the heat of the moment and with total disregard for his own safety, Ben Crane shot to his feet, and with his clenched right fist swaying high overhead he cried out, “Run you damn coward, run! Run hard you back shooting trash, but remember I’ll be right behind you and when I catch you, you will pay with your life,” the excited youth bellowed out as he watched the dark figure vanish into Henry Shanks’ ranch buildings.

A bitter taste filled Crane’s mouth as he watched helplessly as the murderous black figure blended into the distance, but he felt his duty lay in helping the wounded man laying down by the road.

Ben Crane was just a youth, inexperienced in the ways of man and his penchant for crime and violence. His brain swam with guilt at allowing the dark figure to escape. Guilt and recriminations filled his head for not rushing to the Sheriff’s aid after being shot. Shame filled his heart for his failure to give assistance to the wounded posse member, he suffered as many people do the trails of self-preservation.

It was just such a befuddled state of mind that told the youth it would be safe to abandon his cover in order to make amends for his earlier regrettable actions. With his empty rifle in hand, Ben began to make his way to where Sheriff Tom Mayhew lay face down in the dirt road. He moved with a purpose as he neared Whispering Tom’s bleeding remains, hoping against hope to find a spark of life in the tough old lawman’s body. A strange reverence filled the youth's senses as he kneeled slowly beside the famous Sheriff's head.

"Are you hurt bad?" Crane inquired softly, not really expecting a reply.

"Get the hell away kid!" the old lawman growled.

His words so shocked the youth that he automatically recoiled back from Whispering Tom's presumed dead body. Ben Crane's instinctive backward movement saved the youth's life as one more shot rang out from the cover across the road. This single lead slug, fired from a rifle, traveled from left to right splitting his shirt wide open and produced a bright red welt in his skin. A yelp of pain announced Ben's surprise at being attacked once more, while the instinctive act of grasping at his chest caused the youth to land on his back where he began to roll away from the Sheriff's body. The youth spun over and over without any sense of direction, his only thought was to find protection from the hidden shooter across the road. Ben's pain and his frantic rolling action prevented him from finding a safe hiding place.

One more turn and Ben's head struck a solid object, the impact nearly knocking him senseless. Still, instinct dictated he scramble behind the head knocking protrusion. The next sound to penetrate Ben's foggy pain-wracked brain was the sound of a heavy wagon rumbling down the hill from the southeast. He hugged the ground behind the rock knowing full well at least one shooter remained, and he was armed with a rifle. The rifle gave the killer pinpoint accuracy, as well as a greater range than the shotguns used previously.

HELP FROM HOME

Ben Crane listened for a moment to the welcome rumbling groan of the approaching wagon; the sound indicated help was on its way. But Ben's elation soon turned to fear when he realized, whoever held the reins of that wagon was rolling into an ambush. Holding an empty rifle, the youth was prevented from firing a warning shot and he doubted his voice would be easily heard over the noise of the creaking wagon.

Many wild schemes popped into young Crane's head, some fueled by youthful enthusiasm, while others were induced by the blow to Ben's head. As the sound of the wagon drew nearer, warning the driver became even more imperative, and yet no safe means of alerting the oncoming rescue party became evident. Still unable to see the noisy vehicle, Ben fretted that his father or some other family member might be a passenger on the rescue wagon. There seemed no alternative, a clear signal must be given, and quickly if he hoped to avoid another ambush by the killer across the road.

Ben placed his right hand atop the head knocking rock, took a deep breath then sprung to his feet on a dead run. The youth moved towards the rumbling sound as he headed across the side hill hoping to intersect the approaching wagon before it came into clear view of the bushwhacker.

The wagon's rattling grew nearer, giving Ben some hope that the shooter might be distracted by the noise, allowing him to warn whoever approached of the danger ahead. Footing on the side hill was poor at best, causing the youth to slip and stumble several times, the last such occurrence ended with Ben sprawled face down on the edge of the hill road. Stunned by the fall and exhausted by the mad dash across the face of the hill, young Crane lay unmoving as if he were struck down by the grim reaper.

Unconscious or not, Ben's brain received and recorded the vibrations produced by the huge hooves of the draft horse team pulling the wagon. Each plodding step's impact was transferred through the hard packed road to his ears. The rhythmic thudding of the steel shod horse hooves kindled a fire in the youth's distressed brain. That small smoldering ember grew to a flame and then to an inferno, which drove him to move to an upright seated position.

Ben's mind began to clear and he began to recall his objective of warning the oncoming rescue party. He shook his head and struggled to his feet. Waving the empty Winchester rifle above his head, he called out a warning in hopes of alerting the wagon driver.

“Whoa stop!” Ben managed to blurt out as the large team of draft horses plodded by. “Tom and George,” Crane whispered when he recognized the lead team of Percherons, his father’s dearly beloved champion pulling horses. The second team moved past Ben as the front wagon wheel rolled to a stop directly in front of battered youth.

“My God son what has happened to you?” Jerimiah Crane inquired, as he jumped down from the high sided wagons driver’s seat. The senior Crane recognized the questioning look on his son’s face, then continued, “you have blood all over your face and shirt, have you been fighting?”

“I’ve been shot father, can’t you tell?” the younger Crane asked in astonishment. “Someone hiding across the road shot the four vigilantes and Sheriff Mayhew before taking shots at me,” Ben hurriedly explained. “I’m not sure if the Sheriff is dead or not, he’s lying in the middle of the road and we must hurry to his aid. Didn’t Emer Plank tell you all of this?”

“Yes Ben, Emer mentioned the ambush, but he didn’t say a word about you being hit. Let me take a look at these wounds,” the senior Crane insisted.

“Never mind that father, it’s just small buckshot that didn’t hit anything important, but Sheriff Mayhew is laying in the middle of the road and I’m not sure, he might be dead. We must try to reach him,” Ben insisted, while pointing to an unseen place on the road below.

“What about the shooter, how can we reach the Sheriff without being shot?” Jerimiah Crane asked, moving slightly to the side in order to get a better view of the ambush scene below.

"We can keep the wagon between us and the shooter while we drive the team from the ground," the youth suggested.

"Sounds like a good idea son, I'll drive the wagon, but I want you and your rifle to get inside the wagon and stay down behind those heavy side walls," Jerimiah Crane's words were those of a father directing his off-spring in a day's work.

"It's not my rifle and it's empty; it's a 32-20 center fire, do you have any bullets with you?" Ben asked, knowing full well that his father used only .44 Winchester Center fire long guns and side arms.

"No, but your 44 carbine plus a couple hundred rounds are under the wagon seat," the senior Crane announced while delivering a warm smile and a pat to his son's shoulder.

"Thank you father, I'd feel better with my own rifle today," Ben beamed as he clamored up the front wagon wheel, eager to retrieve his rifle.

"Did these men really kill Mr. Shanks?" Jerimiah Crane asked in a low mournful voice.

"Yes sir, I believe they killed Mr. Shanks, as well as those posse members lying dead on the shoulder of the road," the youth replied as he automatically inserted cartridges into the loading gate on the right side of his rifle.

"What a shame, he was such a fine man, and you couldn't find a better neighbor," the older man stated with a disbelieving shake of his head. “Are you about ready?” he inquired of his son while sorting out his team’s long leather reins.

“Yes sir, loaded and ready,” Ben replied anxiously. It had been a long day since he watched Doc Walker ride down the lane to Mr. Shanks’ ranch house. In those hours he had seen a man drown, been shot at, swam the Yellowstone at flood stage, and had his first train ride, not to mention four vigilantes shot and the County Sheriff wounded. During that long day he had been unable to strike back at those doing the shooting, but now the tables were turned and he, with his favorite rifle intended to make his displeasure known to the killers.

Jeremiah Crane called softly to his team, as they leaned into their traces and began to effortlessly start the heavy wagon moving. He walked a few feet to the side and behind the front wagon wheel, making sure that the long leather reins trailing on the ground didn’t become tangled or run over by the heavy wagon. A good teamster would prevent any such incident from happening. The experienced old teamster eased his heavy wagon down-slope then turned toward where Sheriff Mayhew lay unmoving, face down on the edge of the road. “Do you see anything?” he whispered to his son, as he stopped the front wagon wheel beside the Sheriff’s head, using it to block the view of the shooter across the road. Crane kneeled down near Mayhew’s head while waiting for his son’s answer.

“They’re gone,” Mayhew whispered through his pain. “They pulled out and ran down the lane towards Shanks' house while you were stopped on top of the hill," he added trying to roll onto his side.

Jerimiah Crane had reared back in surprise at the Sheriffs first words, recovered himself and then hurried to assist Mayhew in his movements. "I thought you were dead sir," the older Crane declared, as he lifted the Sheriff to an upright position.

"I don't see anything," Ben reported. "Do you need my help?" he asked in a low voice.

"No, you stay and keep a look-out, I'll take care of Mr. Mayhew," Jerimiah ordered. "Now sir, let us look at your wound," he said with a confidence inspiring smile, turning his attention to the lawman's injuries. "Do I need to look at the four vigilantes?"

"Three are dead and one was still alive when I was shot," the Sheriff reported.

"You've lost a lot of blood, must have been a shotgun that hit you," the older Crane stated as he examined the Sheriffs chest wounds. "But I think you got lucky, looks like your ribs stopped most of the shot from penetrating into your vitals."

"I thought it was a scatter gun because it hurt over my whole chest. The pain and the thought of being shot again made me lay still and play possum," Mayhew explained with a loud grown.

"Good thinking Sheriff." Jeremiah Crane praised the lawman's actions.

"Now, I'll put you on the wagon's tailgate and wrap a bandage around your chest. I'll lay you down in the wagon and take you to my place 'cause it's closer and my wife is a pretty fair country doctor. I'll leave Ben here to keep watch on this bunch of no account skunks," Crane explained as he bandaged the lawman's chest.

"I don't know if that's such a good idea, your son's the only witness we have who can tie Doc Walker's gang with killing Mr. Shanks," the lawman argued.

"That may be true, but Emer Planks rounding up some of my neighbors as we speak and should be here presently. Ben can take care of himself," the senior Crane stated confidently, then paused before speaking again, "Of course, Ben could drive the wagon home and I can stay and watch this bunch if you think it best," Jerimiah Crane offered.

"What do you think Ben?" Mayhew asked, as he lay back in the wagon bed.

"I agree with father, mainly because I can recognize everyone involved in this affair," the younger Crane convincingly stated his opinion.

"Yes, I see your point, I have no idea what the members of the Doc Walker's gang looks like and you do. Besides, you got a good look at Boston Corbit, who may be somehow involved with this bunch." Mayhew's resistance was waning to the point of consenting to the youth remaining behind and alone.

"Who is this Corbit?" Jerimiah Crane inquired.

"It's a female we met on the train ride down here," Mayhew replied.

"I thought Corbit was a young boy," Ben Crane declare in surprise.

"You may be right, but it was pretty dark and we were under some stress. It's just that some of his movements and words struck me as a bit feminine. I'm probably wrong, but I got a feeling you should keep your guard up if a slender young female happens by," Sheriff Mayhew warned, then paused to think for a minute. "Just stop any young person, girl or boy and just to make it official, I want you to take my badge and pin it on your shirt. Might give you just a little more clout," Mayhew ordered as he painfully unpinned the five pointed star from his own shirt before handing it to young Ben.

"I'll do as you say sir, but I'm not a Sheriff or any other kind of lawman," Ben continued to mildly protest.

"I think you'll make a great lawman but if anyone should challenge your authority, just tell them that you work for Whispering Tom Mayhew and if they have any complaints they can take them up directly with me," the old lawman growled out through his normally raspy voice.

"Yes sir, I'll keep my eyes open," the youth promised sincerely.

"Good, I know I can count on you, but at the same time be careful and stay safe. Remember these people are killers," Sheriff Mayhew added in a much softer voice than Ben had heard before.

Jeremiah Crane hurried to inspect the four vigilante's bodies only to announce all four were dead.

"Then it's settled, Ben will wait here while I take the Sheriff back to our place," Jeramiah Crane declared as he climbed to his place on the driver's seat.

"I'll get back as soon as I can," Tom Mayhew called out to Ben Crane, as the large wagon pulled away.

"I'll be watching for you sir," the youth replied with a wave of his hand, while a great emptiness spread through his stomach. He watched the wagon containing his father and Sheriff Mayhew disappear over the crown of the hill just behind the cross roads. The two men the youth respected most had abandoned him to once again face a gang of killers, a challenge he felt far beyond his ability, not to mention his courage.

RUNNING THE ROAD BLOCK

The brilliant morning sun began to warm the rocks and soil all about the lone guard as he sat quietly watching the north-south road. Ben had chosen an observation point directly opposite the opening to the Rattlesnake Ranch lane. This guard post was not chosen merely by chance but by a good deal of thought on Ben's part. The top of this round red boulder allowed a person to survey all approaching traffic on the main road as well as the ranch lane. Two days without sleep combined with the warm morning sun brought on a powerful drowsiness that gave the youth the sense of being drugged.

Ben Crane fought the gentle relaxing heat that escaped the large red boulder as it penetrated his muscles. The bewitching energy of the sun folded around his body like a shroud, preventing his moving either arms or legs. His eye lids felt heavy as lead and were sealed against opening just as though they were cast in one piece.

A far away grating sound disturbed Ben's slumber for a brief moment, but even that harsh interlude failed to break the trance-like spell the youth had fallen under. The noise grew louder by the moment while creeks and groans joined in the strange symphony but it was the constant reverberation of metal against stone that finally penetrated his haze-filled brain.

Realizing he had broken his promise to Sheriff Mayhew to guard the road, Young Crane's eyes popped open and he sat bolt upright as if an electrical shock had passed through his body. The youth jumped to his feet in time to see the tailgate of a metal covered enclosed wagon disappear down the trail leading to the ranch house.

"Halt! You there in the wagon!" he bellowed out. But the wagon careened on its way as if no one had protested its movement. "I fell asleep like a damn fool kid and let that wagon slip by. The Sheriff will never trust me again when I tell him how they got by me!" Ben exploded in a self-directed rage. The youth stomped and cursed at the top of his lungs but the box wagon had disappeared down Shanks' lane. "I must make amends for my stupidity!" Ben snarled out as he began to descend from his rock guard post. He ran through the rocks and across the main road without looking for any oncoming traffic including his father's returning wagon.

Young Crane continued yelling as he hurled challenge after heated challenge at the fleeing wagon, but no matter what he said or how hard he ran, he could not recall his mistake. "I'll catch you and when

I do you'll pay for ignoring me!" the youth called out with a shake of his fist, his feet became too heavy to lift.

The youth paused for a second as the feeling of total exhaustion swept over his body. It was a combination of extreme fatigue, and the let down from his mad spell. The simple act of walking felt impossible as he tried to force one foot in front of the other. He stumbled and fell to his knees on the rocky main road. Reluctantly, Ben deployed his favorite rifle as a crutch while he struggled back across the road to his original guard post, the sign post.

"Some lawman I'd make," Ben Crane growled out in a moment of self-abuse. His wounds, though minor, prevented him from resting comfortably against the buckshot scarred signpost. "How could I let that wagon get by me?" the youth asked himself. "You dunderhead, you simpleton!" came the youths self-loathing.

The morning sun climbed higher in the eastern sky warming Ben's back, bringing on a welcome change in his mood. But this time the youth was determined to keep his attention on the road and the lane, which led to the Shanks' ranch house. The morning shadows receded slowly, the change indicated time was passing without any sign of activity from the members of Doc Walker's gang. Then far to the east rose the first rattles of a wagon's slow lumbering approach. "I hope that's father coming back," Ben sighed. "*I don't know how much longer I can stay awake all by myself,*" he confessed, but only in his own mind.

Now the clopping of the horse's hooves could be heard over the wagon's creaking and groaning, assuring Ben that the approaching noises were, in fact, his father. Unwilling to divert his attention from the Shanks' ranch house, but still drawn to the noise of the wagon and the relief it could render, Ben turned around to catch a quick glimpse of the eastern road. But strain his eyes as he might, there were no visual signs of a wagon, only the steady clopping of the team's hooves. Realizing his stolen second had turned to a full minute or more, Ben Crane snapped his head around in time to see a dark figure run between Mr. Shanks' house and the windmill tower.

The youth shook his head and rubbed his eyes, not trusting his weary body to report the truth. Had he really seen someone cross the yard, or was it a figment of his imagination? There hadn't been any movement at the ranch house for a couple of hours and then the second he looked away, a ghostly figure, an apparition if you will, suddenly appeared. "But how could the outlaws know to move the first time he looked away?" Ben asked himself, his eyes focused on the ranch house. A small, almost dull reflection from half way up the wooden water tower caught the youth's attention. "Damn!" Ben blurted out so loud that he shocked himself. "They have Mr. Shanks' brass spy glass and they have been watching my every move," the youth snarled out in discuss. "But why are they watching me, they must know they are out of range of my rifle," Ben paused for a long moment, hoping to detect some other movement from the ranch house but when no movements or sounds were forthcoming he relaxed his body's muscles and leaned back against the signpost once more.

Ben Crane's whole being had been on edge for hours and it felt good to lean back and relax for a moment, still he wondered why the outlaws had kept out of sight when they knew his rifle could not reach to the ranch house. "That's it," he thought, fighting to suppress his excitement. "I can't hit the ranch house from here nor can they hit me, but I can hit anything that would try to use the corner below me and that's exactly what they want. They want to bring that wagon up the lane, then take one of the routes, north, south, or east to make their getaway. The river ford must still be too high to safely cross that way, so they have to come to the corner to make an escape. But the outlaws would be an easy target if they were to try to escape by way of this corner," Ben told himself again realizing fatigue and discomfort were impairing his thought process. "But why do they need a wagon? They could wait until nightfall and merely ride very fast by me in the dark. Unless they fear we will summons more help before dark. But why the wagon, unless they have something heavy to haul?" Ben's last thought brought him upright like a bolt of lightning had struck him on top of the head. "Of course!" the youth exclaimed. "They have found the gold at the bottom of the well and they want to haul it out all in one piece. I've got to warn father and the Sheriff!" Ben exclaimed, pulling his stiff pain-racked, weary body to its feet.

The youth could hear his father's heavy wagon nearing the crest of the hill and it was imperative that he stop them before they came into view of the sentinel on the windmill tower. It became a race between the steady plodding of the work horses and a wounded, but determined youth for the second time this morning. Ben pulled and tugged his way around and through boulders and loose rock until finally reaching open ground. By this time he was wet with sweat and breathing hard from exertion, his proper church-going upbringing was beginning to fail him, as one after another colorful words of profanity passed his lips in the face of the task that lie ahead. But preserver he did, finally falling to his knees as he cleared the crest of the hill just in time to flag down his father's team.

"Ben, are you all right?" Jeremiah Crane cried out, as he locked the wagon's brake and jumped down from the high wagon seat in one quick continuous movement.

"I'm all right," Young Crane replied, slowly rising to meet his father's approach. "But I fear we have a problem before us. So gather 'round so I can tell you all the story," Ben suggested as he indicate they should walk back to speak to the Sheriff whose head could be seen above the sideboards of the wagon. "Where is Emer Plank and the help he went after?" the youth inquired as the pair walked to the rear of the wagon.

"He is on his way but we won't have any help for a couple of hours, seems like all the men were gone or already at work. Runners have been sent to recall the men from the fields," Jerimiah Crane explained.

"A couple of hours might be too late," Ben responded sourly after expecting the assistance of several of the local men.

"Hello Ben," Sheriff Mayhew said in a loud firm voice that indicated his wound was not as debilitating as one might have thought. "What's the situation now?" he inquired with great interest. Before the youth could answer Emer Plank galloped up, dismounted and tied his horse's reins to the rear wagon wheel.

"I'm glad you're all here so I'll be forced to tell this only once, for it pains me to tell you I failed the three of you," Ben began. He paused to look each of the older men in the eye. Young Crane sucked in a deep breath then began to tell of his weakness. "I don't have an excuse, but I fell asleep allowing an enclosed metal-covered delivery wagon to sneak by me, then turn down the lane to Mr. Shanks' house. I didn't see who was driving the team as they were going full tilt in an effort to reach the house before anyone could stop them," he reported with a shake of his head and a dejected look on his young face. "However I think the gang is still hold up in there."

"Don't punish yourself Ben, it's been a long difficult chase and it's not over yet," Sheriff Mayhew tried to speak in a powerful consoling tone. Upon realizing that Ben had failed, the lawman placed his hand firmly on the youth's shoulder then with a wink and a smile pronounced the matter dropped. "Now tell me about this wagon."

"I don't know much to tell, don't know who was at the reins of the wagon, but I think I have figured out the why of it," Ben glanced at each of the three older men before continuing. "As I see it, they have found the gold in the bottom of the well. They can't use the river crossing or drive a wagon weighted down with all that gold across Mr. Shanks' rain-softened fields. Clarence Bates used to work for Mr. Shanks and he knows there are numerous wet spots and muddy sinks on this ranch. Their only chance to get away is on the roads that are better drained and will support a loaded wagon's heft."

"That sounds reasonable, so what do you suggest Ben?" Mayhew asked in his normal soft voice.

"Well sir, I think they will make a break soon, so I suggest that father and Mr. Plank ride quietly over the new bridge, circling down to the opposite side of Shanks Crossing. In doing so the gang's escape across the river will be cut off, and since the Sheriff is wounded he and I can use father's wagon as a fortress to block the road and the lane at the same time," Ben quickly laid out his plan of attack.

Sounds good to me," Jeremiah Crane spoke up quickly in support of his son's plan.

"I'm for it," Sheriff Mayhew agreed without hesitation.

"I reckon if you're all in, I'd be a fool to vote no," the mighty railroad worker consented with a wide smile. "But that's at a price," Emer Plank announced with a childish smile. "That being we hit the grub bag your mother sent along, could be a long time to our next meal."

"Agreed," Sheriff Mayhew declared while striking the floor of the wooden wagon box with his clinched right hand, trying to mimic a judge's gavel.

The four men, Ben included for he had suddenly been promoted to an adult this afternoon, shared the contents of the grub bag as they kept their eyes on the Shanks' ranch house. It was a hasty meal with very little talking and a lot of eating, as each man's mind raced ahead to what might be expected of this afternoon's work.

"Is everyone full?" Sheriff asked softly holding the food sack up high. No one spoke up so the lawman took it as an indication the men were finished. "Good, I think it best if we take up our positions as Ben laid them out," Tom Mayhew, who was still in charge, repeated the men's assignments. "I will wish us all good luck, and be careful in this undertaking," the lawman spoke in a stern yet warm voice.

"Yes, take care gentleman, and I will buy supper at my house tonight," Emer Plank offered graciously.

With the final instructions given, Jeremiah Crane and Emer Plank mounted horses and rode into a grassy draw that would screen them from the outlaws in Shanks' ranch house. Ben Crane, in respect for his wounds, carefully scaled the side of the heavy wagon, and gathered up the thick leather reins before calling back to Sheriff Mayhew who remained seated on the floor of the wagon box. "Are you ready sir?" the youth inquired, to which Whispering Tom gave an affirmative reply. Ben released the long steel bar that locked the rear brake in position, spoke firmly to the team of horses and began to move slowly away.

Once past the crest of the hill and rolling down slope, Ben rested his foot on the long metal brake handle, applying just enough pressure to prevent the wagon from crowding the rear of the team. Upon reaching the base of the hill, Ben guided the team across the main road turning sharply to effectively block the confluence of Shanks' lane and the main road.

"Do you think we should unhitch the team?" the youth softly called to Tom Mayhew.

"If you do, we won't be able to move if the need arises, but if you don't one of your animals might get hit if we should have a gun fight," the lawman replied, all the while mulling over what might happen.

"Do you hear something?" Ben asked, turning to look up and down the main road.

A LONE RIDER

The sounds bounced off the low hills, becoming more distinct and both men recognized the rhythmic beat of a single horse's hooves drawing near. It was clear the animal was approaching from the south and if it remained on the road, would soon round the bend of a small hill that jutted out to meet the flat of the Yellowstone River bottom.

As the horse and rider slowly came into view, Ben Crane and Tom Mayhew exchanged questioning glances. The animal was a high stepping satin black gelding, all decked out in the best English riding saddle and bridle. The world of nineteen seventeen was one of rapid advancement in all things mechanical, and it was unusual to meet anyone riding horseback over long distances, especially on a fancy spit and polished eastern rig. Encountering the obviously expensive horse in the middle of Montana was quite a shock for the two men in the wagon, but the appearance of the oncoming rider was even more difficult to accept. The rider was a tall lanky man in his late forty's with hands and face the color of tanned leather. Long uncut white hair escaped from underneath a felt western hat that sported sweat and grease stains, and a couple of holes in the crown. The rider wore a cheap long sleeved work shirt which was faded and torn in places, not to mention, it showed a considerable amount of fraying on the cuffs and collar. A worn leather belt supported his breeches, but the heavy leather shotgun chaps prevented a person from getting a view of the rest of his pants. Just below the chaps were inexpensive, plain, unpolished, leather boots that seemed awkward and out of place when stuffed into the small metal stirrups which hung on two narrow leather straps from the highly polished English saddle.

The rider, surprised by the two men in the wagon, reined in his mount for a moment as he analyzed the situation. The contrasting pair, man and rider, were approaching the rear of the wagon as Ben jumped down from the wagon seat, his favorite rifle cradled in the crook of his left arm. "That's close enough stranger," Tom Mayhew called out, raising up on his knees on the wagon bed's hardwood floor. "What is your business here?" the lawman growled in pain from rising fast enough to irritate his wounds.

"Just who the hell might you be to ask that question of a man peacefully traveling a public road?" the stranger asked, his voice calm but not cowardly.

"I'm Tom Mayhew, Sheriff of Sweet Grass County, and I am the law in this area, and we are here on official business. Now it's your turn to identify yourself," Mayhew stated once more, his low voice reflected his physical discomfort.

"Sounds fair enough," the tall rider responded. "I am Phineous T. Parminter, but folks just call me Phil," the stranger quickly offered up his nickname, leading one to think he didn't care for his real name. I have ridden with the law many a time over the years and before you ask, my Boss sent me here. It's a long story, but if you want to hear it, just say so."

"All right Phil, let's hear your story, but try to keep it short and simple." Mayhew motioned for the stranger to ride forward, wishing to prevent a long distance yelling match.

"My boss is Avery Hiatt, he is the owner of the Hard Luck Mine up north of here. You might have heard, we had some bad luck when four men stole a big block of gold from us. I don't know why but Mr. Hiatt thought the crooks came this way, so he sent me to try to catch them. This here fine animal is King Henry, Mr. Hiatt's private riding horse that he sent by rail to Grey Cliff where he figures to pick up the outlaw's trail. I was sent along to nursemaid this critter, but the railroad unloaded us east of here at Reed Springs, I didn't have any choice but to ride to Grey Cliff, so I can meet the boss when he comes in on the train tonight."

"Run that by me one more time stranger," Sherriff Mayhew demanded.

The lone rider wiggled his bottom around the spartanly padded English saddle, trying to get comfortable after a long ride, he then scratched his beard stubbled chin, as if he were doing some deep thinking before starting his disjointed narrative of how he came to this point in time. "My boss is Avery Hiatt, the owner of the Hard Luck Mine and four men stole a big bar of gold from the mine. Mr. Hiatt thought the thieves had traveled this way, so he told me to load King Henry on the train and go to Grey Cliff. The boss said he'd come along by another train and meet us tonight in Grey Cliff. The boss thought if we came on ahead, King Henry would be all rested when he hit the trail, chasing those no-account gold thieves. Everything went just fine until me and King Henry were forced to leave the train at Reed Springs. I sent a telegraph message to the boss, and he told me to ride this hobby horse of his to Grey Cliff on this road, and I should go by way of a Mr. Shanks' ranch. The boss said I should use the water crossing at Mr. Shanks place and that would take me to the town of Grey Cliff. Is that right?" the stranger asked obviously unfamiliar with the country around Grey Cliff.

"Well, it will and it won't," Whispering Tom's voice cracked, so he paused to clear his throat. "It's true, there is a water crossing on the Rattlesnake Ranch, but the river is too high to cross there. But you're in luck 'cause just up the road a couple of miles is a brand spanking new steel bridge where you can cross for free and it will take you right into the town of Grey Cliff," the lawman explained.

"Is this the Shanks ranch?" Parminter asked a bit sheepishly, while pointing to the land near the road.

"Yes, this lane leads to the Shanks ranch, but like I said, the crossing's under water," Mayhew tried to explain, but his voice sounded gravely from too much talking.

"Well, maybe I should ride down there and have look-see for my own self," the stranger stated, as he started to rein King Henry towards the lane leading to the Shanks ranch. But just as he did, Sheriff Mayhew drew his revolver from its holster and pointed it at the impetuous rider.

"Reckon you don't understand stranger, my patience is wearing as thin as the seat of your pants, so I won't tell you again, Shanks crossing is closed for now," Mayhew growled out in no uncertain terms.

"But you can't do that," Parminter shouted defiantly.

"This Colt and this badge say's I can, besides this ranch is private property and the owner doesn't want you on his land. Now I'll give you to the count of three to get on up this road, before I shoot that horse you're so almighty proud of," Sheriff Mayhew warned, moving the revolvers muzzle to a point where he could not have missed King Henry's head.

"Take it easy mister, I didn't come here to cause trouble," Parminter declared, trying to rein King Henry to back up. "I ain't under arrest or anything like that am I?"

"No, you're free to go, if you rein over and head up the main road, otherwise I will be forced to shoot you off the back of that high stepping nag," the Sheriff warned with a sharp growl, then paused to think. “Hold up there a minute Parminter,” Mayhew ordered the stranger. “I make it a rule to part on good terms if possible, and I’d like to do so in this matter. So I’m going to ask you to do me a favor, if you’re of a mind to,” Sheriff Mayhew stated with a wide smile, as he placed his Colt back in his well-worn holster.

“I feel the same way Sheriff, you just name your favor and I’ll see that it’s done,” the now nervous stranger replied.

“Good, good, Mr. Parminter I do appreciate a cooperative citizen,” Whispering Tom began. “You are going to Grey Cliff anyway, so I wonder if you’d ride to Emer Plank’s house and tell them where we are. Their place is easy to find, it’s on top of the hill on the other side of the railroad tracks but if you have trouble, anyone in town can point you in the right direction.”

“Why yes sir, I’d be glad to give those folks the message, and if you don’t mind I’d like to be moving along now,” Parminter half stammer out.

“Thank you friend, I do so appreciate your kindness,” the lawman praised in a soft smooth voice, and the wide smile of a slick talking horse trader.

“I’m glad to be of service sir,” Parminter called out, as he hurried King Henry past the wagon and on up the main road.

“Do you really think he will give your message to Mrs. Plank?” Ben asked with a tinge of amusement in his voice.

"I don't care if he delivers the message or not, just as long as he stays out of our hair," the Sheriff chuckled. "We don't know who he really is, or what he is up to, but I do know that I don't want him hanging around here when the shooting starts."

THE STAKE OUT

"Let's take turns watching the ranch house," Mayhew suggested, his fatigue from a long night without sleep becoming evident. "I don't think they'll try to make a break until dark so if you don't mind, I'm going to lay down in your wagon box for a few minutes," the wounded lawman didn't ask permission to use the wagon bed, instead he just made himself to home.

"You go right ahead and rest Sheriff, I'll call you if I see or hear anything," Ben Crane assured the now fast asleep Sweet Grass County Sheriff with a slight chuckle.

Once again the youthful Ben Crane was on guard alone, all the while wishing he had somehow missed out on all this excitement and danger. He wished Mr. Shanks was still alive and they were in the hayfield preforming the mundane tasks that all ranchers endure every day. He studied intently the ranch house where Mr. Shanks had passed so many decades and he imagined how the ranch had changed, and grew up over the last fifty odd years.

Ben's eyes moved slowly from the house to the well, and to the barn, then to the swampy wet lands he had used to escape the Walker gang, the very same swamp where Mr. Shanks had hidden from the Indians.

Ben Crane's mind and imagination swept back to the story that Mr. Shanks told of days long gone, when the Indians were after his scalp, and how he had taken to sleeping in the swamp among the cattails for protection, only to awake one morning to find three savages poised in ambush outside his cabin door. When pressed as to the outcome, the mild mannered old gentleman would remark calmly that he dispatched the would-be murderers.

The faint sound of someone knocking or hammering floated on the slight breeze from the ranch house to tickle Ben's ears. The sound seemed to come from the windmill tower, but he couldn't be certain. The youth's eyes moved from the ranch house to the well, to the barn, then to the swamp once more, only to detect the slightest movement, deep down near the roots of the reeds and waterweeds lining the swamp's bank. It was impossible to distinguish from this distance what it was that disturbed the foliage, but it was clear some living creature that was not native to the wetlands was trying to secretly move about.

With his attention riveted on the movement in the swamp's tall grasses, Crane failed to hear travelers approaching from the small town of Grey Cliff. He was alerted to the oncoming traffic only when his team began to move slightly in anticipation.

Crane remembered he and the Sheriff had discussed unhitching the team, but they never arrived at a final decision, so now all he could do was speak gentle consoling words to the uneasy animals. It was only when one of the horses in the approaching team gave out a hailing nicker that Ben fully realized his situation.

The youths head jerked around to the north road, where the sounds had originated, in time to see a small wagon pulled by a team of large dark draft horses. A young man at the reins leaned to one side in order to get an unblocked view of the road ahead. Two women seated to the left side of the driver raised their arms and waved in recognition, it was only then that Ben recognized the Plank family stopped in the middle of the road. He raised his hand and waved as a counter sign, then he motioned them forward, suddenly glad to see another live human.

The powerful Plank team made short work of closing the distance between the two wagons, and it was only after they were near enough to speak in a muffled tone, did Mrs. Plank say a warm hello. "We got your message and decided to drive out to see if there is anything we could do," she explained. "Where is Mr. Plank?" the woman asked, looking all about the area, a bit of nervousness in her voice.

"He and my father are across the river guarding the crossing. Sheriff Mayhew was wounded and is resting in the wagon," the youth declared pointing to the wagon's bed. "I'm sure that the Walker gang is holding up at Mr. Shanks' house. I've seen some movement, but can't be certain they are all there. Say, do any of you have a good set of eagle eyes for far seeing?" Crane asked, turning his attention back to the swamp.

"Why yes, Ann has exceptional eyesight and hearing," Mrs. Plank replied, obviously proud of her daughter's gifts.

"Is there some way I may be of service?" Ann Plank asked, as she stepped down from the wagon seat.

"If you would be so kind as to climb up here beside me in the wagon, and try to spot any movement in the swamp," Ben stated, as he assisted the young woman's ascending the side of the large freight wagon.

"Thank you Mr. Crane," Ann Plank announced with a warm smile as Ben Crane tenderly grasped her hand. "Now what is it you wish me to see?"

"Stand here beside me if you will, and cast your eyes down along the swamp bank, where it meets the barn and windmill. I'm just certain I saw something moving in the cattails that looked like a man," Ben directed the pretty young woman's attention to the suspicious spot.

Ann studied the area very carefully before placing her left hand over her left eye and once again studied the suspect area in silence. "Yes Mr. Crane, I too see an object there. It is most certainly a man and I would estimate it to be a big man. There, I saw him move, and it looks like he is moving in this direction," Ann Plank quickly appraised Ben of the situation before uncovering her left eye.

"That's what I was afraid of, they are getting ready to make their move just at sunset, when the sun will be in our eyes. I believe that man to be one of the Ames brothers, and he intends to crawl through the swamp, using the grass for cover. Once he reaches this end, he will make a break for the vigilante's horses we have tied out back," Crane warned as he cast his eyes across the Shanks' home place in an attempt to spot any of the other gang members.

"Would you be so kind Miss Ann, as to train your sharp eyes on the rest of the area with the idea of spotting anything out of order?" Ben asked in his most pleasant tone.

"Yes, certainly Mr. Crane," Ann replied as she began a visual search of the Shanks ranch place. "I see three saddle horses tied up at the windmill tower. I see what appears to be a large man's body lying beside the corral fence, and another smaller man's body lying near the house door. There is one large wagon and one small delivery type wagon, it's parked by the well," Ann reported, a bit shocked at having viewed two dead bodies at one time.

"The large wagon belongs to Mr. Shanks and has a broken front axle, which we had planned to fix right away. The smaller one must be the wagon that got by me this morning," Ben replied, still embarrassed at his guard duty failure.

"The big one would be Doc Walkers body, and I assume the smaller one is the remains of Mr.

Shanks," the youth's voice trailed off slightly as he pronounced his old friends name.

"I'm sorry Mr. Crane, I'm sure you had the highest regard for Mr. Shanks as did we all," Mrs. Plank said in a soft reverent voice. "I know what you are doing is important, but the afternoon is waning and I would like to be at my husband's side by nightfall. We brought some food and coffee if you would care to start a small fire before dark and heat everything up, we have the utensils for that," Mrs. Plank offered, sure the men would be hungry and more than willing to accept her hospitality.

"Oh yes ma'am, I'm sorry for not thinking of you and your family. I'm sure you will want to hurry around to the other side of the river in time to fix Mr. Plank's supper," Ben managed to stammer out.

"I would like to know how the Sheriff is before I go, besides we have a message for him that came up on the morning flyer. It seems someone stole a Union Pacific delivery wagon and a team of horses from the Reed Springs stable sometime after midnight. I hate to ask, but I wish you would wake him up before we go," Mrs. Plank stated, hoping the lawman was just fast asleep.

"Sheriff Mayhew," Ben said softly, as he knelt down in the wagon box beside the lawman's body. "Come on Sheriff, wake up, we have coffee and hot food," the youth promised before gently touching the man's hand. "Come on Tom, we are going to need you a little later so I can't let you sleep." With that, young Crane shook Tom Mayhew by his shoulder, but received no response for his efforts.

Ann Plank gracefully knelt down and grasped the wounded man's hand with hers, and began probing his wrist with her finger tips hoping to find a pulse. "He still has a heartbeat but it is weak," the young woman announced, placing her small hand on Tom Mayhew's forehead, trying to get a sense of his temperature. "Sheriff Mayhew feels cold and clammy to the touch of his skin," Ann reported, shooting a concerned look at her mother.

Mrs. Plank was at the Sheriff's side before anyone could ask for her help. After a cursory examination she declared for all to hear. "I believe this man to be in critical condition, and his only hope is to get him back to town. May we use your wagon Ben?" the woman asked, moving around to lay the injured lawman's head in her lap.

"Yes, of course you may," the youth agreed without thinking of the consequences. "I feel like a fool for not checking on Tom this afternoon. I, I," Ben stuttered like a foolish child trying to explain his neglect.

"Coe, you get up in the driver's seat and get us to town fast, and Ann you bring our wagon and we will meet you there," Mrs. Plank ordered as Ben jumped out of the back of the moving wagon, only to be nearly run over by Ann Plank racing by in her family's wagon.

MANHOOD

"My God," Ben mumbled out. "What the hell just happened?" He paused a moment to look at the dust being kicked up by the two wagons then spun around in a three hundred and sixty degree circle finally coming to stop with his eyes locked on the vanishing wagons. "Damn!" he exclaimed, tearing his hat from his head and throwing it on the ground in disgust. "All of a sudden I'm here all alone to face at least three murdering outlaws with my fortress, my only protection, our wagon gone to hell up the road." The youth walked around in circles for a moment, watching the sun lowering in the west, knowing that the gang would, in all likelihood, make their break at any moment. "Damn, it was good of the Plank's to leave me my own rifle," he announced sarcastically. "On the other hand, they took the food and coffee," he kicked a large round rock with the toe of his boot in a moment of dejection, then turned to face the swamp, the first place he expected danger to materialize.

The fear of being abandoned once more raced through Ben Crane's body, it was a debilitating sensation, knowing there were at least three cold blooded killers coming his way and that darkness was fast approaching. But suddenly the fear drained out of the youth's body, and a powerful feeling of resolve reinvigorated the inexperienced young man. The adult man, Benjamin Franklin Crane, standing unprotected in the middle of the road had a sudden revelation. He had made several errors in the last couple of days that were easily accredited to age, lack of sleep and painful wounds, but that was over now.

"No by God!" Ben said out loud with a broad smile. "I let Sheriff Mayhew down several times on this manhunt, but it won't happen again!" With that pledge on his lips, Crane took stock of his bleak situation. "I've got to move, and move fast if I have any hope of preventing that bunch of trash from escaping." Ben turned and ran at full speed to the saddle horses tied up on the other side of the road. No one could blame him if he mounted up and rode after the wagons headed for town, but the thought of running out and allowing the murderers of Henry Shanks to escape brought the bitter taste of gall to his mouth. He shook his head and swallowed hard in an attempt to clear the thought and the taste from his mouth, and then proceeded to untie each of the horses and head them towards town with a sharp slap on the rump.

"Now I've really done it, with the horses gone I haven't any way to escape, but then I don't want to escape, and I don't want to give Bates and the Ames brothers an easy way out of here either," Crane continued to talk to himself as he went about preparing for the fight that was sure to follow.

“I know they are watching me, and the rays of the setting sun are illuminating this hillside like the stage lights at the Billings Opera House. There’s nowhere to hide on the west side of the road and even less cover on the east side. I reckon I’ll finish this fight where I started it,” Ben thought, as he turned and walked to the cedar signpost which was situated part way up the east slope. “No use hurrying cause I know they can see my every move with Mr. Shanks spy glass. I’ll just walk slowly and confidently up to the post, then I’ll stretch and sit down like I’m waiting for the milk cows to come home,” he chuckled at the thought of what he must look like to a bunch of nervous killers.

The setting sun began to show streaks of grey and pink high over the western horizon and Ben tried to remember those old rhymes about sunset red, rain comes down on your head, sun set grey helps a traveler on his way. “That didn’t sound right,” he thought to himself. “I may not be here in the morning to care about whether it rains or not if I don’t keep my eyes peeled for the Walker gang,” he scolded himself, then moved slightly so the signpost would provide more cover from anyone firing at him from the end of the swamp. “That’s better, but now I’m sticking out like a sore thumb to anyone who cares to take a shot at me from the south,” Crane argued with himself about where to sit that would give his enemy the least amount of target to aim at.

THE SHOOTOUT

The air temperature was dropping slightly with the lowering sun, making his wait a bit more comfortable but it was to be a short wait. Down near the barn he could see the delivery wagon begin to move forward at a slow pace as if that were the signal for everyone to move.

As the wagon rolled forward, Ben unthinkingly stretched his head around the signpost for a better look; just then a bullet impacted the signpost just above his head. The shot originated in the last vestiges of the cover provided by the east end of the swamp. A large blue cloud of smoke floated undisturbed in the still evening air. "Must be a black powder gun," he thought as he shouldered his smokeless powder firing rifle, and aimed at the most likely spot where the shooter might be hiding. His .44 caliber bullet ricocheted with a high pitched whine, the end result of his projectile striking something hard and flat in the bottom of the swamp. "Now you know why most men going in harm's way have stopped carrying those old smoke poles," Ben stated, as if explaining to a novice shooter the differences between the two gun powders.

A second shot erupted from far down the lane leading to Mr. Shanks' ranch, and although this weapon was using smokeless powder, it was easy to tell from where the bullet was launched. It obviously was fired from the seat of the delivery wagon, which was now picking up speed. A second shot immediately followed the first, but this one looked to be coming from a hole that had been freshly cut in the thin metal skin, which covered the roof of the delivery wagon. Even in the gathering dusk, Ben could see the upper half of a dark figure protruding through the rooftop hole, causing him to instinctively raise his rifle and make an unaimed snap shot at the shooter. The projectile found its mark, causing the shooter to drop his rifle over the roof's edge before disappearing back through the hole.

Ben Crane automatically worked the lever on his Winchester rifle with such gusto that the fired brass casing flipped high in the air, but he pulled the lever back more slowly into battery when he realized he had just taken his first human life. The youth froze for a moment, eyes fixed on the weapon's barrel as if some profound revelation would be found there. Ice water coursed through his veins, making the youths head pound with pain but in the next instant the feeling of burning hot blood chased the freezing sensation from his head to his feet. Crane's head spun and he was sure he was going to vomit, until another bullet from the swamp crashed into the signpost with a resounding thud. The very thought of the men who had killed Mr. Shanks were now trying to also take his life brought Young Crane to a harsh realization, no matter how repulsive the idea of taking human lives affected him, the time had come to avenge Mr. Shanks cold blooded murder.

The thought of Mr. Shanks' death propelled Ben Crane to rise to his feet behind the signpost, and using wild guess-timation fired three quick shots at the last cloud of blue smoke. A wild scream rose up from the swamp grasses, "don't shoot any more, you got me good with the last shot," the male voice tapered off before calling out in a weakened struggling cry, "for God's sake, don't shoot anymore," the almost inaudible voice pleaded.

The next sound to fill Crane's ears was that of the delivery wagon's steel rimmed wheels rattling on the rock strewn lane, that and the sound of a gunshot, accompanied by a distant scream. Mesmerized by the voice of the wounded man in the swamp, Ben had remained upright and exposed to the delivery wagon, coming from the south and west, far too long. A hot burning bullet caught the youth off guard as it bore a hole through his heavy leather belt before crashing head long into the back of his large oval U. S. Civil War belt buckle. The buckle, the front of which was made of heavy brass while the back was filled with lead, had belonged to his grandfather. It was a cherished family keepsake but poor people have poor ways when money gets scarce they improvise or make do. The bullet had struck Ben at the waist on his left side, penetrating his belt, then sliding across his stomach and plowing a deep bloody furrow until impacting with the heavy buckle. The solid lead bullet and buckle's lead backing melted into one, its forward force knocked the youth to the ground, causing him to strike his head on the signpost with enough energy to render him unconscious.

THE RECOVERY

A cooling sensation ebbed over Ben Crane's body, starting at his forehead then moving across his face before spreading down his neck to his chest. "Wake up Mr. Crane," A soft sweet distant voice hailed from out of the enveloping haze. "Wake up Mr. Crane, Ben it's time to eat breakfast," the voice urged gently trying to provoke a clear response as the cooling started over once more at his forehead. "Mr. Crane," the voice, now sounding closer than before continued to appeal for recognition. "Your mother and father are here and wish to speak to you before breakfast so you'd better wake up."

"Mm, what are you saying?" Ben heard himself mumble out. "Who's here, and where is here? Am I dead, I know I was shot, is this heaven?" the youth asked in a weak raspy voice as his eyes slowly opened, then blinked back closed as his brain tried to focus on his surroundings.

"It's not exactly heaven but it's pretty close," the soft voice answered. "You're inside Mr. Shanks' house and you're lying on Mr. Shanks' bed."

"Oh no," Ben stated in a loud voice, as he tried to rise from the bed before falling back to his original place. "I don't think Mr. Shanks would like anyone else sleeping on his bed," Crane blurted out in protest.

"You must stay down for a couple of days, doctors' orders," the soft voice, now a bit firmer than before, admonished him. "Don't you remember anything about what happened yesterday?" the soft voice asked. The sweetness and warmth of the voice caused Ben to turn his head to the side in an effort to discover its origin.

"I'm sorry to say Mr. Shanks is dead, and so are all of Doc Walker's gang members. Mr. Avery Hiatt arrived on the 9 o'clock train last night. He naturally rode King Henry out this morning while Phineous T. Parminter followed in a heavy wagon they borrowed from father to haul his gold bar in. My father and brother, and your father are outside right now helping them get loaded," the soft voice continued to reiterate all that had happened.

"Oh, you're Ann Plank aren't you," Ben stated rather than asked the pretty young woman as the fog began to clear from his eyes as well as his brain.

"Yes, isn't that better when you know who you are speaking to?" the young woman teased.

"Yes Miss Ann, it surely is, but how did I get here and why am I still alive?" he asked obviously confused on the events of the previous evening. "I couldn't see who was driving the delivery wagon because they were sitting in the shadow of the wagon but the setting sun outlined the man protruding through the hole in the wagon top. I remember shooting at that man who foolishly poked his head through the hole in the top of the deliver wagon. I also shot the man who was crawling through the swamp. I figured they were the Ames brothers. Oh yeah, I remember leaving my side exposed to the delivery wagon too long, then something hit me and I can't remember another thing after that. Clarence Bates must have been in the driver's seat of the wagon, why didn't he finish me off?" Ben inquired, completely mystified by the outlaw's actions.

"Well, shortly after we got to Grey Cliff, my brother Coe saw the riderless horses you had turned loose and realized we had run off with your wagon, and left you all alone. He caught up one horse and me another, then we raced across the steel bridge, that's when we heard distant gunfire. We kicked our mounts into a flat-out run, but you had already been shot by the time we got near. When we arrived at the point where the swamp meets the road, we could see the delivery wagon setting alongside the road and a man wading in the water, probably trying to retrieve Ames' body. Coe was armed and approached the wagon on the run. The man in the water fired at Coe with a hand gun but missed. My brother fired back, striking the man in the chest and he fell face-first in the water like a freshly cut oak tree. What happen next was a real surprise, as someone in the seat of the delivery wagon let out a loud scream then turned the rig towards the big man lying in the water. In the midst of all this, the driver tried to use a double barrel shotgun on Coe as he raced by, but she must have been inexperienced in using a weapon in close like that 'cause she only managed to shoot her wheel horse in the back of the head killing it dead. The other horse panicked and tried to turn away while dragging its dead halter-mate. I saw the whole thing and still can't say exactly what happened but everything got tangled up and before we could do a thing, the delivery wagon tipped over trapping the driver underneath. She was dead before we could get the wagon and gold off of her," Ann explained the strange accident as best she could. "Maybe Coe can explain it better than I."

"You said she? Who was the girl? Was she the same person who called herself Boston Corbit who your father and I met on the train? And did she drive the Union Pacific delivery wagon in here yesterday?" Ben demanded of his young friend.

"That's the way we figure it, but when Coe pulled Clarence Bates from the swamp, he asked about her first thing. He explained her name was Boston Bates not Corbit, she was his daughter. He asked Coe to see that Boston got a proper burial with preacher and all 'cause she was a good girl who had never been in trouble before today."

"According to Clarence Bates' last words, the girl had been living back east with her mother until she passed on, and then she came out here looking for her father. They had hoped to make this one last score, then live out the rest of their lives in Mexico. But it didn't work out 'cause Clarence Bates died in my arms in the swamp and Boston Bates came to her end under the delivery wagon," Ann explained further.

"Sort of a sad tale," Ben whispered sadly. "All that work to steal a bar of gold, then all of them dying so tragically." He paused a moment then asked, "how is Whispering Tom's wounds," he jested, using the man's nickname to cover his concern.

"The Sheriff will be just fine in a month or so, Doc Bacon says," Ann replied, being careful to place an emphasis on Mayhew's title. It was clear to Ann Plank that Ben Crane harbored guilt feelings about all the deaths. Ann wrung out the wet cloth and reapplied it to Ben's scraped up head and face. "Now don't go to sleep, remember your parents wish to speak to you in a moment; and here comes your father and mother now, so I'll just excuse myself so that you folks can talk," Ann announced with a smile.

"No please don't go Miss Ann," Ben took hold of the pretty young woman's hand as she began to rise.

"I'll be right outside if you need anything and I promise to come and sit with you while you have breakfast," Ann insisted with a kindly pat to Ben's hand as she exited the room.

Ben's mother and father quietly slipped into the room; Myrtle sat gently on the edge of the bed beside her wounded son, while Jeremiah moved to the foot of the bed where he stood proud and erect, holding Mr. Shanks' homemade treasure box.

"Are you all right Ben?" his mother asked with great concern as she placed her hand lovingly on his scratched and battered face.

"I'm fine now, thanks to the Planks, Ann and Coe," the youth replied.

"Are your wounds very painful?" Myrtle asked, wishing to give a comforting touch to the white linen bandages, but withdrew her hand fearing it might cause her son even more discomfort.

"No mother, they're not too painful, but I sure am getting thirsty," the youth reported.

"I'm glad to see you doing so well son," Jeremiah Crane said, clearing his throat before speaking further. "I think we have some things to speak of, if you are feeling up to it."

"Yes sir, I see you have found Mr. Shanks' metal box. Did the Walker gang get hold of it first?" the youth asked, sure in his own mind that the outlaws had discovered the box in their frantic search for the stolen gold bar.

"No, I don't think they touched it, but you kept talking about it in your dreams last night so following your directions, Emer Plank and I went out to the well at first light and retrieved it. I want you to know we only opened it far enough to see your name written on a piece of paper. We didn't read anything or disturb any of the contents," Jeremiah Crane was very explicit about the handling of the treasure box.

"I must ask you some questions about this box, and what with Sheriff Mayhew wounded and laid up, well there is very little law around to report this to," Ben's father ashamedly began. We hope to keep you square with the law, so I must ask if there is any connection between what I suspect is in this box and this Doc Walker gang. What I'm trying to ask is everything up to snuff, you know, there isn't any question to the legal ownership of this box's contents?" Jeremiah Crane demanded in his most fatherly voice.

"Yes sir, everything is legal and I know many of Mr. Shanks' secrets now and I never heard of him doing anything disreputable," Ben declared in no uncertain terms.

"See, I told you Mr. Shanks would never do wrong, and of course, our Benjamin is beyond reproach," Myrtle Crane scolded her husband for entertaining such dire thoughts.

"Yes, I guess I owe Ben an apology, but a body can't be too careful. With that settled, what do you want me to do with this box?" the senior Crane asked.

"I would like you to ask Mr. Plank to step in here and witness what is to happen next," Ben Crane asked his father.

Jeremiah Crane placed the rusty steel box on the bed at his son's feet, then slipped out the door and could be heard speaking to Emer Plank in the door yard. "I don't know what he wants but it has something to do with the metal box you pulled from the well," the senior Crane could be heard saying. The two men entered the room in silence, Plank first, followed by Jeremiah Crane.

"Thank you for coming Mr. Plank. I am hoping that you would be so kind as to witness what is removed from this metal box that belonged to the late

Henry Shanks?" the youth asked, painfully turning on his side to look his visitor in the face.

"Yes of course Ben, I will do whatever you ask," the huge railroad man willingly agreed.

"Good, thank you sir. Now if you will please help my father remove the contents of the box and lay it on the bed," Ben instructed the two older men who followed his bidding to perfection. Each item was duly noted and discussed by all four of the rooms occupants. Ben repeated what little information that Henry Shanks had time enough to relate before the outlaws returned. The youth made reference to the two bank accounts, but refrained from explaining where they were derived. Myrtle Crane made an itemized list of the box's contents, then all three witnesses signed it.

"I want all of you to know that Mr. Shanks knew that yesterday would be his last day on this earth, and he made reference to that fact several times. He wanted only for me to get away, while at the same time hinder the outlaws from making a getaway with the gold. Mr. Shanks, even though his arm was badly mangled and was in great pain, refused to let Bates and the Ames brothers intimidate him. Henry Shanks was a tough old man," Ben Crane declared in a somber tone that reflected his admiration for the gentleman rancher.

"Mr. Hiatt left you the reward money for the return of the gold bar and I understand there is also some reward money for bringing in the Walker gang," Jeremiah Crane announced proudly.

“I don’t want any reward money, it should be divided up between Sheriff Mayhew, Emer Plank, and Coe and Ann,” Ben stated in a very matter-of-fact adult tone.

“That is very generous of you Ben, but the reward totals up to quite a sum,” Emer stated a bit shocked at the offer.

“I know but it is all yours.” Ben then added facetiously, “don’t share it with Deputy Trimmer. He was the greedy one who was just after the reward. I’ll bet he regrets letting that ghost dog of yours scare him off.” Everyone laughed at the reference.

Emer Plank rose and shook Ben’s hand while saying, “you are a lucky young man Ben. You are lucky to be alive, and you are lucky to inherit one of the best ranches in the area. I don’t say that with envy or jealousy because I know that is what Henry Shanks wanted for you,” Emer Plank said with a wide smile. “I will be glad to testify to that fact in any court or in front of any judge in the land.”

“Thank you very much Mr. Plank, and I know with you giving your word, no one will doubt the facts of this case,” Ben said, as a painful smile spread across his lips.

A gentle knock at the bedroom door announced Ann Plank had Ben’s breakfast tray, and wished to enter. “Here you are Ben, it may not be a meal fit for a king but it will suffice for the newest ranch owner in the Yellowstone Valley,” the young woman decreed light-heartedly as she sat the food tray on the wounded man’s bed.

“Truthfully all I really need is something to drink, but you promised to join me for breakfast Miss Ann, and I intend to hold you to that promise,” the young man said with a wide grin while extending his right hand to the pretty young woman. Ann’s face flushed a soft crimson red as she tenderly accepted Ben’s hand and lowered herself slowly to sit on the bed beside Benjamin Franklin Crane, the newest rancher in the Yellowstone River Valley.

Gary Jay Pool was born July 18, 1946 to a poor southwest Iowa farm family. His family consisted of his father, who was a World War II veteran and a man of few words; his mother, an insatiable reader and conversationalist; and an older sister.

Being raised on a dead-end dirt road very near the Missouri River, Gary spent countless hours hunting and fishing and became an avid outdoorsman. The author's father spent his life trying to raise his only son to survive being a soldier in a war, he somehow knew was coming. This training fell in line with Gary's choice to serve in the United States Army. A tour of duty in Vietnam in Army Bomb Disposal provided the wealth of factual antidotes for his first book, Xuc May.

Having a lifelong passion for writing, Gary has written several other stories which he plans to finalize and publish during his retirement years. Today Gary and his wife Jan live in Tabor, Iowa where they raised four daughters. His wife and daughters all work as a team to help publish and sell his books.

Watch for the latest updates on Gary's website www garyjaypool.com or follow his Facebook page www.facebook.com/garyjaypoolpublishing.com

OTHER WORKS

Xuc May (Never Happen)

Ramblings of my everyday life

while serving in an EOD unit in South Viet Nam

(Non Fiction)/biography

The Captain & The Candles

(Historical Fiction)

Made in the USA
Monee, IL
31 March 2020

24142718R10192